W9-AFF-276

MR ARKADIN

Alex
(27 W46
230 1539

MR ARKADIN

Orson Welles

A STAR BOOK
published by
the Paperback Division of
W H Allen & Co Plc

A Star Book
Published in 1988
by the Paperback Division of
W H Allen & Co Plc
44 Hill Street, London W1X 8LB

First published in Great Britain by
W H Allen & Co Ltd, 1956

Copyright © Orson Welles, 1956

Printed and bound in Great Britain by
Anchor Brendon Ltd, Tiptree, Essex

ISBN 0 352 32177 6

This book is sold subject to the condition that it shall
not, by way of trade or otherwise, be lent, re-sold, hired
out, or otherwise circulated without the publisher's
prior consent in any form of binding or cover other
than that in which it is published and without a similar
condition including this condition being imposed upon
the subsequent purchaser.

Book One :   *Bracco*

7 – 91

━━━━

Book Two :   *Sophie*

93 – 182

━━━━

Book Three :   *The Ogre*

183 – 222

━━━━

Book One

Bracco

CHAPTER ONE

I'D gone on shore to get a drink, but I suddenly realised I didn't want one. That scene with Mily had been really too absurd and the best thing I could do would be to go back on board and patch it up with her. We usually enjoyed our reconciliations. So what was I waiting for? Wandering around the docks like this wasn't much of an idea. I'd no desire whatever to attract attention.

I saw two men of the harbour police, near the wire fence. They were talking loudly, laughing, sometimes turning their heads and spitting on the ground. They had lit a small fire, though the night was warm. It was one of those grey nights, with a faint mist, in which sounds and smells are curiously emphasised. From time to time the foghorn boomed in the distance. They must have been unloading vegetable oil, because the sweetish scent lingered in the air.

I'd best go back to Mily. She was probably in tears. I'm not a hard man. Not hard enough. When I make women cry, I do it only just enough to keep them steady. And even so it worries me sometimes. "You've a soft heart, Guy, my pet," my mother always used to say. Except that I wasn't called Guy in those days—not that that matters. "You're like me, you're too kind. It won't do you any good." And she would give a melancholy sniff. Poor woman. I'd already noticed that she always made a mistake when she gave way to her emotions: her make-up seemed to fall apart, and she became an old and faded doll with hair that was too blonde. I used to find such moments sad and somewhat discouraging. Like the sweetish smell on the docks tonight. . . .

Like Mily, too, for that matter. She was all right, Mily. A good girl. I loved her skin, which was extraordinarily soft and creamy. It had a most delicate perfume, as of polished ivory. Funny the way the scent of that woman could excite me sometimes, while at others, like tonight, I found it insipid and tedious.

The greasy, sugary smell of vegetable oil arose here and there like an unmoving cloud. . . . Not a breath of wind. The sea was invisible, but it was there all right and I could hear the slapping of the black water against the stone walls of the quays. It would have been better to put to sea tonight, since everything was stowed away. We'd sail at dawn tomorrow at the latest. Otherwise Tadeus would be angry.

It was all Mily's fault we were still here. She'd gone shopping. She had this complex that her dollars would buy her anything she wanted, practically free. She'd been done, good and proper, over that pure silk lingerie. And how! I used to dabble in silk myself once upon a time. I know my way about that racket. That's what had started it. One thing leads to another and she'd talked a lot of nonsense. With women everything becomes personal. Mily had this funny idea that because she'd been helpful to me once, when I was in a bit of a jam, she had some sort of right over me. Basically she was made for suburban life, she should have got married, only the sort of men Mily met weren't interested in marriage. They saw her as a one night stand. And she, poor kid, always hoped it would last.

She'd been with me for four months now. I was kind of low and had plenty of spare time. It was through her I'd met Tadeus, and when this cigarette stunt had jelled, she'd insisted on making the trip. I'd given in.

"You're making a mistake," Tadeus had said.

I knew he despised me; after all, he despised everybody. Not that I cared what he felt about me. Our relationship was strictly business. I'd go and see him in the little Arab café, by the Zocco, where he sat, always at the same table, in front of a glass of Pernod which he never seemed to touch but which nevertheless had to be refilled ten or twelve times a day. He worked in broad daylight, while the Arab boys polished his shoes. The hawkers went to the other tables, trying to sell their tooled leather or their packets of pistachio nuts. Tadeus bought nylons, Japanese cameras, cigarettes, guns for all I knew, women, drugs, anything marketable. He always paid in cash, in dollars. He would take the roll of bills from his pocket, and it was always the exact amount, that is to say, exactly what he had decided to pay. There was no point in hoping for a penny more. He said himself that he never did anything for anybody, he wasn't interested in popularity. Strange character, Tadeus. Nobody ever saw him with a woman.

"The ugly ones I can do without. The pretty ones cost too much."

No vices either. Nothing. Not even an address. He'd arrive at the little café early in the morning in his pearl grey suit, his grey patent-leather shoes and his grey silk tie. His hair was grey too, and his eyes were like grey flints. Wonderful face. Sometimes I even envied him it; not that I had any reason to complain. The only thing I ever got from my mother which was any use to me was my looks. As for Tadeus, with that long scar running down one cheek, his narrow mouth and his colourless eyes, I didn't even know whether he was handsome. I wondered if women would go for him, and I asked Mily once. She hesitated, then said:

"He's a man."

I'd felt strangely humiliated, but all the same I couldn't help seeing what she meant.

Tadeus was on the level. He'd decided what he wanted to be, and that was what he was. He didn't boast about it and he didn't apologise either. He played one hand at a time. If he'd come to fetch a shipload of Chesterfields, he'd certainly never have brought along a pretty girl as passenger.

Well, we all have our own way of doing things, and after all it was Mily who'd got me the *Queenie* as well as the original capital for this cigarette business. She had useful contacts in Tangier and Marseilles and I could look forward to a steady income, travelling all around the Mediterranean. I only held one joker, which was my U.S. passport.

And that I also owed to my mother, incidentally. I believe in being grateful when it's due. She'd been smart enough to persuade a Detroit businessman that I was his son, and she'd even got him to pay for my education and upbringing. Though I changed schools no fewer than fourteen times, and usually lived in a boarding house at one or other of the spas and fashionable resorts scattered across Europe, it wasn't his fault. It was due to the social life, if I may so put it, that my mother lived. In any case I'd learned several languages with no trouble at all. This had come in most useful, in 1942, when I decided that I was sick of having no proper nationality. I volunteered for the American army and they gave me a job as interpreter. Without taking many risks I won an honourable discharge and a first-class passport.

But this passport did not immediately solve my problems, for America did not exactly take me to her bosom. I preferred to come back to Europe, because for me the Boulevard des Capucines, Piccadilly or the Gran Via spells home. And as it happened I managed to make out all right, with ups and downs naturally. Until I got in the cigarette game, which looked such a snip to start with.

Still, I couldn't hang about here all night, inhaling rancid peanut oil and thinking about my past. I lit one more cigarette and decided to go back on board. And then I heard, so close to me that I was startled, the uneven footsteps of the man with the wooden leg. He must be walking along a passage parallel to the one in which

I was standing, on the far side of a wall of packing cases. His wooden leg made a sound like the blows of a hammer in the damp silence of the night. For a moment he was caught in the crude light of a naked bulb, then he scuttled away like a rat into the dense shadow of a warehouse. There was something grotesque and pathetic about that hobbling figure. I'd thrown away my cigarette. I did not move, but I tried to follow him with my eyes. He must be walking on soft earth now, because I couldn't hear him. Then, suddenly, a piercing whistle broke the silence and almost at once I could hear the clop-clop of his wooden leg against stone paving. The two policemen had left their fire and were running after him. But the cripple had the lead on them.

He was hurrying clumsily along beside the white wall of the customs house. The lights along the waterfront cast his shadow, long, crooked and enormous, before him. He vanished behind the massive outline of a watercart which was moving slowly into a shed. The guards were blowing their whistles furiously, sharp noises uselessly piercing the nocturnal fog. The only echo was the stupid, impotent booming of the foghorn.

I hadn't stirred. I watched this strange game of cops and robbers, as though I were solely a spectator, as though it was something I was seeing on the movies. My sympathies were, I suppose, on the side of the fleeing man—because he was the quarry, I guess. And also because of that heavy wooden leg which he was dragging along with such obvious effort.

He must have run up against the steel fence, because now he was coming back towards me, having perhaps lost his way among the piles of cases and crates that made the docks a labyrinth. I didn't want to be seen, and I flattened myself against a pile of cement bags. Then I began to run, doubled-up and keeping in the shadows, towards the little jetty where the *Queenie* was tied up.

I had almost reached it when another man reared up out of the darkness in front of me. He was huge, a real giant, or so it seemed to me, perhaps because I was running crouched, or perhaps because he was so close. He staggered. His great body lurched wildly, crashing against the pile of sawn timber which formed one side of this alleyway. Then, with his head lowered, like a charging bull, he brushed past me, and collapsed two yards farther on. I took it he was drunk, or rather I had instinctively assumed he was drunk so as not to have to bother about him. But now that he lay groaning at my feet, terrible, low groans, I couldn't just go on and leave him there like that. I had to lean down, touch his shoulder, say something. It was then that I saw the handle of the knife sticking out of his back. The entire blade was buried in the flesh between his shoulders. Blood was pouring from the wound. . . .

I stood up and realised I was bathed in sweat. Over by the customs house the guards were still chasing the cripple, their whistles piercing the darkness.

"Listen . . ." gasped the man at my feet. "Listen to me. . . ."

I kneeled down beside him. He was panting. I scarcely dared touch him. And at that moment I saw Mily standing before me. She was in pyjamas and was staring at me stupidly. I was annoyed but also relieved that she was there.

"Go get a doctor. . . . Quick !"

She was trembling beneath her thin pyjamas, from fear rather than from cold. Her expression, as she looked at the wounded man, showed more disgust than pity.

"Who is he?"

I shrugged my shoulders. She said:

"Look out. You know we've got to be careful. Tadeus said . . ."

I seized her arm and shook her roughly.

"A doctor. You must get a doctor. . . ."

But the wounded man, with a terrible effort, had half risen.

"Too late for a doctor. . . . Not worth it."

Meanwhile the absurd game of cops and robbers went on, across the docks with their thousand hiding places. It was strange that the guards had so far received no reinforcements despite all the strident blowing of their whistles. From far away came the rumble of rolling stock, and on the landward side of the docks not a light was to be seen. All Naples seemed to be asleep, save only the man in flight and his pursuers, save only Mily and me and the man dying between us. Now I could see his face: his thick lips quivered horribly and his inky eyes seemed to search for mine.

Mily pressed her hand against her teeth and tried to stop trembling.

"Guy . . . the police. . . ."

The wounded man made yet another attempt to get up, but could not, collapsing heavily on the ground, face down. Mily, through chattering teeth, repeated stupidly:

"The police . . . look out . . . the police. . . ."

I was leaning over the wounded man, I could smell the odour of death, that thick mixture of sweat and blood. He gripped my wrist, and his hand was already cold.

"Not the police. . . ."

He groaned.

"I don't want to die . . . with the cops. . . ."

Blood gushed from his mouth. Blood had poured down between his coat and his shirt and now it was running out of his sleeve. I thought for a moment that I was going to be sick. I turned towards Mily again.

"We can't just leave him to bleed to death like that, on the ground. . . . We must . . ."

I would have been hard put to say what we must do.

Suddenly, on the far side of the little harbour where the yachts rode at anchor, a shot rang out. Then there was total silence, like a blanket. Even the dying man seemed to hold his breath. Now came the answer, a furious answer. There were three shots in rapid succession. I saw the clumsy silhouette of the cripple teetering high on a narrow bridge. He toppled and fell into the water with a dull smack.

"Was he the one who stabbed you? Don't worry. They got him."

It was the only consolation I could offer this poor man: the other man's death. He had raised his head again, and he might have been trying to smile.

"You're a good fellow. What's your name?"

I told him: "Van Stratten . . . Guy van Stratten. . . ."

He shook his head. My name meant nothing to him.

"I'm Bracco. You call me Marcel. That way I'll feel I'm dying among friends."

He pressed my hand, clung to it and now and then, as a spasm racked him, he would dig his fingers into mine. My feelings of nausea and disgust had almost gone.

"Steady, old man. Easy does it. I'm with you. . . ."

It was a stupid remark, but it did him good.

"It's awful. I think of all the friends I used to have. . . ."

He could hardly speak, yet he had to talk. I leaned down in order to catch his words. Mily had come closer too. She was more frightened of the encircling blackness than of the dying man.

"It had to be you . . . you I've never seen before. . . . You're a good fellow. . . ."

The blood gushing from his mouth made his words thick and hard to understand.

"I'm going to do something for you, I am going to . . ."

"That's okay, old man. . . . Don't fuss yourself. . . ."

I found my handkerchief and wiped his lips.

Police reinforcements had arrived at the wire fence around the docks. Two motorcycles with sidecars. Followed by a whole lorry-load of cops. Time to pull out!

Mily was trembling again.

"It's the police. . . . They're coming this way. Look!"

I could hear their boots on the paving stones and voices talking loudly in Italian. In minutes they'd be here.

Bracco said: "What do I care? There's nothing they can do to me now."

A flicker crossed his face which already seemed to be decomposing in death.

"I'm going to die," Bracco went on. "But not before . . . not before I've done something for you."

Why hadn't I simply left him to bleed to death between the two mounds of sawn planks? On board the *Queenie*, if I didn't make a sound, I might have had a faint hope of getting away with it. Whereas now . . . Mily had the shakes. Maybe they were catching.

"Bracco never forgets a pal."

Among the warehouses torches were flashing, pencils of light stabbing into dark corners. One almost reached as far as us. Mily was deadly pale, so that her lips looked black. Bracco went on mumbling stubbornly: "Got something for you."

"Forget it, old man."

He was beginning to get on my nerves too. The police had seen us. We were in the soup.

"Something better than money . . . much better. . . ."

Mily was on her knees, pressed up against me. The smell of her skin reached me through her pyjamas. I saw her firm little breasts, and their nipples thrust against the tight silk.

"The police!" she whispered once again.

Bracco drew me towards him. His breath was disgusting.

"A present for you, my boy. . . . Worth a fortune to you. . . ."

He can hardly have been conscious of what was happening about him. He clung to this one idea, as he clung to my hand. He half raised himself, his face distended with pain.

"Listen. . . . Listen carefully. . . ."

I glanced at the two policemen who were walking towards us. The beam of their torch picked out Mily's body, then her face, then the face of the dying man.

"It's Bracco," one of the policemen said.

He did not sound as though he were particularly surprised to find him there, dying, a knife between his shoulder-blades. The beam was turned on me.

"Who are you? What are you doing here?"

If I answered in good Italian, quite calmly, maybe I'd still have a chance . . . a tiny one, but still a chance. . . . If only Mily weren't here looking as though she was about to faint and obviously terrified.

"I happened to be passing by. I'm just a tourist. My boat is over there."

I'd done it all wrong, of course. I should have pretended not to understand and produced my American passport. That would have made me look much more innocent. Too late now.

The steely eyes of the policeman were fixed on mine. He saw how upset I was. I think he enjoyed what he saw.

"This kid's got nothing to do with it. . . ." Bracco tried to say.

The policeman was not interested. He said: "So you've got a boat, have you? I think we'll just have a quick look at this boat of yours. Come on."

In the soup. Ten thousand dollars' worth of fags on board. What would Tadeus say? He was expecting me at Tangier, without fail, on Wednesday next.

"Well, are you coming?"

I squeezed Bracco's sticky hand. I pushed off Mily.

"Stop here and wait for me."

If she came on board too she'd put her foot in it again somehow.

Not that there was anything to lose, as it happened. There's not much place to hide stuff in a little boat like the *Queenie*. And those bastards knew where to look.

"Just cigarettes? Nothing else? No snow?"

"I swear. . . ."

It was child's play. And I was acting like a kid. Tadeus would give his nasty one-sided smile, on the side without the scar. They'd go through the *Queenie* with a fine comb. Well, they wouldn't find anything except the cigarettes. But that was enough to put me in the lock-up.

"You're coming along with us."

The cop looked very pleased. And so he might. He'd got all the evidence against me he'd need.

I fetched myself a clean handkerchief, rubbed my face with eau de Cologne, brushed the hair back off my forehead. I didn't feel anything, either disgust or anger. I was simply tired, terribly tired.

I walked up the gangplank. The policeman was right on my heels. I saw Mily still kneeling beside Bracco. I said:

"You needn't worry the girl. . . . She had nothing to do with it."

The policeman said nothing.

Bracco was still talking. It was Mily's hand that he now clutched in his big, sticky one. His lips were very close to her ear. I saw the poor kid's face, nauseated, almost green. I thought she was about to pass out.

"Don't forget the name . . . his name . . . and the woman's too. . . ."

I wasn't sure if I'd heard correctly, but that was what it sounded like.

"What's that you're saying, Bracco?" the policeman asked. "Go on, talk!"

He too was leaning over the wounded man. But Bracco collapsed. His grip on Mily's hand loosened. He was dead.

The policemen were busy for a moment, dealing with the corpse. I took advantage of this to draw Mily aside quickly. She was icy cold, her expression haggard.

"What did he say to you? Tell me, quick. We've no time to lose."

She stared at me from sightless eyes. I shook her.

"What name did Bracco say? Tell me. . . ."

The policemen had satisfied themselves that he was in fact dead. Carefully they let the body fall back into the pool of blood. Nothing must be touched before the doctor arrived, and the homicide experts. Within a few seconds they'd have turned back to me.

"Mily . . . I beg you . . ."

She shrugged her shoulders:

"He didn't know what he was saying any more. . . . Poor devil. . . ."

She was probably quite right. All the same I insisted:

"But he gave you a name? What name?"

The police had finished with the body for the time being. They beckoned me to follow them. I just had time to catch Mily's answer.

"Arkadin," she said. "Gregory Arkadin."

CHAPTER TWO

No, Mily was not waiting for me by the prison gate, when I walked out through it three months later. In fact I had no earthly idea what had happened to her. She'd never written to me. Which hadn't hurt me, or even surprised me. That had been the agreement between us when she insisted on making the trip with the *Queenie*. I like sharing my pleasures with women, and they're all right in minor difficulties too, but not when things get really tough. Mily had everything to lose in sticking by me, and I had nothing to gain.

A girl like her, living from hand to mouth—everyone knew very well what she lived on, though it hadn't ever been written down in black and white—a girl moving from country to country, sometimes alone, sometimes not, depending on a whole heap of bureaucrats working more or less hand in glove with the police, from the consulates to the vice squads, she couldn't afford to have any sort of black mark against her name. I assumed they would have kept an eye on her for some time after my arrest. Then, since she'd apparently forgotten all about me—a chance meeting that had come to a bad end—they'd have dropped her. It was logical enough.

It was wise too, as I'd often said to myself when I was inside. All the same, now that I was out in the hard streets with nothing except a handful of crumpled lire I'd found in the pocket of my raincoat, I missed Mily. I missed her badly.

Of course I knew plenty of people in and about Naples. But I wasn't in any too great a hurry to look them up. Some of them worked for Tadeus, and I couldn't tell quite what sort of a reception I might expect from that quarter. I'd done three months and lost the *Queenie*. But they'd confiscated the cargo, which was a net loss to the boss.

So I went to see the head waiter at the Hotel Vesuvio and touched him for the price of a first-class ticket to Monte Carlo. He gave it to me willingly enough. He'd known me during some of my palmy periods, and when I was flush I never skimped the tips, knowing it was money well invested, a sort of insurance against bad times.

The Riviera was home to me. I'd grown up on that coast. I called the croupiers in the casinos by their first name, I could rely on the bar-tenders and the hotel porters, and many of the women who looked after the ladies' lavatories had once been friends of my mother's.

And as a last resort, there was always my mother herself, now living somewhat modestly in a tiny two-room flat at Beausoleil with Myrtle. Myrtle was an Englishwoman who, thirty years or so ago, had spent many a gay evening with my mother at Deauville or Lugano. Now they lived together, off bitter-sweet memories and the meagre earnings of laborious roulette 'systems'.

I knew that they went to the Casino as soon as it opened, the way businessmen go to their offices. So I looked in on them early one morning, and found them, their faded hair still in curlers, down-at-heel slippers on their feet, in cotton dressing-gowns. Their narrow rooms were crowded with pretentious ornaments and filled with the smell of turnips boiling on the gas-ring.

"You look well," my mother said.

I could hardly return the compliment. She had spent so many anxious hours in the shuttered halls of the casino, crouched over the roulette tables, that her complexion now seemed to reflect the green baize. One of her false teeth had lost its crown. I recalled the care with which she had had her original set made, by one of the finest dentists in New York. She had remarked to me at the time: "My smile, honey, is my fortune."

She still smiled, but it was a mechanical grimace which belied the perpetual anxiety of her eyes between lids reddened by cheap cosmetics. A small tear seemed ever on the verge of trickling from these eyes that were still childishly blue.

"At least you've got no worries, have you?"

It was a cry from the heart. She had seen my expression, which was one of pity for her. But being a rampant egoist, it had not occurred to her that one might feel sorrow for others. So she had immediately assumed what was in fact the truth: that I was in trouble and that I had come to her for help.

I reassured her with a smile. I knew my mother far too well to expect the least assistance from her, should she guess that I had just come out of a prison and had nowhere to hang my hat. Thank heavens, I've always been careful to make sure my clothes are smart. And having grown up among women determined to display their beauty at its best, I acquired at an early age the gift of wearing my last shirt, and spending my last thousand franc note, with the ease of a man who knows that there are plenty more where that came from.

I held out a packet of Chesterfields—which had cost me a small fortune. Infuriating—or comical, according to your point of view. I flirted with Myrtle whose English-style beauty—a complexion like a wild rose, with hair and eyes the colour of October leaves— had suffered even more from the ravages of time than had my mother's looks. I accepted their invitation to share their simple meal, filleted anchovies and a mass of re-heated vegetables. I adopted the cheerful manner of a dutiful son who gives up two hours of his valuable time to visiting his mother.

"No, I'm only passing through. I've got rather an interesting idea, which I think I can build up into something. . . ."

23

My mother never asked me any questions about my means of livelihood. She had told so many lies about her own that she had acquired the wisdom—reinforced by laziness—not to enquire too closely into those of others. She thus willingly accepted my apparent optimism and the external evidence of my prosperity without even wishing to know what basis these might have. I was glad of this. Had she made such enquiries, I should usually have been hard put to find an answer. My sources of income were usually, if not exactly crooked, at least somewhat special. They were fluid, often dependent on chance, on indiscretion, or even a sudden reticence.

And on this occasion how could I tell her that my plans for the future, for starting again from scratch, were founded simply upon a name? Even though it was a notorious name. Everyone had heard of Arkadin.

Yes, everybody had heard of him, but nobody knew much about him. Who was he? What sort of a man was he? The stories told about him were endless and legion; were they not produced by the fertile brains of those gossip columnists who must daily dish up a ration of rumours, jokes, slanders, insinuations, sly digs for the anonymous multitude concerning whom nobody ever bothers to write anything? It was known that Arkadin had a complex about cameras. There was the occasion when he had smashed one over the head of a photographer who had refused to take "no" for an answer, an incident which had caused Arkadin a certain amount of trouble with the Press. A large cheque made out to a journalists' charitable organisation had solved that little trouble. Since then the editors had given up testing their cub photographers by demanding a shot of the terrible Arkadin. They now sent them after Farouk instead.

In the absence of photographs, the newspapers had had to rely on caricatures of Arkadin. All the world knew his huge bulk, his square-cut beard, his bristly hair, his vast furcoats, his great, broad-brimmed hats, all the accessories which seemed specially chosen to emphasise, weighten and widen his massive figure.

His cutting epigrams were widely quoted. Long descriptions were published of his parties, some of which were remarkable for their splendour, while others were little better than squalid orgies. His love-affairs were a constant subject of speculation and discussion. It was all good copy. He frequently changed his soul-mate, or, more simply, acquired another. Large though his appetites might be, there was always plenty of new, even of untouched, flesh at his disposal. To be seen with Arkadin was one certain way of being written about in the newspapers. Furthermore, such liaisons always ended with a handsome present. What will a girl not do for a diamond clip, a white fox fur or even an astrakhan coat?

I had heard people talk of Arkadin in New York, London and Hamburg. I knew that he was deeply involved in all that is really big in big business. He had plantations in Brazil and in Borneo, mines in Alaska and South Africa, he owned oil wells, railways, power stations. He had fleets of fishing boats and of steamers, research laboratories—was he not financing experiments in interplanetary travel? He had schemes for fertilising the Sahara and for extracting food from deep-sea plants. He supported museums, mental homes, institutes for cancer research. He was everywhere, behind everything, or at least his name was. And that was all that was known about him, his name: in the bottom right-hand corner of a cheque, or at the foot of a contract.

And that was all I had, this name which everyone knew. That and the fact that it had been spoken—as a matter of great importance and with tremendous effort—by a dying man, three months ago, on a foggy night in the Naples docks.

"Something for you. . . . I don't forget my pals. It could be worth a fortune to you. . . ."

How many times during these past three months had I not examined and re-examined Bracco's words? Was he delirious, as Mily had thought? No. And even if he was . . . there must be a reason, a profound and deliberate reason, for the fact that this dying man had been preoccupied with one thing and one thing only—Arkadin.

But what connection could there possibly be between Bracco, a rather pathetic small-time crook who dealt in cocaine and women, and the tremendously powerful Gregory Arkadin? This was a problem to which I did not even possess a clue. In my prison cell I had passed the time by elaborating possible solutions, a harmless mental exercise. Now, however, I had to do something rather more positive. But what?

I had tried in vain to pull off one or two little deals in Rome, among the movie people. Nothing complicated or even particularly difficult. I knew plenty of people in that world, and it should have been easy enough for someone like me; but my heart wasn't in it. I couldn't stop thinking about Arkadin. And whenever I thought of him, I felt again the clammy darkness of that night on the Naples waterfront, I smelt the sticky smell of vegetable oil, I heard the useless whistles of the port police, the tap of the cripple's wooden leg, Bracco's death rattle.

And I saw Mily's hard nipples pressing against the silk of her pyjamas, I felt the familiar warmth of her body against mine, I wanted to find her again. Was it her that I desired? Or was it simply because she had lived through those minutes with me, because she too had heard Bracco's last words?

Finding Mily turned out to be easier than I had expected. I discovered that she was dancing at a night-club in Juan les Pins. Yes, she was a dancer. That was her alibi, and if nothing better turned up it was always a small source of income. Her principal act was posing, naked, with an enormous transparent balloon as her only prop. Since she was a wonderful shape, her act was usually well received, particularly towards three in the morning when the ice in the champagne buckets was getting pretty watery.

I'd got enough to stand myself a Scotch and soda in the joint.

Myrtle had lent me twenty thousand francs. The old thing had hit a lucky streak on the roulette wheel. Poor old lady. There'd been something between us once upon a time, when I was fifteen and she was . . . well, let's say twenty years younger than she is today. She'd never forgotten. Little acts of kindness of that sort are sound investments. All the girl-friends I've been able to oblige throughout my life have always kept a soft spot for me, a credit of affection on which to draw if need be, a sort of human collection of traveller's cheques. That's my private fortune. Not everyone can be a millionaire like Mr. Arkadin.

But on this particular evening my whisky and soda was eight hundred francs straight down the drain. Not a single familiar face in the joint. I had to waste a further five hundred on the porter in order to be told that my friend had gone to the party. What party? Why the party everyone was talking about all along the coast. I must have just arrived. . . . The party Mr. Arkadin was giving on board his yacht. He had been at Cannes for a week. Last night he'd come to this club, and had liked Mily's act. He paid a large amount of money so that she might break her contract and dance for his guests, on board.

I listened with an expression of disinterest. The porter was a talkative fellow. He went on and on about Mr. Arkadin, Mr. Arkadin's yacht, Mr. Arkadin's guests, the tremendous tip Mr. Arkadin had given him the night before. It's the size of the tip that always impresses them the most.

I felt humiliated and angry. Because of the distinction this jerk so clearly drew between the regal tip that Mr. Arkadin had given him and my wretched five hundred francs. And even more so because of Mily. Jealousy? Of course not. Nobody could be jealous about Mily. Annoyance rather that she should already have established a link with Arkadin. It had taken her three months, true enough, but still she was a long lap ahead of me. It was perhaps this twinge of irritation which made me make up my mind to unravel the mystery so sketchily outlined by Bracco. Mily's action

27

showed that she too had decided to take a gamble on this remote and tiny chance which Bracco had bequeathed to us.

I took the next bus to Cannes. It was an extraordinary co-incidence that Arkadin should be there of all places. Because Cannes was, in a way, my home town. La Croisette had been my play-pen.

I went first of all to the Jockey. Jennie was an old pal. Why not? I've nothing against women of that sort. I'm not scared of competition. Even though, when it had come to a struggle with Jennie, it was she who had won. It had all been about a little Aus-trian girl, pretty as they make them. Friedl belonged to me, but one night I'd brought her to the Jockey for a spin round and Jennie had made a dead set for her. Eventually I'd bowed out, gallantly enough. I'll try my hand at pretty well anything, but I've never cared for mixed grills. Jennie had been grateful. It had remained a link between us rather as though we were relations by marriage, brothers-in-law perhaps.

At the Jockey I didn't have to bother about the bill. It was a good observation post. One saw plenty of people there. Except tonight. Dead as mutton.

Jennie wasn't feeling talkative. She'd got the hump. And she wasn't getting any younger either for that matter. Beneath the hairline of her Eton crop, I saw that the skin on the back of her neck was wrinkled. Her white blouse was as well-tailored as ever, as well-laundered and well-pressed, but her narrow waist now had a desiccated look to it, her body was no longer firm so much as stiff.

Her club was gloomy beyond belief. No customers at all. By which I mean nobody in any way interesting. Parisians on holiday with the skin peeling from their red noses, one or two girls not sufficiently worth while for Arkadin to have mobilised them for his party, a couple of silent old Englishmen. Francis, the pianist, played on without trying to conceal his boredom. His pale brown fingers moved over the keys lethargically, now and then strumming out an unexpected melody or a sudden caprice, then suddenly stopping altogether. Anyhow, nobody was dancing. Nobody was listening. The mulatto threw back his pretty little head so that the gold dust glittered among his curls, closed his eyes as though enraptured by his own playing, but his thick lips were curled into a sneer. I never could stand Francis but I carried my glass across and stood by the piano. He always knew everything worth knowing, from Palm Beach to the Casino.

"He wanted me to go on board his yacht too. I told him to go to hell. I know what they're like, those little family parties. They last two, three days. Then up anchor and away. And every joint on the coast tells you thanks very much. . . . Me, I've got my regulars. Anyhow, I couldn't do a thing like that to Jennie."

He bullied Jennie, he tyrannised her with his swinish character, his laziness, his fancy ways. Sometimes he'd simply get up from his piano in the middle of the evening, with a full house, and walk out. Or else he would try the effect of his velvet eyes on some girl accompanied by a young man. Nasty little piece of work in fact.

All the same, I buttered him up:

"Quite right. One's got to remember one's position. That man must think he can get away with anything."

Francis sat with his pomaded hair on one side, humming a Chilean melody. Was there any point in my saying disagreeable things about Arkadin to this disgusting ill-tempered mulatto?

"Yes, he's a tough fellow, Arkadin. I agree with you. . . . All the same, there's one person he can't order about."

The fat fingers, with their violet fingernails, caressed the keys, gently, cruelly, like a cat. Francis licked his blotting-paper lips. I was wasting my time. He was going to tell me the story of how he'd given Mr. Arkadin his come-uppance.

"Someone who can give as good as she gets. Raina. . . ."

I'd emptied my glass again. I'd have to ask Jennie for another drink. Or maybe it would be better to move on somewhere else and see what I could find out.

"Raina? That's what he calls this famous yacht of his, isn't it?"

29

The mulatto was whistling now. I saw the bluish whites of his eyes, beneath the crêpe lids.

"It also happens to be the name of his daughter."

So he had a daughter, had he? That was interesting. How old? Eighteen, a bit on the young side. It was always trickier with the young ones, and riskier too. I specialised in the early thirties myself. Women who had lived a bit, who knew what they wanted, who appreciated certain delicacies, a certain skill. Eighteen. . . . Still, nowadays, there were eighteen-year-olds . . .

"The joke is, he wanted to bring her up in a convent. Won't let his daughter out of his sight."

"Is she on board too?"

"On board? Not on your life. She's never set foot on board the yacht. He's set her up in a villa, up in Super-Cannes. She sees her friends there . . . friends selected by her pop. . . . But she never goes out. Never alone, that is."

This girl was an altogether new aspect of the problem. Funny that nobody ever talked about her, at least not so far as I knew. It's true that I'd been out of touch with society gossip for the last three months, tucked away in a cell in Naples. I didn't want to show too much interest. Francis was canny.

I wandered about. In the lobby of the Carlton, at the Majestic bar, visiting a pub down by the waterfront—I found out what I wanted to know.

The sudden appearance of Raina in Arkadin's life had surprised everybody else just as much as it had surprised me. She'd been educated in Switzerland and then at an American finishing school. On her eighteenth birthday she had made her début, in the apartment which Arkadin rented by the year at the Waldorf. She had been with him ever since.

Everywhere they went a great fuss had been made of this girl who must eventually inherit one of the largest fortunes in the world. Miss Arkadin had bought dresses, furs, the most expensive headwear. But the only thing she really cared about was her car.

She drove it alone, and at a tremendous rate. In all other matters she apparently did as her father wished. But as for the car, he had to give way. He admired her stubbornness, anyhow. He'd rather see her driving at ninety-five, in full control of her nerves and her machine, than at the mercy of young fortune-hunters who clustered around her the way wasps cluster around a pot of honey.

Miss Arkadin was extremely well-guarded. All the same she struck me as the only loophole through which I could hope to reach her formidable papa. Mily had her secret weapons. Well, I had mine too. . . .

CHAPTER THREE

I HAD to admit that luck was on my side.

Two days later I was sitting in the bar of the Sporting, busily making a gin and tonic last as long as I could, despite the barman's cynical glances—or maybe I imagined those glances. Twenty thousand francs don't go far. But at least I'd found Mily. So I'd got somewhere to sleep.

She'd seemed overjoyed to see me again. She'd proved it too. Her warm and velvety skin was delightful as ever, and her familiar presence a comfort. At the same time there was almost a sort of tension between us. Things weren't as simple as they used to be. We liked each other, helped each other, were real pals, but nevertheless . . . It was the shadow of Arkadin.

In the first place she had almost no spare time. She'd come back at five or six in the morning, sleep a little, put on clean clothes and go back to the yacht, 'back to the job' as she put it, with a rather sour smile. On board the Raina the gaiety was permanent, and almost non-stop. There were about thirty guests, some of whom were always at the bar or dancing on deck to the gramophone. Drinks and snacks were brought around ceaselessly between the meals. In a small stateroom a perpetual poker game was in progress. Some of the guests never came ashore at all, simply dossing down on the foam rubber mattresses or taking cat-naps among the coils of rope on deck. The butler had to step over them as he carried round the early morning cups of tea or the last whisky to those who had not yet gone to bed.

Their host put in an appearance now and then, wandering from group to group, usually silent. He seemed almost a stranger in the midst of his own party, on board his own yacht. Conversations would fade away as he approached and despite the large number of guests—despite, too, their easy manners and varying degrees of intoxication—he seemed always face to face with his loneliness. A laugh, a wisecrack, a stale joke which was given more applause than it had deserved even when new, and then silence—the silence of school children when the teacher approaches and wants to know 'what all the fun's about'. Sometimes he would disappear for hours on end. Or else he'd call for drinks, strong, brutal drinks, neat whisky, vodka, kummel. He'd want music. He'd grab at the first girl he met, laughing, singing, slapping the women's behinds.

"That's when it's worst," said Mily. "Terribly sad, because it's obvious he isn't really having any fun at all."

I found it hard to envisage a brooding melancholy Arkadin. Nor was Mily's picture a convincing one.

"Do you see much of him?"

"Yes. No. That is, never alone."

He had paid the night-club at Juan les Pins. He had promised her twenty thousand francs a day. But he'd never asked her to do her dance. Or anything else for that matter. . . .

"Nothing. . . . He's never even touched my hand. I swear. . . ."

I shrugged my shoulders. Why did she insist so? It was rather to our disadvantage if he was really so uninterested in Mily. Still, she went back to the yacht, where nobody took any notice of her. I suggested she take me along too, but this she refused to do. There was a sailor permanently posted at the end of the gangplank. I saw her point. It would be too silly to be turned out as a gate-crasher. Mily would have to nurse this contact along on her own for whatever it was worth. Meanwhile I'd see what I could unearth elsewhere.

What I hoped to unearth was, of course, Arkadin's daughter.

Mily lent me her car, and I had money in my pocket. Enough, that is, to keep me going provided I was careful. Enough for three or four bars each evening. And now, on this second evening, at the Sporting . . .

She walked in with that self-assurance of girls who have always been rich, who have never been snubbed. That was the first quality I noticed about her, that and the way she moved like a swallow on the wing. Light, graceful, certain. She must have taken ballet lessons at some time. I'd heard that ballet was often included nowadays in a really super-de-luxe education for girls. It seemed that the doors opened on their own at her approach. Even before the barman nodded his head in her direction, I had noticed that it must be she.

It was a moment or two before I realised that she had an escort. The young man was too fair and too thin. He looked like a stick of celery, but a highly distinguished one. The barman leaned across his bar and whispered to me:

"The Marquis of Rutleigh. . . . Scottish nobility."

They were alone, which was contrary to the story I'd heard that she never went out unless her father or a whole group of upper-crust friends was with her. She looked as though she was used to paddling her own canoe. She chose the table, ordered pink champagne, told the waiter to move a lamp which displeased her. The young man did his best, but was always a few seconds too late: by the time he was ready to speak, she had already given the orders in her calm, imperious voice.

She had thrown back her stole, and the simplicity of her clothes was too complete not to be premeditated. Fantastically smart. On any other woman her little dress of raw silk, without any jewellery or other decoration, would probably have looked like nothing at all. But then on most other women it would almost

34

certainly not have come from Dior's workroom. I knew all about the importance of dressmakers, because I'd spent my childhood with a woman permanently torn between the necessity of possessing beautiful clothes and the difficulty of paying for them. But Raina seemed as though born with that dress on her back. One could not imagine her having to be fitted for it or even choosing it. Everything about her was inevitable. That was it, and that was the way it had to be. For example, if her eyebrows hadn't been slightly too heavy and slightly too dark, if her straight little nose hadn't ended in that slightly arrogant tilt, she would have been less pretty than she actually was. And she'd never have allowed that.

Pretty? I'd decided she was pretty before I'd really looked at her carefully. Usually I can gauge a woman's beauty the way an expert can judge the value of a picture, with a certain indulgence mixed with shrewd realism. I knew that a pretty leg—I mean really pretty, from hip to ankle—or the way a woman holds her head can compensate for a very great deal. I knew too that it's easy to exaggerate the importance of a pair of beautiful eyes or well-placed breasts. I'd learned as a child how much can be done by skilful make-up or a cleverly constructed brassière.

Usually, when looking at a woman, I would tot up the good points, cancel the bad ones against them, reach an average. Raina had deprived me, temporarily, of my critical sense. She had forced her looks upon me. Pretty? Not the right word, too cheap and too hackneyed. Mily was pretty. There were thousands and tens of thousands of pretty women. Raina was something else again.

Which was obvious. She was Arkadin's daughter. A thing like that gives tone to a girl. Eighteen years ago was her father so impressively rich? Probably not. People had only really begun to talk about him during the war. And rather vaguely at that. Raina had been born in Berlin, her mother dying in childbirth. Mily had told me this, and she had got it from a cabin boy on board the yacht. Funny that Arkadin should have been so devoted to the child, or had he arranged for her to be brought up far away and out of sight, with no paternal responsibility beyond that of signing the cheques, as my father had done with me?

In that case why all the jealous care with which he surrounded her nowadays? As an investment maybe? A pretty, marriageable girl who was also an heiress might, in certain circumstances, be a trump card to play in a business deal. Arkadin had no need for cards of that sort; wherever he was, whatever he did, he was always the one who called the trumps.

More likely he was simply frightened that his young daughter would fall for the first man who made eyes at her. It was hard to envisage Arkadin in the role of doting father-in-law, willingly paying his daughter's husband's debts. Or did he wish to choose Raina's future himself? A title perhaps? That would explain the presence of the pale little Scottish Lord.

Rutleigh, was that the name? Time I set to work. I wasn't here in order to admire Miss Arkadin from afar, I was supposed to get to know her. Thank heavens I was on the best of terms with the little girl who worked the switchboard at the Sporting. We'd even had a bit of a tumble together, two summers or so ago. She remembered the incident with pleasure, and so did I. Now she understood at once what I wanted her to do.

A page boy came across and told Lord Rutleigh that he was wanted on the telephone. Long distance from London. He looked annoyed, but got up and went out to the booth. He had asked Raina to excuse him. She seemed quite uninterested and gazed about the room with an expression that combined childish curiosity with disdain. The rich traveller observing the quaint habits of the natives. I wasn't the man to be put off by the attitude of the princess driving through the slums. I asked her, quite casually:

"Shall we dance?"

She raised her slightly heavy eyebrows, eyebrows which underlined each fleeting expression that crossed her face even as a pencil can underline the key words on a printed page. It was her turn now to be somewhat taken aback. She decided to cover it with a smile.

"I'm sorry, but I . . ."

She glanced towards Rutleigh's empty chair. I leaned a little closer to her.

"Don't worry about him. His call from London will keep him busy for quite a long time."

She arched her eyebrows a little higher.

"How do you know Bob's talking to London?"

I saw her close to, now. An expert can detect the brushwork of a master at a single glance, and has no need to examine the signature. Looking at the face of this unknown woman I saw beyond doubt that hers was a deep and complicated nature.

Raina Arkadin was proud, prickly, stubborn and distrustful. She was her father's daughter. She was accustomed to solitude, to living alone in the shadow of nurses, governesses, elderly tutors. But there remained in her a trace of childishness . . . of that childhood which she had never really had. Nobody can ever have played with her properly, no other child had been allowed to teach her what fun childish games can be.

I looked her straight in the face:

"I put the call through."

I thought she was going to burst out laughing, but she quickly controlled herself. She hesitated, and I must say that this hesitation took me by surprise. I went on quickly:

"Do you want to be stuffy, or shall we just skip that part and get on with the dancing?"

I was holding out my hand. I felt a certain dryness at the back of my throat, the way a poker player does when he doubles a big pot on a pair of tens. It works, sometimes. . . .

It worked this time. She decided to let herself laugh and, ignoring my proffered hand, got up and made her way between the tables to the edge of the dance floor. Only then did she turn and wait for me. Like Rutleigh, I was a fraction of a second too slow for her. I realised that this was her way of showing who was the boss. I hadn't been quite quick enough to stymie this one.

I foresaw a lot of fun, with this little girl. The future looked rosy enough.

How light she was! It wasn't just her narrow waist. Tightly though I held her against me, I couldn't feel the weight of her in my arms. It was like holding a little bird in one's hand, warm, silky —alive, but without weight, without reality. A kitten, or even a mouse, is a concrete object. With a bird it is fragility that you notice, a fragility that is also a declaration of freedom. No matter how tightly you hold a bird, it remains a stranger, it never belongs to you.

Calmly, without looking up, Raina had loosened my grip around her waist. There was at least a quarter of an inch of space between her body and mine. The hand I held was relaxed, impersonal, and I could not even feel her other hand on my shoulder. Her eyes continued to move about the room, with that somewhat irritating expression of patronising curiosity. Did she regard me, too, as part of the spectacle, something brought in for her amusement? All the same, she followed my steps obediently. Dancing with a woman who exactly understands and anticipates your every movement is itself a sort of intimacy, a sort of communion. A pleasure enjoyed together.

Raina loved dancing. She no longer held her proud little head quite so high. I saw her neck curve sensuously. Her cheek brushed mine. I looked into her eyes. They were sparkling.

Never have I studied a woman with such intensity nor so anxiously. This was my chance, probably my only chance, of getting at Arkadin, and if I missed it . . . Or would I have been precisely as interested if she'd had another surname, if she had been simply Raina? . . .

I held my breath. Women had told me that nothing is more ridiculous than a man who pants with emotion, like a dog. I was careful not to draw her body close to mine again, though I was beginning to be aware of her soft warmth under the silk dress. I thought it wiser not to talk, and in any case the band played one tune after the other, moving subtly from one rhythm to the next as good bands do, from tango to rumba to blues. This was all right, our bodies were learning to know each other, and she was relaxing like a swimmer on a cold day who gradually grows accustomed to the temperature of the pool. Something was being created between us, the unspoken complicity of shared and absolute pleasure.

I had almost forgotten that Rutleigh could not be permanently kept away by a false call from London. She had forgotten Bob's very existence.

The porter walked across the room, straight towards us.

"Mademoiselle Arkadin?"

She raised one dark eyebrow, in eloquent expression of her annoyance at being thus disturbed.

"Monsieur Arkadin says that it is getting late."

Her expression had changed. She was a little girl, though one who had surely never been scolded. It was not fear that I saw. But already she was as far away from me as if we had never met. She left me, even as she had dismissed Rutleigh twenty minutes ago. Her face betrayed a question which the porter answered before she had time to utter it.

"He's outside. He's waiting for Mademoiselle."

She went across to her table, and I followed like a spaniel. She picked up her bag, her fur.

"Thank you very much."

A completely impersonal phrase of gratitude. Thus might she thank a porter, a bar-tender, a policeman who holds up the traffic at a busy crossing. She walked towards the door without another glance in my direction. But I went on following her, though to do so now was probably useless and almost certainly tactless.

Luckily, in the hall, she almost bumped into Rutleigh, who was emerging from the telephone booth, his pale hair in disorder, his face flushed. He thought, silly fool that he was, that she had become

39

bored by his long absence, and he attempted to apologise, to explain the inexplicable mystery of this telephone call.

"I really can't understand it. . . . They told me three times that London was on the line. . . . And each time I was cut off. . . . There must be a typhoon in the Channel. . . ."

Was Raina listening? She was still walking towards the door, and hardly any slower than before. I drew back with calculated tact. I could hear every word they said and through the open door I could see the glistening bonnet of a Rolls Royce.

" . . . and you're off tomorrow!" said Bob in tones of tragic disappointment. "I wonder if there's any chance of meeting in Spain, before the party?"

She had regained that polite and worldly manner which she had no doubt been taught, but her whole attitude contradicted her words:

"Do try to come. I think it should be quite fun. Daddy thinks a lot of you, you know. . . ."

They were two yards away from where I was standing. Outside, the horn of the Rolls was tooted twice, softly. A curious summons, such as I had never before heard. Brief without being brutal. A melodious horn, gentle but insistent. I saw Raina raise her eyebrows.

Bob went on with the heavy-handed insistence of those who have made fools of themselves.

"I'd love to drive with you. It's such a lovely road."

"I like driving alone," Raina interrupted, and her tone showed slight impatience. "Anyhow, I'm planning to start at dawn. . . ."

He was being dismissed.

"Damn! That's a horrible time of day. . . ."

He tried to take her hand again, but she shook his off quite sharply.

"My father is outside. I'd sooner he didn't see us together."

And with that she was gone. His expression was hang-dog as he stumbled back towards the bar, so clumsily that he bumped into me. He was almost as tall as me, but colourless, feeble, nothing. Not the sort of rival to worry about.

I hadn't wasted my evening.

I knew that very early next morning Miss Arkadin would be driving, alone, to Spain.

CHAPTER FOUR

NEXT morning, at first light of course, I was on the Marseilles road, standing beside Mily's car, the bonnet of which was open. It was a childish trick, but there are occasions when subtlety is pointless. People do not ignore a driver in distress on a deserted stretch of road.

Raina drew up before she recognised me. When I walked across to her car she may well have been annoyed at being taken in so easily. At least she pretended to believe the yarn I now pitched her.

"I've got to be in Marseilles by noon. A big deal. . . ."

She did not bother to answer, but simply nodded towards the empty seat next to her own, and as soon as I'd climbed in she let out the clutch, still without speaking.

I had one hundred and fifty miles ahead of me, and I'd better make the most of it. It wasn't very easy. The Alfa Romeo had bucket seats, so we were not in physical contact. Also Raina concentrated entirely on her driving. Her eyes were fixed on the winding coast road. She drove at an insane speed, with careless ease, her body supple and relaxed, her head straight, exactly as she had danced the day before. But her little gloved hands must have been firm as steel.

I wouldn't have made much progress at this rate by the time she dropped me, with my suitcase, in the Canebière. How could I start a conversation, with a ninety-mile-an-hour wind blowing between us? She treated me exactly as she would have treated a little poodle or a parcel on the seat beside her.

All the same, it was a wonderful drive. The beaches were deserted, the water rippled against the red rocks, the pines, still damp with dew, exhaled an aromatic freshness.

I was worried. I'd left Mily penniless and with a touch of quinsy. She'd spent too long on the deck of the yacht, with one of Arkadin's secretaries, wearing only a thin evening dress. On the other hand, she had extracted a considerable amount of useful information from him for her pains. I now knew that Arkadin owned a castle in Catalonia, stuffed with treasures which incidentally he only enjoyed for one week in the year when he gave his annual ball at San Tirso. No one knew what this ball was supposed to celebrate, though it always took place at approximately the same date, a few days after the *fiesta* in the little village at the foot of the castle. There were hundreds of guests, international financiers and characters out of the *Almanac de Gotha*, important politicians rubbing shoulders with music-hall celebrities, and writers, famous painters and infamous ones, officers and officials from all the great capitals of the West, the cream of the diplomatic corps.

Nothing had ever persuaded Arkadin to cancel or even postpone his ball, neither private business nor public crisis nor even an intrigue. This would be the first one at which Raina was present.

Mily was already running a temperature when she proudly brought me this intelligence. She found me buckling the strap about my suitcase. When she learned that I was off to Spain, to San Tirso to be exact, she was bitterly disappointed and in her usual, somewhat basic fashion—her reactions were typically feminine—she rapidly transformed this slight to her pride into sexual jealousy. While she was compromising her reputation and wrecking her health on board Arkadin's yacht, I was happily flirting with his daughter on shore. And now I proposed setting out on an amorous escapade in Spain!

It was a bad start to the conversation. Particularly as I had only a few hours in which to calm Mily down and persuade her to advance me the funds I would need for this project of mine. It's no use running around with the daughter of a multi-millionaire if you haven't got enough cash to buy her a drink. I couldn't hope to scrape an invitation to the castle ball without a certain preliminary outlay.

I'd managed to deal with Mily. Raina was an altogether tougher proposition. The needle of the speedometer never sank below sixty. The sun lit up her face, smooth, bare, with a jade-like texture. Neither the bright Mediterranean light, nor the wind, nor the dust seemed to trouble those clear and steady eyes, though she did not wear an eye-shade or dark glasses. I tried to decide what colour precisely her eyes might be. Yesterday I'd thought they were the colour of tobacco. Today they seemed to be tinged with green. A strange girl. She didn't even paint her lips. From time to time I stole a glance at those lips, firm and plump, scarcely pinker than the skin of her cheeks now gilded by the rays of the morning sun. It occurred to me that I had never tasted lips without lipstick. Or else hot and bruised, the rouge washed away by a torrent of kisses. I tried to imagine how Raina's mouth might taste, pure and clear as the lips of a child. Or, who knows, passionate perhaps? Already experienced?

She whistled like a boy. Her hair was shorter than mine. Last night it had been black, now it seemed to me a warm brown with hidden reds when the wind blew its tresses apart. I hadn't been mistaken, yesterday. I can see through a woman's evening dress. This morning her sweater clung closely to adolescent breasts, her tight toreador's trousers outlined slim and nervous thighs. I was completely at a loss to know how I should begin with this strong-willed and disdainful young person, and my entire scheme struck me as quite ridiculous.

Luckily we had a puncture. High up in the mountains and miles from the nearest village. Raina, without swearing or even making a face, jumped out and calmly opened the tool chest. I let her set about the wheel, but it was almost red hot. She couldn't help giving a small cry of pain. I came across, without any exaggerated enthusiasm, without saying a word, and since I was wearing heavy motoring gloves I soon had the wheel off; I put on the spare, still in silence, and not even glancing at the girl. She stood behind me and I sensed that she was somewhat taken aback by my polite and competent silence. I felt that she was almost convinced that my car had in fact broken down, that I did have an important engagement. It was she who broke the silence, with a schoolgirl's laugh:

"It's lucky it happened this side of Marseilles. The only trouble about driving on one's own is changing a wheel way out in the country."

I screwed up the last nut. Careful, precise, totally preoccupied with this little job. She said:

"We'll still be in Marseilles by eleven. Will that be all right for you?"

I put the tools tidily away in their box, each in its proper place.

"Perfectly all right. Particularly as my business doesn't happen to be in Marseilles . . ."

I didn't look at her. I was busy rubbing the grease off my hands.

". . . but in Barcelona."

At last I'd finished. I stood in front of her, simply, without pride or humility, smiling, waiting for her answer. And none came. Presumably she couldn't find any words which seemed to her suitable. She stared at me for a long time—yes, her eyes were green, green as old bronze, green as the pine forests above us, where the summer sun cast flecks of gold and the trunks gleamed red in the shadows. I didn't hurry to resume my seat. I even dawdled a little, to keep her waiting.

And we set off again, faster even than before, through the forest of Bormes with its delicious scent of resin. We roared through Toulon in a cloud of white dust, now Marseilles was behind us, and the Nîmes road pale between the sea and the cypresses. Was she not thirsty? Or hungry? We sped through Montpellier.

She stopped the car on the road that winds between the Mediterranean and the marshes. Sète was behind us and Agde in front. Calmly, without bothering to hide among the yellow reeds, she stripped off her tight trousers and her sweater, and appeared in a black swimsuit, very simple, with an almost ridiculously high neck. And as she ran towards the sea she became once again a woman, modelled in firm wax but delicious to watch, her figure delicate and modest and astonishing as an Eve by Cranach. She swam and I stood on the shore, as stupid as a dog who sees the otter he has been chasing take to the water.

The heat was crushing, the countryside empty. I threw off my clothes and dived in. I caught up with her far out to sea. It was just as it had been yesterday, when we were dancing. We did not touch one another, but our gestures were completely attuned. We both tasted the delicious bitterness of the water, the waves caressed both our bodies. When our eyes met, she smiled. It was once again the secret complicity of pleasure shared.

At precisely the same moment we both turned inland, at precisely the same moment we stepped ashore. The sand was so hot that it stung. I threw myself down on it, was dry in a second and overwhelmed by irresistible sleepiness. Raina slept beside me, equally exhausted, and sleep made her younger: like a child, neither her eyes nor her mouth were completely closed, and I saw the moisture of her lips and eyelids. It was touching that she should lie there like that, delivered to my gaze. Trust or contempt? It was far too hot for me to bother my head with questions such as that.

When she opened her eyes I saw that their pupils were golden, the colour of topaz, and so bright, so big. She jumped to her feet.

"Lord, I'm hungry," she said.

Half an hour later we were eating bouillabaisse and mussels in a little restaurant I knew.

It was very late when we reached San Tirso. A stony, frozen moon lit up the many pot-holes in the road. Raina had let me take the wheel. Maybe she'd drunk a little too much of the Frontignan wine. She put her head on my shoulder and slept half the way. Now she was showing signs of nervousness. She kept glancing at her watch. I said:

"Somebody waiting for you?"

"Yes, my father. I'm frightened he'll be worried because I'm late."

For more than an hour we had been bumping over a shocking road. The engine was beginning to complain. Cliffs reared about us.

"It's always like that here," Raina explained. "The pass is narrow and stuffy."

I felt a bit worried myself. Why should I be anxious to arrive? Nobody was waiting for me. Not even a dog. Raina would leave me, would pass under her father's control again. Well, wasn't that exactly what I wanted? Wasn't it her father I was after?

At last the pass opened up, the headlights lit up a copse of chestnuts, and there was the castle, high upon its rocky pinnacle between two rushing streams. A real fairy-tale castle, with turrets and a winding road and ramparts draped in ivy. A fairy-tale, but not the one in which the princess marries the prince and lives happily ever after. This was the castle of the magician or the wicked ogre.

The moonlight picked out every detail of the rough stone, shimmered on the tiles that roofed the turrets, cast deep shadows across the gorges where we could hear the tumbling waters in the still and silent night. The village slept. Lights still burned in the castle.

Raina laid her hand on mine.

"Leave me now, please," she said.

It seemed to her perfectly natural that she abandon me in this sleepy village where I knew no one, in the middle of the night. She thought of nothing save her meeting with her father. She hardly bothered to answer my somewhat sour 'Good-night', before setting off up the steep road that led to the castle. I watched until the car disappeared through the massive gates of carved oak.

CHAPTER FIVE

ARLY next morning I was breakfasting at the inn beside the aqueduct. I had slept very badly. The *fonda* hadn't been too bad nor had I, as I feared, been eaten alive by bugs. But the din had been beyond belief. From first light a tremendous hubbub had begun in the paved courtyard on to which my bedroom windows opened. The shouting of the muleteers and the rumble of the carts had mingled with the smell of eggs fried in oil and of black olives. I realised that there must be a fair in San Tirso. There was no point in trying to get any more sleep. Besides, I had to organise my life.

The innkeeper was very busy, but the muleteers were a talkative lot. They were full of the procession which was to take place on the following Friday. As for the castle, the guests up there and the celebrated ball, that was all as remote to them as the man in the moon. All the same, in the bright morning sunlight, as last night under the moon, the frowning, feudal pile was omnipresent, crushing the countryside beneath its weight, dominating the little town in which one felt that there could be no corner so remote, no secret so well kept as not to be apparent to the powerful building up above: it overshadowed the little squares and alleyways, the courtyards, balconies and gardens. Was the castle beautiful? Or hideous? It was hard to say. It must have been haughtily majestic in the old days, when it was an ivy-covered ruin. Arkadin had bought it, restored it, decorated it. All in the best of taste and no detail was wrong. Yet somehow it was all wrong. Maybe one was too conscious of the vast amount of money which had been spent on it, and which contrasted so strongly with the rocky roughness of the countryside, the dilapidated little town, the simple poverty in which the people of San Tirso lived. They were not to be impressed by millions, nor by all Mr. Arkadin's power. They simply ignored him, with that superb pride which makes Spaniards only the more contemptuous of wealth the poorer they happen to be themselves.

The owner of the castle might summon to his remote mountain all the most important and famous people in the world. The muleteers stepped aside just enough to let the cars of his guests pass by. And at night down in the inn beneath the aqueduct, the men drank their jug of wine and talked of crops and cattle and women, their backs towards the castle.

It was a refreshing attitude. It reduced Arkadin's stature to almost human proportions. At least I thought so as I drank a glass with the parish priest and the blacksmith. But on second thoughts I realised that this total gulf between castle and village was not at all to my advantage. Because I was in the village, and Raina had not invited me to visit the castle.

There was no point in walking up the hill and ringing the doorbell. I'd be met with a volley of arrows. . . . Or rather with the answer that Miss Arkadin was busy. No point in contemplating a visit to her window. . . . It probably opened twenty yards above the roaring stream. Indeed, there was no hope of even approaching the castle without becoming enmeshed in the net of Arkadin's secretaries and guards. I knew from Mily that these latter were legion, some of them disguised as chiropodists or as court jesters, but all, to a greater or lesser degree, spies or bodyguards.

I might telephone. I could try it, hoping that a Spanish servant would answer. But Arkadin didn't employ any Spaniards up at the castle. He travelled with his entire staff, down to the humblest pantry-boy and garage hand.

So there was nothing for it except to wait. . . . Watching the sun revolving slowly around the arches of the aqueduct, listening to the braying of the donkeys and the songs of the children, drinking *anis* in the deep shadow thrown by a convent wall, munching olives for lack of anything better to do, when suddenly . . .

Yes, it was she. In a cotton dress and rope-soled shoes such as the peasants wore, her hands in her pockets, a leaf between her teeth, betraying not the faintest surprise.

"You're still here, are you?"

Had she really believed that I had a business appointment in Barcelona? Why had she come down to the village if not to find me? There was no sense in going into all that.

"I like this spot. I've been wanting to have a few days complete rest for a long time. This seemed a good chance, so I've taken it."

"The devil finds work for idle hands."

He found work for mine often enough, God knows. But her remark sounded completely innocent. Or did she distrust me? I had no idea what she thought of me.

She did not seem worried as we scrambled down the rocky path which led to the stream. Up above, the village was baking beneath an indigo-coloured sky, but down here it was like being in a cool cave and the air was almost misty from the water that leaped and twisted among the rocks. The sheer walls of the castle seemed even more remote, even more inaccessible.

"That's the place where San Tirso tried to jump out into space," said Raina, pointing at one of the chapel windows with a blade of grass she had been nibbling.

Her eyes had changed colour again. Maybe it was the shadow of the gorge where the ferns grew so thickly, or maybe it was the reflection of the water. In any case they were almost grey, the colour of agates.

"What did he want to do that for?"

Raina was lying on a flat rock which hung over the boiling torrent. Droplets sparked about her head, like a halo of tiny diamonds. Her throat was really exquisite. She gazed up at the castle as though it were nothing to do with her, and told me its legend.

San Tirso was a monk who had sinned greatly and who, doubting Divine Grace, had wished to throw himself down into this gorge. But Our Lady of Despair had caught him in her arms and had laid him, unhurt, upon the bank of the stream. Then she had said to him: "You tremble and are afraid because you have sinned against God. Yet you commit another sin, and that the most unpardonable of all, in doubting His mercy. You will spend the rest of your life in repentance, in regaining that mercy of which you had doubted." The monk had passed his life in repentance, had won Divine Mercy and died, at a very advanced age, in the odour of sanctity. This was the miracle which would be celebrated on Friday evening in the village that now bore the monk's name.

"You've never thought of jumping out of the window?"

She answered:

"Me? Why should I?"

But I was quite right. From where we were sitting Arkadin's castle did look like a prison fortress. Indeed, Maria Mancini had once been locked up in it for several months. Raina said: "Which served her right for being so stupid. She thought it amusing to be loved by a king, and she wanted to be as happy as a grocer's wife."

Raina was pitiless. Or maybe this was a warning addressed to me.

"I love the castle myself. It suits me. Of all Daddy's houses it's the one I like best. I feel sort of protected. . . ."

She let one of her arms hang down over the edge of the flat rock. The cotton dress was tight across her breasts, which were like little apples. Why should she want to feel protected?

"And then I love Spain. And the Spaniards. They're clean . . . hard . . . stern . . . fatalists. I love . . ."

What chance was there of her ever loving me? But was that what I was after?

As a matter of fact, by this time I was after nothing else. True, I might still try to fool myself. Each evening, in my room at the *fonda*, I might well draw up a sort of balance sheet of the day's achievements, noting with affected coldness the progress I thought I had made during the day. Raina came to find me every day. I never knew when to expect her, because she could never be sure when she'd be able to slip away.

"They haven't got much to do here. So they watch me. They imagine that Daddy would be grateful to them for spying on me."

'They' were the satellites, the Ogre's attendants. It was she who first called her father 'the Ogre', in a tone of mingled sarcasm and affection. Sometimes on our walks she would stop and search the skies, or give a sudden start at the sound of an aeroplane engine. Then she would interrupt whatever she was doing until she had located the plane, which she would then follow with her eyes until it was out of sight. Because it usually contained her father, going to Tangier or coming back, making a quick trip to London, but always so arranging these visits that he would be back at the castle in time for dinner with his daughter. They dined at the Spanish hour, of course, so that we could prolong our days together until the light became that extraordinary, shimmering radiance which occurs just before dusk in the summer in Spain. We had hired bicycles, and we bumped over the rutted roads, stopping for naps on mossy banks beneath the short and scanty shadows of the juniper trees. We wandered about the village, deciphering ancient inscriptions and drinking from the fountains, climbing up the old aqueduct where the brambles grew and the lizards lived.

"They built it without mortar or cement, and it's lasted two thousand years," said Raina.

Sometimes she was as serious as a schoolgirl.

"I love that. Something absolutely self-supporting. Kept up by its own equilibrium, its own weight, its own strength. . . . I love . . ."

It was a word she often used, and not gently, but with a passionate intensity. I loved hearing her say: 'I love'.

The days passed, slow and thick as olive oil, days filled with cries and songs, laughs and smells: the smell of apple fritters, of ripe apricots, of mule dung, of the barrels of Rioja unloaded outside the inn.

Though Raina was strong, firmly built and daring, she would occasionally take my hand when climbing over a pile of rocks or would jump down into my arms from a tree or a wall. Such physical contacts were, for her, without reserve or flirtation. I had never spent so much time alone with a woman without something happening between us. At times this worried me, but I felt strangely shy.

One day I talked about the forthcoming ball up at the castle. I assumed that so important a function must require feverish preparations, but from outside at least there was no sign of any such activity, and Raina seemed equally uninterested in her costume and in the guests.

"It's a masked ball, isn't it?" I asked in the most casual tone I could muster. "A domino would do, I suppose?"

She looked at me and her eyebrows shot up like a couple of little snakes.

"You . . . you're planning to come to it?"

We were munching the little cakes which we'd bought from the old man who sold sweetmeats in the square. Raina's lips were covered in sugar.

"Of course I am. . . . You want me to, don't you?"

Her small face looked worried, almost hostile.

"I don't send out the invitations."

Once again I felt as though I were walking a tight-rope. Suppose she asked me not to come to the ball? Perhaps I'd made a mistake in mentioning it at all.

"And I don't think you'll get one."

Was she scheming? Was she thinking how to outwit her father's control? Did she wish to construct an obstacle between us, ensure herself of a retreat into which I could not follow?

The blood-red sun tinged the white walls of the castle with a pinkish glow. Through the beautiful curved arch of stone under the aqueduct the eastern sky was the colour of mother-of-pearl. It was time Raina was going home.

"Beauty must get back to her castle before the sun sets. . . . That's the fairy-tale. . . . Or else the Beast will eat her. It seems strange though, that Beauty should take refuge in the Ogre's own castle."

Raina was clearly in a bad mood. She threw what was left of her cake on the ground and trod on it with the heel of her sandal.

"I must ask you," she said sharply, "not to talk to me in that way. Sentimentality doesn't suit you, or me either for that matter."

Contemptuous. Like my mother, like Tadeus. Too soft to be good, too soft to be wicked. As insipid as the cake she had thrown away and crumpled under foot. Raina loved granite, speed, Spanish harshness, her father.

Evening had fallen, Raina had gone, and the mountains seemed suddenly to have become great piles of cinders.

CHAPTER SIX

ON the following Friday I was wakened by a hullabaloo more violent even that that of market-day. All San Tirso was in the streets. The men were dragging leafy branches down from the mountain to decorate the walls. From the windows the women were hanging carpets and old, brightly-coloured counterpanes. Holy images, too, were brought out of doors, statues of saints, bleeding Christs, Saint Isidore in his workman's tunic, the Madonna with her seven-pierced heart, and of course countless reproductions of the local saint, falling straight as a candle down the castle wall with Our Lady of Despair hovering at his side.

Children carried baskets of rosemary, to be scattered over the cobbles which had been cleared of the vegetable peelings and mule dung in honour of the occasion. Little altars had been erected here and there, with many paper flowers and candles and much white linen. The inhabitants of some houses had even brought their mirrors out into the street. Faded and none too well silvered, instead of the dark and drab interiors to which they were accustomed, they now reflected the cheerful hubbub of the streets, occasionally catching and tossing out again an entire, blinding sunray.

I wandered idly through the gay tumult. I did not think there was much chance of my seeing Raina today. She had told me yesterday that her father's yacht had docked at Sitges and that the first of his guests had already arrived up at the castle. But she would certainly come down to watch the procession.

The day, all too short for the busy citizens of San Tirso, seemed very long to me. At last darkness came and the candles were lit. Their flames fluttered like yellow butterflies against the deep blueness of the night. With the darkness silence had fallen, and suddenly the streets were empty. I found myself alone with the garish images of saints and martyrs, and occasionally I was surprised to meet my own reflection, usually distorted and weirdly lit by candlelight in one or other of the mirrors. A thick and greasy smell was now mixed with the fresh aroma of the green branches and the delicate scent of scattered rosemary: it came from the oil lamps burning beneath the crucifixes, and it suddenly took me back vividly to that other night, in the Naples docks, the night that Bracco had died.

I saw the castle, high on its rocky pinnacle, its windows alight and its white walls glistening softly like a lantern in the darkness.

At last the bells began to ring frantically and the penitents poured out into the streets. In a matter of seconds they were crowded. I saw the headlights of several cars coming down the winding road from the castle. But it was already almost impossible to move, for solid ranks of pilgrims lined the route which the procession would follow, first to the church and then to the saint's own chapel built on the very spot where the hermit had died, deep in the woods.

The bells rang and rang, tolling a knell. The penitents formed two long files, unrecognisable and indistinguishable beneath their heavy robes and high capes. Each one carried a torch of resin, and they chanted as they went.

With difficulty I managed to push my way through the festive crowds, slipping down side alleys and climbing over barricades, until at last I reached the cemetery where I hoped to find Raina. The village was full of strangers, pilgrims come from all the surrounding countryside and also tourists who whispered together.

Some of these foreigners were presumably friends of Arkadin's. Why did I suddenly feel a tendency to panic? Simply because I couldn't find Raina? Or was it the funeral chantings, the monks' robes, the flickering torchlight which so depressed me? Or this smell of oil and the memories it evoked?

"Hullo!"

As usual she had taken me by surprise. She was standing beside me, slim as a pencil in her black dress. She wore a mantilla on her head. She took my hand.

"Raina. . . . At last. . . . I was frightened. I . . ."

"Sh!"

She made me keep silent. The procession almost touched us. From the monks' robes there came a heavy smell of mildew, sweat, saltpetre, the smell one associates with the crypt of a church. The men were barefoot, and the pebbles cut the feet which crushed the rosemary and the scattered petals. A rope belt was knotted about their waists. Some wore a wooden crucifix upon their chests.

Raina's expression was intense, her face very pale. All about us the crowd was praying. A woman sobbed and beat her breast. I attempted to shake off the feeling of discomfort that oppressed me. I said:

"Now's the time to examine one's conscience. . . ."

A glance from Raina silenced me again. I stood motionless, hemmed in by this crowd in its frenzy of contrition, with the strangely silent and attentive girl at my side. And suddenly, facing us and also lost in the weird crowd, I saw Mily.

She was obviously looking for me. But when she saw me her face, instead of relaxing, assumed an expression that I knew only too well. She had recognised Raina at my side.

It was again a lengthy business to reach the other side of the procession. The penitents streamed past, the spectacle grew more and more tragic. Many staggered under crucifixes made of two roughly hewn tree-trunks nailed together, while others dragged heavy chairs, and now and then one would strike himself and groan aloud.

I joined Mily at last.

"What's all this . . . this Ku Klux Klan stunt?" she asked in a raucous voice.

I drew her back into a dark corner.

"It's nothing. . . . Nothing to do with us. Penitents."

Mily did not know what this meant.

"They're repenting their sins. They're hoping for forgiveness."

Mily could not take her eyes from the strange spectacle. She kept on staring at the greasy yellow torches and the huge shadows that the men's capes cast on the walls.

"They must have sinned awful badly. . . ."

But suddenly she remembered my own wickedness and turned towards me angrily:

"Incidentally, I saw that little Arkadin girl with you. I can't imagine what you see in her. . . ."

It's curious how anger can distort a vulgar woman's face. Raina's features seemed unaffected by the emotions they expressed. Mily's jealous fury, on the other hand, quite destroyed her beauty.

"What's that girl got that I haven't got? Don't tell me. I know. A few million bucks."

I was afraid someone would hear. This was no time for half-measures. I drew Mily to me and put my arms around her.

"You fool. . . ."

And at once she melted like butter, burying her face against my chest and sobbing:

"Oh, Guy . . . if you knew, if you only knew."

I knew all right. And I didn't want to know. I stroked Mily's hair, as one strokes an animal to soothe it.

"Did you arrive with Arkadin?"

She was crying, with nerves, with love, with exhaustion.

"Yes. No. With his people . . . the others stopped at Sitges. But me, I wanted to see you. . . ."

The moans of the penitents grew more harrowing. The crowd replied with a long wail of lamentation. Was this the moment, as I had jokingly remarked a little earlier, to examine one's own conscience? To repent?

"Listen, Mily," I said sharply. "I think it would be better to drop it. . . ."

She had stopped crying.

"You see. . . . It's all so absurd. . . . And dangerous, too. . . . Let's forget it."

Mily's eyes had hardened, and I did not like the way she was staring at me.

"I see," she said at last.

She had moved away from me.

"You've worked out how to get your feet in the trough. . . . That nice big trough of Arkadin's. . . . Easy as pie. Simply a question of seducing the girl. Right?"

How could I make her understand? She was stupid, ignorant, impervious to all reasonable arguments. Not that there was much that was reasonable about this business, or at least nothing seemed so in this delirious night filled with the clanging of bells, the rattle of chains, the shouts of the penitents.

"But you listen to me, Guy. . . ."

From time to time her face was lit up by the glare of a passing torch.

"You watch out. . . . I'm warning you, just you watch out. . . . Or else I'll have a little word with Arkadin. Not about Bracco. . . . Not about this whole absurd racket, as you called it. But about something that will interest him much more, unless I'm mistaken. About you. . . ."

Suddenly I was face to face with an enemy. Funny. Still, I preferred it that way. It fitted the whole tragic set-up much better.

"You're threatening me, Mily?"

My voice was icily calm. For a moment she was shaken.

"I'm just warning you to stop running after that . . ."

I'd already turned away and was making my way back to Raina.

Both sides of the great church door stood open. The Host was being carried out amidst a brilliance of white candles. There was always a remission for the sins of man. So long as man did not despair of God's love. Love . . . Tirso had been forgiven. The penitents poured out, chanting the *Te Deum*. A great burst of fireworks lit up the mountainside. All was gaiety, and Raina, when at last I found her again, gripped my hand tightly in her little one and smiled at me.

Next day the village was enveloped in a happy exhaustion. The statues and the sacred images had gone back indoors, but the branches of greenery, now fading, still decorated the walls. The street cleaners were lazily brushing away the torn flowers and scattered leaves, spotted with burned resin. Raina and I walked happily through all this debris. She seemed to wish to forget her exaltation of the night before, of which she appeared to be somewhat ashamed. She adopted an easy, light-hearted manner, telling me a funny incident that had occurred up at the castle. A woman guest, infected by the spirit of repentance after seeing the procession, had decided that she absolutely must tell her husband that she had been unfaithful to him with his closest friend, who also happened to be staying up at the castle. The only way they managed to keep her quiet was by dropping two sleeping pills in her champagne.

"Which only goes to show you shouldn't pay too much attention to popular beliefs," Raina said with a laugh.

It was very hot and we went down to the cool shadows under the aqueduct. Raina was a little weary; there were shadows under her eyes, which made her appear softer, more womanly. Her lips were pale, without any make-up, which was the way I liked them to be.

"I must get back," she said, stretching. "One of the secretaries saw me go out. He'll be on my trail."

60

We were not far from the spot where Mily had declared war on me.

"What fun does your father get out of acting Othello to your Desdemona? I'd have thought he'd have other worries. He's worse than a jealous husband."

She was leaning against the warm stone of the aqueduct. Framed in the high arch I could see the castle.

"It's true. . . . If he had his way I'd never get married."

She raised her head.

"But after all, why should I get married?"

The question was directed at me, or so I thought. Was it a trap? I side-stepped it easily.

"Don't worry. I give you my word of honour I'll never ask for your hand in marriage."

She looked at me with that slight expression of distrust I knew so well, and then burst out laughing.

"Oh, Mr. van Stratten," she said in an affected tone. "This is so sudden . . . I don't know what to say. . . ."

And standing up straight she did a little pirouette, like a ballet dancer. Her skirt swirled about her hips, and I saw her elegant legs. She tripped over a pebble and fell on to my chest; it wasn't now, as it had been on that first evening, a body without weight and therefore untouchable. She pressed herself against me, warm and living, her breath somewhat rapid, her great amber-coloured eyes fixed on mine. The shadows beneath imparted a touch of pathos to those eyes. Her lips trembled. My God, this was love!

I held her tight, brutal and demanding. I kissed her lips frantically. Yes, they tasted good, those pale, fresh lips. And they were so hot. Docile, greedy, hotly demanding.

The sunshine poured down on us. I thought for a moment I was going to faint.

"Oh, Raina," I stammered. "Raina. . . ."

Her eyes were close to mine. Her eyelids fluttered.

This slim body against my own was mine to do with as I wished.

I had only to take it. After a moment she slipped easily from my embrace, out of my arms that had held her so tight.

"I would like . . . I would like. . . ." she said. And there was a challenge in her voice. A man says 'I want'.

But I saw that her eyes were still troubled.

I had completely forgotten Arkadin.

CHAPTER SEVEN

O N the Sunday night I went to the ball.

When I woke up that morning I found an invitation pushed under my door. A note was pinned to it: "A domino will do." Raina had not signed this, nor had she explained why the invitation bore the name of a certain Count Torregon. I've used quite a lot of names in my time, but I've never been so rash as to adopt a title. I wondered who Torregon might be. Not that it mattered very much compared to the fact that this piece of pasteboard would enable me to spend the evening with Raina. In Arkadin's castle.

So far as I was concerned Arkadin was now simply Raina's father. When I told Mily that I thought it better to drop the whole obscure and probably dangerous business of Bracco's legacy, I had been saying exactly what I thought. And I was glad I had taken this decision. It destroyed a barrier between Raina and myself. My feelings for her were now free of any motives of gain or self-interest. Free even of those motives which the mercenary Mily had thrown at my head. I did not suffer from those foolish delusions which Raina had ascribed to Maria Mancini. I didn't want to marry my beautiful heiress. I didn't want her money, all I wanted was her love. I wanted that so much that when I received Mily's note, shortly before going up to the castle, I simply crumpled it up and tossed it in the waste-paper basket. It said: "Guy, I beg you, don't see that girl again. Or else there's likely to be a tragedy. I'm warning you."

A postscript stated that she had not gone back to Sitges. She was waiting for me at the Hotel Fronton, at Vila Hermose. I knew the place, because I'd often been there with Raina.

I had no time to worry about Mily's troubles, or her threats. I knew that a woman will threaten quickly but will usually act slowly. I had seen my mother fake two suicides, one, incidentally, in order to persuade my father to pay for my education. I was therefore rather unresponsive to emotional blackmail.

So as I set off in a remarkably good humour, with a name not my own and disguised in my domino.

I've crossed many frontiers in my time but I do not remember ever having been as excited as I was when I crossed the imaginary line beyond which Raina had not previously allowed me to accompany her. All the other guests were in cars, and I felt rather like a poor relation as I climbed up the winding road. On the other hand, I thought with a smile, it was our host's own daughter who had arranged to smuggle me into his house.

In the entrance hall, lit by twenty torches held by footmen in livery, the first person I saw was Rutleigh. He was wearing a velvet cap on his blond head, and his thin calves were encased in white stockings. He was the centre of a group of idiots exactly like himself.

I stared at him, smiling slightly. He noticed me, remembered vaguely that he'd seen my face somewhere or other, and was all the more affable since, for obvious reasons, he could not recall my name.

"Hullo, old boy! Topping evening, what!"

Arm in arm we passed the major domo, who collected our invitation cards.

There was an immense crowd. Almost everyone was dressed as a character in one of Goya's pictures, for that was the theme of this

64

year's ball. The guests had not yet grown accustomed to their fancy dress and there was considerable shoving and pushing in front of the mirrors. The room was a mass of velvet, cloth of gold and delicately coloured silks. But I couldn't help noticing that some of the guests, with their boleros and their scarves, their wigs and their parasols, resembled the great painter's characters perhaps rather more closely than they might have wished. Beneath the social veneer I detected the outlines of selfishness, greed and envy, and I wondered what costume I would have selected had I had the time, and what I would have looked like in it. In any case it was safer to be in tails. A tailcoat is really a sort of uniform, so far as I am concerned, and one that suits me extremely well.

"Put on your mask," said Rutleigh. "It's compulsory after the second drawing room."

His was of red satin, with a ridiculously long nose. I put on mine. I had recognised Elsa Maxwell, disguised as Goya himself: her knee breeches and scarlet sash seemed in imminent danger of bursting asunder. The Begum looked lovely as the Duchess of Alba. Had I dressed up, I might have come as Godoy, the Queen's favourite. No. His character was distasteful. Rather one of those jolly boys flying kites or taking part in the sardine's funeral. But where was Raina?

I saw her talking to a loathsome old woman whose ashen complexion was accentuated by her grey scarf. But my sweetheart's face was glowing beneath a mantilla intertwined with peals and spikenard. Her petticoat was richly embroidered, her pink and silver skirt hooked up to reveal her legs which, in cream-coloured stockings, looked both rounder and more delicate than usual. Through the slits in her sky-blue satin mask, her eyes glittered like a wild creature's. I recognised the elaborate and beautiful costume: she was the young bride in *La Boda*.

"Long live the bride!" I whispered, as I passed close to her.

She smiled and soon joined me.

"I was waiting for you. Let's go in."

Two enormous men guarded the entrance to the ballroom, with heavy halberds crossed in front of the open doors. They were stripped to the waist, their torsoes oiled, and on their heads they wore Moorish turbans.

"A whim of the Ogre's," Raina explained with an apologetic smile.

The guests were goggling at the rippling muscles of the two giants.

"What am I supposed to do? Fight a duel with these two characters to the death?"

It wasn't quite as bad as that, but almost equally lethal. No guest was allowed to pass until he had drunk three large glasses of vodka.

"It's my father's idea, to get things going . . . these high society functions take such a long time starting. Usually people aren't in the right mood until it's just about time to go home."

I swallowed the first glass willingly enough. The second was a draft of liquid fire.

"It's rather a savage custom," Raina admitted. "But then he's a bit of a savage himself. It's his way of eliminating the weaklings."

I had drunk my third glass. I knew that my cheeks were glowing, and my head felt quite hollow. I glanced at the corsage of tuberoses trembling on Raina's breast.

"He should like you," she said. "At least I sincerely hope he will."

Now I was allowed through. The Moors had raised their halberds for me. Raina had turned back to greet her other guests.

I no longer felt the slightest desire to meet Gregory Arkadin. I wanted to dance with Raina. I wanted to lead her out on to one of the balconies. I wanted . . .

The collar of my domino suddenly tightened about my throat. Somebody had stepped on the trailing end of my cloak and I was caught as though I had been lassoed. I turned, expecting an

apology. The man kept his foot firmly on the end of my cloak, and
it was I who said:

"I beg your pardon."

Like me, he was wearing tails beneath a huge cloak, but his was
of heavy cloth with a triple tippet. There could be no question of
who he was despite the mask, despite the three-cornered hat. That
deliberate massiveness was quite unmistakable. I tried to think of
some polite phrase.

"Mister Ark—"

He interrupted me.

"This is a masked ball. No names, please."

He had taken his foot off my cloak, but had moved so that I was
more or less pinned against the corner of the door. The vodka seemed
to have paralysed my brain. Also I was horribly thirsty.

"I saw you talking to Raina," Arkadin began.

This was a situation which was quite new to me. The conversation with the girl's parents. It was essential for me to regain my
equanimity.

"You've been seeing a lot of her, lately."

There was no point in denying it. Anyhow, we hadn't been
meeting in secret.

"Yes. Almost every day. We met by chance. . . ."

"By chance?"

Arkadin's short sentences fell like the blows of a sledgehammer.
I had a splitting headache. The elimination of the weaklings. . . .
So far as Raina was concerned, I was no weakling.

"Well, a series of lucky accidents . . . not altogether unpre-
meditated. I . . ."

"You . . . and Rutleigh . . . and so many others."

He was completely motionless. A black and faceless mass. I saw
his celebrated square beard above the frill of his linen shirt.

"There are hundreds of you. . . . It's inevitable. . . . She's
rich. . . ."

Raina wanted me to make him like me. She can't have seriously believed he would. He was entirely hostile. Worse than that, he despised me. But I mustn't let him win the day as easily as this.

"Men who chase heiresses, you know how it is."

"Yes, of course. . . ."

How could I stand up to a man like Arkadin when everything seemed to be swimming before my eyes? Had he given me drugged vodka? Hardly. I'd seen the other guests swallowing the idiotic compulsory drinks with a laugh. And I knew how to drink, after all. But three vodkas, of that strength, on an empty stomach. . . .

He repeated my own words back to me, in a tone of insulting mockery.

"Yes, of course. . . . Of course you know."

They were dancing in the ballroom now. Raina circled past, on Rutleigh's arm. She had noticed us, and her face was turned in our direction. Arkadin saw this. He said: "Come this way."

He pushed open a door and led me down a corridor. We had left the part of the castle where the ball was being held. We went through a dressing room which though empty had an atmosphere of intimacy. A bedroom opened off it. It was huge, shadowy and silent. I saw a great fourposter bed beneath a lace canopy. Raina's scent enveloped me, and I almost felt her presence here.

"This is her room," said Arkadin.

He was standing on the threshold, looking at this room which managed to be both luxurious and simple. There were huge vases filled with hellebore and white roses.

"That is her bed."

He walked across to Raina's bed and beckoned me to follow. Her maid had already turned down the sheets, which were of satin, embroidered with her initials. On the pillow lay a yellow folder.

"She'll find it when she comes to bed," said Arkadin. "I put it there, because I want her to read it."

I felt as though a steel band was tightening about my brow. My temples throbbed painfully.

"You can read it now."

The bedside lamp shone softly beneath its parchment shade. I read the name inscribed in a round and flowing hand on the cover of the folder. It was my own. *Guy van Stratten.* And underneath, the words: *Confidential Report.*

I was beginning to understand, and at the same time I felt anger rising within me. The anger cleared my head. I was ready to fight.

"So what?" I said with a laugh.

Arkadin had picked up the folder and was thumbing through it. His fingers were square and spatulate.

"You're called van Stratten on the cover," he said, and his voice remained extremely calm, like that of a schoolmaster carefully explaining something to his pupils, "because that has been the latest alias you have chosen and also because that is the name by which Raina thinks she knows you. . . ."

"My father is Samuel Streeter," I said, adopting an equally casual tone of voice.

He shrugged his massive shoulders slightly, beneath the heavy triple cloak.

"Your father's identity has never been established with anything like complete certainty," he corrected me. "Let's say that Samuel Streeter accepted your paternity."

He held out the folder to me. It was open.

"Have a look at it. Read it. You'll see that it's a first-class job of reporting. Very easy to follow."

I saw names, dates, places. Everything was exactly correct, even down to the smallest details.

"Be so good as to put it back on the pillow, so that Raina will find it there after the party," said Arkadin.

"The party's over, Mr. Arkadin."

I threw the folder down on the pillow and tore off my mask. He removed his own, deliberately, and at last I saw his face. Broad, powerful, framed between his hair and his beard which was thick and carefully trimmed. His heavy eyelids half concealed his eyes, giving them an air of weariness, even of boredom.

"Who gave you this information about me, Mr. Arkadin?"

Once again that disdainful shrug of the shoulders.

"A firm of private detectives. A dull way of getting it, but a sure one. Also extremely expensive."

The monotonous quality of his voice, the insulting indifference of his manner, were intolerable.

"You may well wonder why I should waste so much money on a person as dingy and insignificant as yourself. Little more than a gigolo. . . . A very small-time crook. . . ."

The sweat on my forehead was icy. He was insulting me at his leisure, and I had no valid answer.

"But for me," Arkadin went on, and his voice was harsh now and menacing, "for me it was worth the trouble and expense. Because Raina is very important to me."

There was something on which I could not quite put my fingers in the way he said that. I felt that somehow he had nearly revealed to me the one chink in his armour of money, the one crack in the granite of his power.

"More important than anything else on earth."

Yes, a note of sadness, even perhaps of fear. Maybe he was a man, like me, after all. Once again I did not feel completely defenceless. I had weapons with which I could fight him, or at least hurt him. And yet those last words which he had uttered, which almost put him at my mercy, were pronounced in a way that touched my heart deeply. My childhood had been lonelier than that of a true orphan. My mother had always regarded me as a nuisance. My father, or at least the man who was presumed to be my father, had felt that his obligations towards me were completely fulfilled when he had signed a few cheques, when he had paid my school bills as another might answer an appeal for charity. Family feeling was a closed book to me. And Gregory Arkadin, this man who could do anything, or almost anything, had stooped to a trick which was unworthy of him in order to separate me from Raina, because Raina, to him, was more important than anything else on earth.

It happened that she was equally important to me, and I could not forgive her father, this blow which he had struck below the belt in order to knock me out once and for all. Nor could I forgive him the string of insults he had thrown at me so coolly. A bastard. Dingy. Small time-crook.

"How about you, Mr. Arkadin? What exactly are you? Would it surprise you if somebody were to say that another yellow folder existed, with your name on the cover?"

He had thought the game was over and appeared surprised by this belated come-back of mine. He was about to reply when another voice startled us both. It was Raina's.

"What are you doing in my bedroom, you two?"

She had opened the door silently and was standing close beside us. The lamplight caught on the pieces of jet sewn into her skirt. She was still flushed from dancing, she was acting the perfect hostess, pretending with a friendly smile that she had interrupted an amicable conversation between her father and me. But she saw the expression in our faces and she went slightly pale.

Arkadin picked up the folder and handed it to her, but without taking his eyes from mine.

"Would you please repeat what you just said?"

I remembered the horn of his car. His voice reminded me of it. Nothing unusual, yet absolutely determined. Almost inhumanly soft. Thus, I imagined, did savage priests chant their spells when carrying out some bloody rite. Neither spite, nor pity. Complete attention combined with a curious detachment.

Still with his eyes on mine he had ordered Raina with an imperious gesture to read the folder. I saw her turning the pages reluctantly.

Once again my anger enabled me to defend myself.

"Yes . . . yes, it's true . . . it's all true, Raina. . . . I've been mixed up in all sorts of things. . . . Currency deals, smuggling. . . . I've lived on women, done a bit of forgery. Three months in jail, and lucky it hasn't been more. Does all that make any difference to the . . . the way we feel about each other?"

She had put the folder down on the table. The roses at her breast and the flowers in her hair were already beginning to fade. She looked withdrawn and hurt, with the haughty silence of the woman whose costume she now wore.

"The bride is too beautiful," said Arkadin. "Too beautiful for you. Get out."

He was sending me away. He was within his rights to do so. This was his house. And his daughter. He was Arkadin. I was frantically miserable, furious, powerless as a boy who is being spanked, but who still wants to hurt the man who is punishing him, who tries to kick and scratch and spit.

"I'm not worth much, all right, I admit it. But how about you, Mister Gregory Arkadin. Have you nothing, really nothing, on your conscience? Nothing that would make you blush to think of Raina seeing it written down in black and white? How about a confidential report on your past . . . with no details left out. . . . How about Bracco, for instance?"

I threw this name at him as David threw the pebble at Goliath. He did not tremble. That imperturbable calm of his completely paralysed me. My headache was worse. I was afraid I was going to be sick.

"This is disgraceful," said Raina.

I saw her little nose quiver. It was the only indication of how angry she was. Her voice remained as calm and controlled as her father's.

A man who is being stoned to death can hardly feel the impact of the final rock. I was too badly hurt to react.

"He *is* disgraceful . . . that is what I had to show you."

I must go. Far away. Never see them again. Him or her. I walked towards the door.

"No," I heard Raina say. "It's disgraceful . . . what you have tried to do, Father. It's disgraceful what you have done."

I plunged into the masked crowd as into a hot and sticky sea. I pushed past the stupid Moors with their halberds. I ran out into the cold night, high on the mountain, alone with my anger and my grief. . . .

CHAPTER EIGHT

MILY was asleep when I forced my way into her rather wretched room at the Hotel Fronton. I can't think why I hadn't broken my neck on the bad Vila Hermosa road, particularly as I'd been almost running in the dark. Exhaustion had exasperated my rage.

She was frightened.

"Don't be scared . . . I won't touch you. Because if I did I'd probably wring your neck. Jailed for murder would make a pretty entry in the yellow folder, wouldn't it?"

A feeble light hung from the ceiling. I can't have been a pretty sight, my face running with sweat, covered with dust, scratched by branches. . . .

"What's the matter, Guy?" she stammered. "Are you drunk?"

She was crouching against the wall, at the far side of her bed. I was gasping with exhaustion. But I had to know:

"What did you tell Arkadin?"

"Arkadin?"

Mily was a liar like everybody else. But she was a bad actress and I saw that her astonishment was genuine.

"What did you tell him about me?"

She folded her pyjama jacket across her chest, shaking her head of chestnut hair.

"But Guy, I haven't even seen Arkadin since I arrived in Spain. He's been up at the castle, and I—"

I gripped her wrist roughly.

"You haven't seen him? Do you swear that . . .? How about your threats the other evening? And your letter. . . ."

She was beginning to snivel, as usual.

"I was so unhappy. . . . That girl. . . . You know how much I . . ."

I interrupted her: "Well, you've got what you wanted. She's through with me, that girl. I've lost her. I'll probably never see her again."

Mily threw her arms around my neck, crying:

"Oh, darling. I'm so happy. . . ."

But I pushed her away:

"You are, are you? It makes no difference. At least not so far as you're concerned. What I want to know is . . ."

What did I want to know? I'd come straight to Mily because I was certain she'd revenged herself by denouncing me. I was determined to make her admit it, and I planned to make her pay for her treachery. Fury, a longing to make somebody else suffer, somebody I would have at my mercy, that was what had driven me along the bad road at such a rate. If I'd stopped to think even for ten seconds I'd have realised that Mily simply hadn't had the time to see Arkadin and that even if she had somehow done so, Arkadin would not have had the time to prepare his horrible confidential report. Besides, the report contained incidents of which Mily knew nothing.

I collapsed heavily into a dusty armchair.

"Okay, you haven't seen Arkadin then. You haven't told him about me."

"Or about anything else. I went on board that yacht every day, as you know. That secretary I told you about, the one with spectacles, kept on making passes at me. Obviously I didn't discourage him too much, because if I had . . ."

I interrupted her impatiently:

"All right, I know all about that. So what?"

"So nothing. One evening four or five other girls and me were invited to go on a cruise round the Mediterranean. Of course I accepted. We left next morning. The others . . ."

"The others are at Sitges. You told me. And you . . ."

"I wanted to see you, Guy. I'd been thinking of you such a lot, and the last time I saw you. . . ."

I'd stopped listening. I tried to think. She'd got out of bed and was brushing my hair back off my forehead.

So Arkadin had told me the truth. He'd got a firm of detectives to check up on me. If you're prepared to spend enough money, those private eyes can do a pretty damn thorough job. But as I'd remarked to Mily a few minutes before, how he'd got his information didn't affect the situation in any way. Except that I was glad Mily hadn't played such a dirty trick on me after all. Because she was really the only friend I had in the whole wide world.

She was rubbing my forehead with eau de Cologne. She gave me a clean towel and a glass of water that had the earthy taste of alcarazas. She was, in fact, quietly re-establishing possession of me.

"And, Guy, that other name, I remembered what it was."

"What other name?"

It required an effort on my part to take in what she was saying:

"The other name that Bracco said . . . the woman's name. . . . It was Sophie."

She announced this with a certain triumph.

"Sophie? Sophie what?"

She was immediately deflated.

"Sophie . . . something or other . . . a foreign sort of name. I didn't hear it properly. I think it sounded kind of Russian."

I shrugged my shoulders:

"A lot of good that does us. You can't handle this alone. And me, I'm absolutely out so far as Ark—"

There was a knock at the door. We were probably making too much noise, so late at night in this one-eyed hotel.

76

"All right, all right," I shouted crossly.

But the knocking went on and I opened the door.

An old night porter, unshaven and bleary-eyed with sleep, said I was wanted on the telephone. It was absurd, but there was no use arguing with the moron. I followed him down a long, damp corridor till we reached an ancient telephone, the sort with a handle, screwed to the wall.

"Hullo. What do you want?"

The voice at the other end of the line was courteous and precise.

"Mr. van Stratten? Mr. Arkadin would like to speak to you."

I couldn't have misunderstood. But how the devil could Arkadin . . .

Still, it was his voice right enough that I now heard. He wasted no time on preliminaries and spoke with his usual crushing calmness:

"I've a mind to talk business with you."

What could he mean by that? Again my mouth went dry, and I could feel the beads of sweat forming on my forehead.

"I said I've a mind to talk business with you."

I had to say something. I swallowed awkwardly but at that moment I heard a distant click. Mr. Arkadin had rung off.

Mily had followed me down.

"What's the matter, Guy? What is it? . . ."

Mily had followed me down the corridor after hastily slipping on a house-coat. I was totally confused.

"It was Arkadin. . . . I don't understand at all. What did he mean?"

It was chilly in that dank corner. All the same it did not occur to us to go back to Mily's room. A cat we had awakened, as sad and grimy as the old night porter, rubbed itself against Mily's legs. She was awaiting some sort of explanation from me, or maybe a decision.

It was then that I heard the sound of the car outside. The front

77

door opened and a little man with a toothbrush moustache walked in. He touched the peak of his cap.

"Mr. van Stratten? If you are ready . . . the car is here. Mr. Arkadin is waiting."

All I could do was nervously, timidly squeeze Mily's hand, for she had taken mine. Then, without saying a word, I followed the toothbrush moustache out into darkness.

A glorious dawn was breaking over the castle. Its dark walls were tinged with pink, the roofs of the old village below shimmered like ancient gold, and the sky was as pure as on the day of the creation.

But the atmosphere inside the castle was still that of night, reinforced by the smell of guttering candles in the chandeliers, of lobsters and game pie, of the breaths of several hundred people who had spent these last few hours talking, dancing and drinking.

The drawing rooms and the ballroom were more or less empty. the floor was littered with paper hats, roses fallen from ladies' dresses, confetti. Arkadin was leaning against a huge chimneypiece, surrounded by the last dozen or so of his guests.

He saw me come in and waited till I'd walked across to the group by the fire. He was telling a story. The very old story of the frog and the scorpion. He held a glass in his right hand, and the butler was filling it with champagne.

"'I've got to cross the river,' the scorpion said to the frog. Give me a ride on your back.' But the frog knew all about the scorpion and refused. 'If I let you climb on my back, you'll sting me, and everyone knows it's fatal to be stung by a scorpion.'"

Had he looked at me when he said that? I did not think his eyes had moved, yet I had felt his glance cross my face with the swiftness of a lizard's tongue.

"'Don't be silly,' said the scorpion. 'If I sting you, you'll die, and if you die, I'll drown. That's logical, isn't it?' Because the scorpion is an intelligent beast, and therefore logical. The frog had

78

to admit it was and let the scorpion climb up on his back. But when they were half-way across the river . . . Suddenly . . ."

He had only raised one finger, the spatulate little finger of the hand holding the champagne glass, on which there glittered a heavy gold ring. His other hand was buried in his pocket.

". . . the frog felt an atrocious piercing pain. The scorpion had stung it. Its limbs became paralysed, and as it sank below the surface, taking the scorpion with it, it cried out with its dying breath: 'Is that logical?'"

The butler handed me a glass of champagne.

"'No,' said the scorpion, 'it's not. But what would you? I can't help it. It's my nature.'"

One or two of the guests laughed, nervous, sycophantic laughter. I felt that Arkadin was looking at me once again.

"Let us drink to those who, as Shakespeare had it, can to themselves be true . . . no matter what their nature may be," said Arkadin, raising his glass.

Was it a challenge directed at me? I drank the toast. The champagne was icy cold and so dry that it burned my throat. Arkadin had relapsed into silence, nobody else spoke, and the tiny flame of gaiety which had flickered among the guests about the fireplace was extinguished. Despite the insensitivity of these last revellers, even they realised that they were no longer wanted.

"If you would come this way, Sir."

It was the voice of a footman at my elbow. I put down my empty glass. He led me out on to one of the terraces and left me there. The morning was as radiantly clear as ever, but from the kitchen there arose a greasy smell of frying. Doubtless the exhausted staff, disdaining lobsters and tongues-in-aspic, were enjoying a dish of nice, thick tortillas. I was as conscious of the smell of oil these days as if I had been a pregnant woman.

Luckily Arkadin did not keep me waiting long. He led me out on to the ramparts. He was still in tails, but had got rid of his heavy cloak. He seemed to me even larger than before, overtopping me by a good head and a half, and so broad that we could not walk abreast. I had to follow behind, like a servant.

He did not speak, and I found nothing quite so nerve-racking as those heavy silences of his which he used with scientific deliberation for just that purpose.

"You said you wanted to talk business with me. What sort of business?"

Beneath our feet the stream was boiling over the rocks at the bottom of the steep castle wall. I've always had a bad head for heights.

"The only sort of business you know anything about, Mr. van Stratten."

He deliberately stressed the name which he knew was not my own.

"You said it might be possible to compose a confidential report about me . . . leaving out nothing. . . ."

Had I not been as stupid as the frog in his story, to let him lure me out on to the parapet of the castle in this fashion? Accidents are quick affairs. Of course I might, like the frog, drag him over the edge with me. But then he had obviously foreseen that . . . and it wouldn't stop him striking . . . like the scorpion. It was his nature.

Anyhow, if we spent much longer walking along this narrow ledge I would throw myself over the edge. My head was spinning. I had to close my eyes.

"Of course you yourself are already well informed concerning some of those . . . interesting details. . . ."

To regain my self-control I had to fix my eyes on that massive back which moved ahead of me like a black screen. I began to feel a return of confidence.

"Yes . . . some of them. . . . A man like me, who gets about . . ."

"And where exactly have you got to, Mr. van Stratten?"

Thank God we had reached a sort of platform. I leaned my back against the wall of a sentry tower.

"Among other places, to Naples."

I was feeling definitely better. The morning breeze dried the sweat which had been streaming down my neck. Arkadin was facing me now.

"And now to this castle of yours," I went on, with mounting self-assurance. "After all, it's not everyone who's invited to a private interview with the great Gregory Arkadin."

Had I succeeded, as I hoped, in injecting a note of sarcasm into my pronunciation of his name? I had to make the most of this temporary sensation of courage. I went on:

"Bracco is dead. . . . But before he died, he talked. He said something which you would not like to have generally known."

This was my masterstroke. I'd lunged, the sword had gone home. I watched for his reaction. There was none.

"But why did this man . . .? What did you say he was called?"

"Bracco," I said, loudly and angrily.

"Why didn't this Bracco come to see me?"

I was beginning to feel impatient again. No doubt that was a tactical trick of his, to irritate his opponent, to make him act or speak rashly.

"Bracco's dead. I already told you. He died three months ago in Naples. Murdered."

"By you?"

The question was asked in a gentle, slightly shocked voice. It made me laugh.

"Do I look like a murderer?"

Arkadin took a step towards me. His black suit, his beard, his appearance of patiently taking part in a conversation which he found tedious, all this made him look not unlike a priest. The shrewdness of his eyes, too, and the certainty of his judgments added to this effect:

"No, you don't. Because as it happens you're not a murderer, van Stratten. You're simply a fool."

The wind stirred his greying beard, but his face remained as immobile as though carved out of granite.

"I shan't try to buy your secret, because you have no secret to sell. All the same . . ."

Those eyes half hidden beneath their heavy lids, that unmoving hand so easily capable of violence. . . .

"All the same, I'm going to make you a proposition. I'm going to give you something to sell . . . and I'll buy it from you. At a good price."

Jackdaws were quarrelling about the castle turrets. The village huddled down below seemed as though buried beneath a layer of dust, ridiculous. Everything in fact appeared pitifully small in comparison with this black and grey giant who dwarfed the whole landscape.

"Come this way," he said.

Once again we passed along arched and draughty passages, through huge and echoing rooms where heavy pieces of dark furniture and sumptuous tapestries were lost between acres of polished parquet and high pointed ceilings. Occasionally a portrait would give me a cold, inscrutable glance as I passed by.

"You tried to impress me with a secret that doesn't exist. . . . In exchange I shall present you with one that does."

He was striding along now, and I had a hard time keeping up with him, but still he preserved his appearance of deliberate slowness.

"The great secret of my life, Mr. van Stratten."

He pushed open a door studded with huge nailheads, and we were in an office. It was modern and bare, the walls lined with metal filing cabinets. There were dictaphones, typewriters, calculating machines, a short-wave transmitter and receiver, but nothing that was not strictly functional. This room was in remarkable contrast to those ostentatious and useless apartments through which we had just come.

Arkadin sat down in a swivel chair, behind a bare table. Had he not been in evening dress, he was now the man whom I had imagined before ever I met him, a magnate seated behind a battery of telephones, among the files and graphs and equations which contained the latest secrets of the world's affairs. It was only this total absence of decorations, this complete austerity (for even the blinds were green, as in a post office or a public building), which gave the room its unique and personal quality: it was the deliberate bareness of a monk's cell or of an operating theatre. In this room, without any external distraction, to the muffled rhythm of the typewriters broken only by the ring of the telephone, Arkadin worshipped his god: Mammon.

He gestured me to take a chair opposite his own. He had suddenly become cordial.

"This is where my secretaries work. It is rather cluttered, forgive me, but we won't be interrupted while we talk."

He had taken a bottle of Spanish brandy and two glasses from a cupboard in his desk.

"Carlos Quinto. . . . Excellent stuff. Now then, where were we? . . . Oh yes, now tell me this . . ."

He had handed me one of the glasses filled with a golden liquid, as though he were anxious for my views as to its merits.

". . . if I had something to hide, what would it be likely to be, in your opinion?"

Was he making a fool of me? I might have thought so if I had not been convinced that he was not the sort of man to waste his time in such futilities. If he'd sent all the way to Mily's to find me, he had had a good reason for doing so. I'd soon learn what it was. Maybe after I'd left, he and Raina had had a violent quarrel. Maybe she'd insisted . . .

I mustn't let myself become carried away by this supposition, nor by the vivid heat of the brandy which I could feel pulsing through my veins. Perhaps Arkadin had sent for me in order to study me more carefully and at his leisure. Perhaps he was saying whatever came into his head, so as to observe my reactions. I'd have to watch my step, take it all as lightly as I could. The best course would probably be to imitate his mood of general friendliness and complete sincerity.

"Perhaps I don't know what exactly it is that you have to hide, Mister Arkadin, but it's obvious you have something . . ."

"Really?"

His manner was one of interest, as though he were listening to an intriguing story.

"Everything points that way. Take your hatred of photographers, for instance. . . ."

He was carefully warming his glass of brandy between the palms of his hands. He sniffed it and took a small sip. He said:

"Vodka has to be drunk in one. A virile, brutal drink. . . . Cossack's tipple. Brandy and port are civilised drinks, full of subtleties which must be savoured very, very carefully."

Then he said, suddenly:

"Van Stratten . . . how old do you think I am?"

It was so unexpected, despite the fact that our conversation was already extremely erratic, that I couldn't restrain a nervous laugh:

"What a question!"

He repeated it.

I said: "How on earth should I be able to tell?"

"I don't know. There you are, that's my secret. *I don't know how old I am.*"

He had leaned back in the chair which seemed almost too small for his great bulk. All of a sudden he looked tired, and old.

"You think I'm crazy, don't you?"

My passing feeling of well-being had vanished completely. I tried to recapture it, but without success. This man was full of devilish tricks.

"I assume you didn't have me brought here at six in the morning so as to ask me to guess your age."

He was gazing at me from under those heavy lids, taking my measure once again. And once again his tone changed, without any transition:

"Do you know what the Americans mean by an 'Intelligence check'?"

He put down his glass, his forearms rested on the table with the hands, palm down, towards me. They were huge, calm hands which did not need to fiddle with a paper clip or clasp a pencil. He said:

"Yes, it's a sort of investigation. And a remarkably thorough sort. They dig up everything, absolutely everything. Not just facts, but intentions and motives. They take the circumstances into account. And there's no sort of time limit either. It doesn't matter how long ago something happened. It doesn't matter what you may have done since. There's no cancelling out, no forgiveness. An event in a man's past remains for them as decisively important if it happened twenty years ago as if it happened yesterday. . . ."

He explained this carefully, once again, as though he were a painstaking teacher with a rather slow pupil.

"The reason being that the Americans have never digested Freud. Your longing for the breast as a baby influences your actions as an adult, and so on. . . . Now it happens . . ."

I was leaning back in my chair with a friendly, relaxed expression on my face. I too was enjoying my Carlos Quinto.

". . . that the Americans are thinking of building important air bases in Portugal."

So that was it. It was simple and obvious as this. He wanted to get the contract for the bases. He was afraid of the American security agents. What I had learned about him—and he did not yet know that I had in fact learned nothing—those others could also discover. By getting me on his side he'd be killing two birds with one stone. He'd be making sure that I held my tongue, and he could employ me to make equally sure that certain other people held theirs. Not bad, not at all bad. Though maybe a little too simple.

He listened carefully to what I had to say, and I watched his thick thumbs, which remained motionless as ever.

"What you've just said, Mr. van Stratten. . . . Are you asking me a question, or are you making me a proposition? . . ."

I refused to be put off by this. I said:

85

"I've been advancing a hypothesis, neither more nor less. But there's something I still don't understand. What makes you think you can trust me?"

A shadow of a smile crossed his lips. . . . Or perhaps I imagined it. It was hard to tell, because of that beard of his.

"I think that you will do what I tell you to do."

The brandy, and this latest turn to our conversation, had revived my feeling of annoyance.

"Another question: why?"

He waved one hand vaguely.

"We'll come to that later."

I banged my fist on the table.

"No, Mr. Arkadin. I want to know now."

He shot a brief glance at me, sharp and swift as the click of a camera. Yes, there was a definite half-smile there.

"You're a fool, van Stratten. But a . . . shrewd . . . fool. And me . . . I know how to pay handsomely."

So there we were. Undoubtedly some sort of a dirty job. I'd have to accept. It was the only way of maintaining some sort of contact with Arkadin, with Raina.

"Ten thousand dollars," Arkadin went on. "Tax free, naturally. Payable in gold, in Liechtenstein."

He spoke like a businessman clinching a run-of-the-mill deal. I interrupted:

"Let's make it twenty thousand."

He resumed his sarcastic superiority:

"As a businessman you're quite pathetic, van Stratten. You're trying to bargain without even knowing what it is you've got to sell."

My reaction was automatic. I was annoyed at my own annoyance as I said:

"What I don't know I can find out."

"Exactly."

He gave a brief and patronising laugh. How had I imagined I

could deal with him as with an equal? He was completely in charge of the conversation and was totally contemptuous of my childish outbursts.

"What I am willing to pay for, and pay for well, is your specialised knowledge of the international underworld."

I wanted to protest. He silenced me.

"You'll carry out an investigation and prepare me a full report. . . ."

I knew that I was beaten.

"A report on what?" I asked, almost humbly.

"On Gregory Arkadin."

He had drawn back his elbows, so his hands, still motionless, were now closer to his chest.

"On Gregory Arkadin and everything about him. I want you to investigate ME."

He seemed somewhat less in charge of the situation and I tried to take advantage of his temporary indecision. I said, in the tone of voice one uses to calm down hysterical women, the victims of road accidents and abusive drunks:

"Very well. You want me to investigate YOU. But tell me, quite between ourselves, what is it you're so afraid the Americans may find out about you?"

It was then and for the first time that Arkadin really looked me straight in the face. It was the first time I actually saw his eyes, eyes like Raina's only larger, more beautiful, of a subtlety and a depth that were truly disconcerting.

"Van Stratten. . . . On my mother's grave I swear to you . . . I'd give anything to be able to answer that question of yours."

His anxiety, even fear, was revealed by the tone in which he spoke, but even more so by those wide open eyes which seemed to fix on a point far, far away.

"I'm going to tell you a story. A strange little story."

The heavy lids had dropped, half hiding his gold-green pupils, giving his face once again its usual mask-like imperturbability.

"It's 1927. In Zürich. The depths of winter. Do you know Zürich? A terribly cold place in winter, particularly on the banks of the Limatt where the church steeples point at the sky like icicles upside down."

I listened enthralled and I felt that I had been infected by the almost superstitious fear which I had seen in his eyes a few minutes earlier.

"I can see myself now as I was on that particular night, walking through the snow, my ears frozen, my fingers numb, and alone. Entirely alone, a young man in a strange city with no idea where he is going."

He stopped and drew a long breath.

"My solitude was far more total than anything you could imagine, van Stratten. I walked through black and white streets, along the banks of the frozen river. I had no overcoat, only a jacket with a bulging billfold in the breast pocket. In the billfold were two hundred thousand Swiss francs."

He stopped again for a moment.

"Those two hundred thousand Swiss francs was the basis on which I subsequently built up my fortune. Well, I told you my little story would be a strange one."

He fell silent and I decided not to speak. I wanted to see what he would say next. He said nothing. At last my impatience overcame me and I spoke almost despite myself:

"Well?"

He looked as though I had awoken him from a dream.

"What do you mean—well?"

I was irritated at being caught out like this. I became aggressive:

"Well, go on! Tell me about her. . . . Because that's what you're working towards, isn't it? Who was she?"

Again I was becoming too excited. He shrugged his shoulders heavily.

"She? Who was she? You seem to have missed the point completely, van Stratten. The question is: Who am I?"

There was enmity between us again, the result on my part of an incredulity which was my only defence, on his of his desire to convince me.

"Okay, Mr. Arkadin. I give up. Who were you?"

He drew his hands back, a little closer to his chest. In self defence?

"That's exactly what it's all about. Who was I? What was I doing on this icy quay in my thin suit, with wet shoes. Where had I come from? What had I done before that winter's night of 1927?"

His greenish eyes were wide open now, and deeply troubled.

"That is the real secret, van Stratten. And you're the only human I have ever told it to. *I don't know who I am.*"

I couldn't take my eyes from his. This man who had every reason to distrust me, whom I had every reason to hate, and now all of a sudden I felt sorry for him. I pitied him, as I would have pitied him, automatically, had he told me he was suffering from cancer. Only this was worse, and far more mysterious. I murmured a few vague words, the sort of things one says to people with incurable diseases:

"Amnesia. . . . You're sure it was quite total? . . . You remember nothing? . . . Really nothing at all? . . ."

Suddenly I realised that there was something not quite right. I said:

"In which case, how do you know your name is Arkadin?"

Now it was his turn to be taken by surprise.

"Don't be a fool. I wouldn't forget my own name."

But he was being the fool. He fell silent.

"You say you don't know who you are, but you're quite certain your name is Gregory Arkadin. How? Perhaps that's the name of a cough mixture you'd been taking that winter before you lost your memory? Or the name of the man you'd killed and stolen those two hundred thousand Swiss francs from. . . ."

I'd thrown this out at random, to strengthen my hand. He took it without a murmur, gave me an even more searching look and asked in a voice that trembled slightly and yet was terribly calm:

"You really think that's how I got the money?"

I was already relenting my brutality:

"Or maybe you simply stole it. . . . Who can say?"

There were footsteps in the corridor outside. A glance from Arkadin silenced me.

I heard Raina's voice on the far side of the door.

"Is Guy in there?"

I did not move, silenced by the expression in Arkadin's eyes. The same foolish obedience with which the lion obeys the lion tamer, though the lion is far the stronger of the two.

"Raina, my child, you know I don't like to be disturbed when I'm working."

Impatiently she rattled the handle of the door. It was locked on the inside. I could see the key.

"I want to see Guy," Raina said. "He's come back here. I know he has."

All I had to do was to speak her name, to get up and turn the key in the lock. But I neither spoke nor moved.

"Mr. van Stratten has gone away, Raina."

His voice was now his usual one of masterful detachment.

"He told me he was leaving Spain. I don't think you'll ever see him again."

Raina's hand must have closed tightly over the doorknob. She was clutching at one last hope, I supposed. Then she let go of the knob. For a moment or two she went on standing outside the door, waiting—waiting desperately. At last we heard her footsteps move away.

Arkadin now had sufficient proof of my submission to his will. We discussed the details of our arrangement. He was practical and precise.

"This will be enough for you to get on with, I think. Get in touch with my secretaries for your running expenses. Don't worry about costs. I want results and I want them fast."

I put the banknotes in my pocket, and got my final orders.

"Incidentally," said Arkadin at last. "It's obvious—and I see you've realised it yourself—that Raina must have no idea of the deal between us. You'll see to it that you never meet her again."

He was insistent, and I didn't argue.

"Above all she must never have an inkling of the nature of the . . . little job you're doing for me. Or she might imagine that I thought it up simply to keep you away from her. . . ."

A last flicker of anger and resentment made me snap at him:

"Isn't that precisely what you're doing?"

He ignored this.

"I misjudged you to begin with. I thought you were a black-mailer."

His lips parted in a disdainful smile. I noticed those lips now. They were thick, sensual and red as a woman's. Like Raina's lips that needed no rouge.

Arkadin had refilled his glass to the rim with brandy. He got up and I knew I was being dismissed.

"Don't forget what Shakespeare wrote, Mr. van Stratten . . . to thine own self be true."

That was how I came to sell my soul.

Book Two

Sophie

CHAPTER ONE

I COULD not attempt to give all the details of that crazy investigation which I carried out to try to pick up the lost threads of Gregory Arkadin's life, all the minute shreds of evidence, the way money talked. It would be long and tedious, almost as discouraging to read about as it was to live through.

I started from Zürich, certainly, but it was a childishly symbolic idea, as Arkadin had given me nothing to go on but a date, and a vague one at that, and a picture in my mind of shivering solitude on a snow-covered quayside.

I re-established contact with twenty or more dubious characters, run across by chance in the course of my chequered career: I loaded them with whisky, made various proposals to them, with the sole object of bringing into the conversation at a certain moment the name of Arkadin. But it was too well known a name to evoke any reminiscences which were of the slightest use to me. The noise of it smothered the dead echoes of a past nearly thirty years old. Arkadin. . . . Everybody had some story to tell about Arkadin. How he had sold armaments to the Chinese of both sides; guns without ammunition, torpedoes without fuses. But that was run-of-the-mill stuff. So many others had done as much. How he had feathered his nest in Ethiopia, building roads for the Fascists with sweated labour; how the natives were tricked, the water polluted, the food contaminated so that an epidemic broke out. The same accusations are made against all big contractors. And the money he'd taken from the Nazis, promising to invest it for them in South America. No more was seen or heard of it. There weren't even any receipts. But could you blame him for that? There's no sin in deceiving scum like that.

All these stories, I knew them by heart. They were of no interest to anyone, least of all to me, because they concerned the Arkadin of today. Even my best informed contacts knew nothing of the Arkadin of the past, who was not yet in a position to sell dud munitions to the Chinese, to build bad roads for the Fascists, nor to inspire confidence in rich Nazis.

I changed my tactics. From the starting-point of Zürich and the year 1927, I was up against a blank wall. As a jumping-off place I had to get some solid, concrete basis. To find the Arkadin of the past, I must first get a line on the Arkadin of the present, and not rely for my information on talk picked up in bistros, or in the newspapers. Investigate Arkadin in his normal surroundings. Have him judged by his equals. I was quite aware that the pillars of high finance were unlikely to lean my way, that buried secrets were fiercely guarded with that scrupulous care which protects great families from their indiscretions. But I thought that there at least I would escape idle babbling, easy calumnies. If I could only retrace, with sure steps, the career of Arkadin, it would lead me inevitably to his beginnings. It was the easiest way to get back to Zürich, and perhaps beyond it.

My contacts in the higher spheres of finance were less extensive than in those of the movies, the demi-monde, the smuggling racket and de-throned royalties. In order to penetrate into this world I had to get myself a false identity. I succeeded with an assignment from an American magazine to investigate the "big money" men and women in Europe. I started on a series of interviews which I conducted conscientiously, and which, sandpapered by an impoverished young writer, were published with some success. These enabled me to present myself to Sir Joseph, whom I had kept as my trump card. Sir Joseph, almost as rich as Arkadin, if not more so, knighted for services rendered to the Crown during the last war, was quite a mysterious character himself. A Levantine, or of some other obscure origin, he had not reached the key position which he occupied in 1940 without having been mixed up in a few intrigues. On more than one occasion he had found himself up against Arkadin and I found out that they hated each other. Or rather that Sir Joseph had never let pass an opportunity of delivering ferocious, if pompous, judgments on Arkadin. The latter, to my knowledge, had never bothered to reply to them. He had the last word in the end. Sir Joseph, crippled by a stroke which attacked him on the floor of the London Stock Exchange, lived in Switzerland, semi-paralysed, and, some people said, already in his dotage.

His enforced retirement and the slackening of his intellectual faculties would make my job easier. Living alone, retired from the world, Sir Joseph would be flattered by my visit, which would give him back some of his importance as one of the great financial bosses. I was counting on his senile vanity to make him more inclined to talk. As it turned out, I was wasting my time and money.

I spent almost a week in a lost village in the Engadine, insensitive to the beauty of a lake fringed by dark pine-trees, exchanging circumstantial notes, by messenger, with Sir Joseph, in which I had to explain the object of my enquiry, ask the prearranged questions and give the replies made by other personalities already interviewed. Finally I was told he would receive me at Belvedere, which was his home. But I only met a secretary. Pretty, but glacial, protected by her tortoise-shell glasses and of undoubted efficiency. She read me the long reply to my questionnaire which Sir Joseph had dictated "out of respect for the magazine I represented and in spite of his bad state of health." I had to swallow the views and suggestions of the old fool on important present-day economic problems. There was a lot of wordy nonsense and a frequent tendency to leave the subject and start lashing out into vindictive comments, which gave me some grounds for hope. In this I was to be disappointed. When asked to comment on certain of his fellow-financiers, Sir Joseph, prolix, and ready to preach about everything concerning Onassis and the late Gulbenkian, contented himself with flaying Arkadin in the following terms: "One of the shrewdest of all adventurers in high finance, and certainly the most un-scrupulous is Mr. Arkadin. In another epoch such a man might have sacked Rome or been hanged as a pirate. But today we must accept him for what he is—a phenomenon of an age of dissolution and crisis."

I listened patiently to this diatribe, into which the severe-looking secretary put a note of personal conviction. I waited for her to continue:

"As to his place of origin, and the source of his first capital—the most painstaking personal investigation has shown that these are quite impossible to trace; no reliable evidence could be collected."

The secretary gave me the typed copy of his statement, and I was able to study the contents—which were disappointing, alas!—in the funicular railway which took me down again from the heights where the dying old eagle had his eyrie.

"The most painstaking personal investigation." There was all the frustration of a self-made man who had been taunted so much about his origins. He had tried to attack Arkadin with the weapons by which he himself had been hurt so often. But he hadn't been able to get beyond that "no reliable evidence could be collected." Here was no news-hungry journalist, quite satisfied with rumour, more especially because it is more sensational. Cold, calculating, clear-headed, Sir Joseph had collected all the bits of gossip spread around about his enemy, had rejected them one after the other. No foundation. The way he stated with a childish despair: "Nothing satisfactory." He certainly ought to have been pleased by one or other of these tit-bits, when the haul was so meagre. But he affirmed that he had drawn a complete blank.

What hope did I have? I chewed it all over, slumped down in my seat by the frozen window-pane, and felt about as lonesome and chilly as Arkadin in the winter of 1927. . . .

Finally, after a long, expensive and useless detour, I went back to that point. Zürich was not far away. I returned there, for want of anything better to do, out of stubbornness and because I didn't know where to go any more, like Arkadin.

I found the quayside again. The snow there was hard as granite. The sea-gulls were mewing, scavenging for food. The people were hurrying past, their coat-collars turned up, well protected with scarves and woollen gloves, and with ear-flaps of cloth or otter-skin. I went on repeating to myself, like an incantation, the words of Arkadin. ". . . in my thin suit and my wet shoes. . . ." Didn't he have an overcoat? I took mine off, and deposited it in a café, to the amazement of the cashier. I went out again, my ears frozen, my fingers stiff with cold. Superstitiously, I had put in my bill-fold two thousand Swiss francs in small change. I was going to be as like Arkadin as possible and, I stopped for a moment, in 1927 he must have been just about my age.

I went all along the quayside, tortured with cold which made me gasp for breath and there wasn't any doubt that my major pre-occupation, despite the mental effort I tried to bring to bear on my problem, was the need to get myself warm.

A hot drink and an overcoat. That's what I needed, before anything else. And it certainly must have been that way with Arkadin. Desperate as the cold must have made him, he would have attended to the most urgent matter first. He had money. He had to have some more clothing. In the first place, so as not to freeze up with cold, and also so as not to attract attention to himself. Consequently, he would go into the first tailor's shop that he saw.

I followed the quay along as he had done, shivering as he did, looking for a shop, just as he had looked. Fate ordained that I should find one—the same one. . . .

CHAPTER TWO

FROM Zürich, I went on to Copenhagen. My first success, flimsy though it was, made me dizzy. I saw it as an encouraging omen. After those months of sterile marking-time, fate at last was favouring me. Otherwise I should never have found that old tailor. I should never have known that Arkadin was Polish, or at least that he came from Warsaw.

The old man remembered quite well having noticed the label sewn into the jacket pocket. He was not then the owner of the shop, but a cutter. The man who had come in without an overcoat had wanted to buy and have let out for him an enormous pelisse which was in the shop, and which they had given up hope of selling. The salesman had offered him other, more elegant models. But the customer stuck to his pelisse. While the necessary alterations were being made—for he was very big, very wide in the shoulders, a fine figure of a man—he sat near the porcelain stove. He seemed tired. The salesman had insisted on selling him a suit as well, for the one he was wearing was old and dirty, and in the end he agreed. That's how it was that the cutter managed to read the label. He was glad to be able to get confirmation of his perspicacity. Owing to the obstinate insistence of the stranger on having a pelisse, and from his accent, the cutter recognised the man as a Russian. "Or a Pole perhaps, it's the same thing, if that's the way you want it."

I was too excited to discuss this legal point. I was basking in the luxury of a vast cashmere overcoat. "You were frozen, too, weren't you? You're not going to take a pelisse, like he did. You've done better. You know they call these coats like yours 'gentlemen's mink'."

He laughed at this sally, as he must have laughed, all by himself, at the label in the pocket of the Pole with the pelisse. The man who was Arkadin. Who couldn't be anybody else but Arkadin.

"And you say this happened more than twenty years ago? Your memory is good. . . ."

He bridled: "As to that, sir . . . I know the measurements of all my customers. And when I say more than twenty years. . . . Wait a minute. It was in 1927. I remember. Because it was a colder winter than normal that year. And I remember saying one evening: 'Pity the Pole has taken the pelisse. . . . I could have done with it myself.'"

So, Arkadin came from Warsaw. I couldn't go there to trace his history but that wasn't very serious. They say today that Poles are everywhere, except in Poland. I knew a bit about them, and in different spheres of life, in different countries. I hardly hesitated a moment. I knew where to find the Professor.

In Copenhagen it was nearly as cold as in Zürich. The winter had come early that year. The amusement park was half empty. Most of the stalls were closed. Lena, the headless woman, and Hortense, half-Venus, half-monster, were warming themselves and drinking something hot in their caravans. Marco, the king of the jungle and his Bengal tigers had been put under cover, also the fakir's sacred cobras. But the professor's trained animals were tougher.

The 'Greatest Flea Circus on Earth' occupied a modest corner, behind the chocolate machines.

The Professor must have been kind of sour about this. He who, according to the placards, had "been applauded by all the crowned heads of Europe." But from long and bitter experience he had acquired a dignified resignation.

The Professor received me in the booth itself. It was circular, very small, and contained a metal table flooded with pale light from a projector. The spectators would be grouped around this table, for the talents of the Professor's pupils could only be appreciated at close quarters. For the moment we were alone.

I don't know whether he recognised me. The first time I met him, just before the war, I was only a kid of twenty without enough money. It was at Estoril, where my mother had pursued a Brazilian who was blacker than his own cigar. She hoped to marry him, and I was used as a chaperon. I spent my days sailing in the Bay of Cascais, but the evenings found me in the Casino, prowling around the tables. The Professor was playing for high stakes in those days. He was already terrifyingly thin, and the colour of his face was grey, matched his pointed beard. It would have been impossible for him to waste away any more, but the years seemed to have covered him with a kind of moss. He still had his monocle, and the tangled hairs of his little beard fell, as they used to do, over his tie, which was a knot of black cord. He was wearing a tail-coat, just as he always had. I never saw him in anything but a tail-coat, even very early in the morning, when I once surprised him on the beach, bathing. I had been struck by the gnarled muscles of his long legs and arms. There was something horrible about the vigour revealed in the skinny body of this man.

I saw his muscles again now, slackened with age and projecting from a network of arthritic veins, for his arms were bare; the sleeves of his tail-coat were cut above the elbow for professional reasons. He also had his top-hat, and although he had a celluloid dicky held together by brass buttons, I noticed on the table, among the minute ladders, swings and paper harnesses used by the performing fleas, an enchanting tortoise-shell snuff-box, encrusted with gold, which I had seen placed near him in the old days at the gaming tables. I didn't know exactly what disappointments had dragged this rich playboy of Estoril to the flea-trainer's booth in a Danish amusement-park. For I always knew his title was perhaps not authentic—he preferred, moreover, to be addressed as 'Professor' rather than 'Count'—and, above all, that the riches he tossed around with equal indifference were not inherited. It was whispered that he dabbled in important international undertakings. Or that he was in the Intelligence Service. In fact, he was a big-time crook, well known in Warsaw, Vienna and Berlin for the dazzling coups he brought off, coups, however, which obliged him to spend some time on the lovely Côte des Deux Printemps. It was not on account of having known him in Portugal that I was able to approach him. We had several mutual friends, whom I had met since then. He appeared moderately surprised at my visit; no more interested than that. He was infinitely more preoccupied by the time. His little performers had firmly regulated habits, and gave their performance in accordance with a strict time-table. There were no spectators in sight, and the Professor naturally wondered whether to make his pupils work for my sole benefit.

"Exactly what do you want to know?" he asked in his cavernous voice. "I'm a very busy man. You have five minutes. . . ."

It was not a very encouraging start, particularly as what I wanted to know couldn't be condensed into a few precise questions. I talked to him about Poland. His round black eye, buried under the crinkled skin of his eyelids like that of an anxious hen, watched the clock.

"In your opinion, Professor, what would be the reasons for a man suddenly quitting Warsaw?"

He gave a little dry chuckle. His bony hand fiddled with the objects on the shining table.

"In the last fifteen years my country has offered its citizens the most complete choice of urgent reasons for wanting to get out . . . must I enumerate them? Invasion, siege, occup—"

I interrupted him. What was the use of letting him finish?

"Professor, I'm not talking about the usual incentives. But there's a particular thing that happened in the winter of 1927 . . . a criminal matter. . . ."

I caught his eye, black and glistening behind his monocle.

"You yourself were mixed up in certain activities. . . ."

He chuckled again. It was clear that he hadn't been afraid of the cops for a long time. He had given up at the same time the perquisites and the anxieties of his old grandeur. He took the snuff-box, and switched on the projector, so that we were bathed in a blazing light.

"They are cold," he whispered, opening the tortoise-shell box.

Fleas swarmed like particles of red snuff in the box. They jumped on the professor's arm. He looked at me severely.

"Move away a little. You're worrying them with cigarette smoke. They hate it."

Then, leaning carefully on his wrinkled forearm, he contemplated his charges grouped on the most tender part of the bend of his arm, which was livid white.

I was becoming quietly exasperated.

"Professor," I started again, firmly, "try to remember something . . . it's very important to me. . . ."

He was obviously fooling me. What could I offer him? He was miserable and enjoying it. Didn't smoke. Didn't drink. Because of his little charges, who didn't like it. I pretended to be interested in their activities. He picked them up on the point of a little ivory stiletto, dropped them on the various pieces of apparatus, and the most amazing part of it was that they stayed where he put them. Now he was smiling, with paternal pride.

"They are astonishing, aren't they?"

We were leaning over the table. I was holding my breath so as not to cause a panic in this minute circus.

"Look, Professor . . . there was somebody called Sophie mixed up in this affair."

Because I was very close to the Professor, and under the fierce bright light which showed up all his wrinkles, I noticed that he had flinched slightly. I hung on to this Christian name. . . .

"You knew Sophie, didn't you, Professor?"

He had straightened up. The fleas were jumping on his hand.

"Why don't you find another Pole? There are plenty of them. Why pick on me?"

Anyhow, I had hit the jackpot, and the name of Sophie was certainly more effective than that of Arkadin.

The Professor picked up his performing fleas, and replaced them quickly in their little box. He hadn't the heart to continue the performance. There was something pathetic about the pains he took to hide his nervousness. I stammered:

"As I knew you slightly, Professor, I thought . . ."

Just the same I wasn't going to let myself be impressed too much by this poor, sunken old man, as I was when I used to greet him awkwardly in the hall of the Estoril Palace. His rough skin had been mellowed by the light from the projector, but the flesh underneath was frozen like a lizard's.

"If you could put me on to someone who might help me. . . . Someone who, as far as you know, had an idea what was going on. . . ."

He broke away, and looked at me with suspicion, with hostility.

"Why haven't you tried to find Tadeus?" he said, pursuing his own thoughts rather than answering my question.

I was taken unawares by this. Did he know I had once worked with the Tangiers Pole? Was he really as cut off from things, as exclusively preoccupied with his performing fleas as he wanted me to believe? I tried evasive tactics:

"Tadeus. . . . The guy that's mixed up in the smuggling racket. . . ."

The Professor had recovered his poise. He picked up one of his straying charges from his celluloid shirt-front.

"Why don't you ask *him* some questions?"

His black and troubled gaze rested on me again, point-blank.

I was always uneasy about anything to do with Tadeus. Above all, after the Naples business. Above all, now. . . .

"He is much too young to have known anything about it."

It was really no good trying to reject Tadeus in this careless way. The Professor's eyes, opaque like metal behind thin, greyish lashes, were always watching me.

"Tadeus knows everything worth knowing. What's happening now is what happened before, and often what's going to happen again some time or other."

There was perhaps a touch of secret malice in his voice when he spoke of Tadeus: the spite of the ageing boss against the younger fellow who has taken his place. There was, at any rate, respect in his voice.

Then he made a gesture of contempt, as though sweeping away useless regrets. Hadn't he had the sense to give it up in time. . . .

"All the scum of the earth collect around him, swarming and struggling . . . like my fleas. Except that my fleas are much smarter."

He smiled. His large nostrils quivered, showing the dark, hairy cavities, as he sniffed the fragrance of some secret revenge. I took the initiative again.

"Tadeus didn't know Sophie, at any rate . . . as you did, Professor."

I'd no sooner said this than I regretted it. Going forward into the totally unknown, as I was, I couldn't allow myself to be so categorical. It wasn't proved that the Professor had really known Sophie, nor that she wasn't still working, perhaps even with Tadeus. But the Professor was still smiling, only his smile wasn't so crafty.

"Sophie," he murmured. "Sophie. . . ."

I felt that he was going to give something away. But he went on:

"No good looking that way, boy. A woman like Sophie, if she's still alive, must be legitimate by now. Respectable, maybe."

Did he figure that he himself was respectable, behind his platform of performing fleas, with his tail-coat and the cut-down sleeves, with his grotesque appearance like an undertaker?

"How come you're so sure Sophie would go straight?"

He eyed me contemptuously:

"Simple, she was intelligent."

Then he condescended to explain:

"Did you ever stop to think why cops are supposed to be dumb? Because they don't need to be anything else. You don't have to be intelligent to outsmart crooks; they're even stupider."

His voice was penetrating, and convincing.

"You don't have to be bad to be a crook; but you must be stupid. The proof is that most of them come to a sticky end."

I sniggered: "Crime doesn't pay."

He had that dull look again; his smile was cruel, bitter.

"It's twenty thousand years since Cain, my friend, and murder's a business that's still mainly in the hands of amateurs."

Two kids with snotty noses lifted the entrance flap of the booth, clutching their money.

With an imperious gesture he gave me to understand that the interview had gone on long enough. It was time to get on with serious matters. Enthusiastically he picked up his precious tortoise-shell box.

CHAPTER THREE

Amsterdam smelt, like it always does, of herring, smoke, rotten fruit, and that penetrating, unforgettable flatness of still water. . . . I had some trouble locating Trebitsch's shop, behind the old synagogue. It was amazingly narrow, huddled between two fine houses with stone steps, shut in between them like a cockle in its shell. The Jew's shop was sunk down on a lower level, and its window was so dark and dirty that it was hard to read the name and the words: "Antiques—Curious Books—Exceptional Bargains." Going down the slimy steps which led to the door, one came on a notice, half obliterated:

> English Spoken.
> Se habla Español.
> Man spricht Deutsch.
> Si parla Italiano.
> Man spreekt Hollandsch.
> Gavarutze po Ruski.
> Movi cie po Polusku.

But would Trebitsch want to talk in any of these languages? I paused for a moment before pushing open the dusty door. Burgomil Trebitsch. That was certainly the name Tadeus gave me. This was certainly the kind of place, too, where I might hope to find some trace of Sophie. For it was her I was keeping after now. "Cherchez la femme" as they say in the cheap crime novels. She was the one who would lead me to Arkadin. It's true I was in the habit of counting on women; they brought me luck. And women, furthermore, have that inestimable quality of attaching themselves to you exactly according to what they do for you; and the more weak, defenceless and ungrateful they think you are, the more they'll do. At any rate the women I'd been used to—Mily, for example.

I'd gone through everything with Mily; foolishness, infatuation, jealousy. But these sentiments weren't humiliating for me, they could even be flattering. She didn't condemn me, and all she demanded of me—that I should be around, and be faithful to her—it was easy enough and pleasant enough to give her. I kept straight with her. It was restful, and comforting.

Secretly I was counting on Sophie, as I'd been used to counting on Mily. Of course, she'd be of an uncertain age now—about Arkadin's age or more—but being fifty doesn't prohibit women from having their little weaknesses. On the contrary. Myrtle, for example. . . .

But Myrtle wasn't important. Nor was Sophie. It was Trebitsch. I decided to prepare myself rather carefully for this meeting, and climbing up the worn steps again, I went to collect my thoughts a little way off in a small seamen's bistro. The varnished oak panels were impregnated with tobacco-smoke, and a porcelain stove roared gently in a corner, glowing in the thick mustiness of pickled food and aniseed. I was alone there, my mind dulled, and I read for the twentieth time a letter I'd got from Mily: "Dearest, I have seen Tadeus. Don't worry. I don't think he really wants to get you over that dirty business in Naples."

For I hadn't had the courage to face Tadeus. He had learnt from Mily about my arrest and the confiscation of the *Queenie* and its cargo. When I came out of jail I had been drawn into this strange Arkadin affair, and my haphazard wanderings hadn't taken me near

Tangier. Or rather, I had carefully avoided the Moroccan coast. When the Professor advised me to go and see Tadeus, I had made the first excuse I could think of—that I was on the track of something hot in Belgium—and made Mily see the Pole in my place. The devil had taken a hand, too, tempting me that way.

Returning to my hotel in Copenhagen, after my rather depressing interview with the Professor, I found an interminable letter from Mily, hellishly written, on very thin airmail paper, almost illegible, full of words put one on top of the other, sentences added in the margin; and the style was even more careless than the writing. "I write same as I talk" Mily used to say; in other words, any old how. I had kept in touch with her. Before quitting Spain, we saw each other again in Barcelona. The proposed cruise did not take place; Arkadin changed his mind, and sent his guests away somewhat unceremoniously; and my brunette girl-friend was sulkily facing the prospect of returning alone to France. I assured her, by way of consolation, that I wasn't going to run off with Raina, that I wouldn't even be seeing her again for some time. Isn't that what Arkadin had ordered? So I had to obey his orders, if I was going to make anything out of the job he had given me.

Mily saw in this break with Raina a proof of my love.

Raina and her father had to leave for England, and Mily came with me herself to the plane which was taking me to Zürich. We had organised our own mail service, using the offices of American Airways, and her letters wandered around a long time before reaching me.

She'd fixed herself up in Paris, living with a girl-friend who had a mezzanine in the Rue Victor Massé. When it was known she'd come back again, she hoped to find a little night-club job, or some photographic modelling. I preferred that she didn't leave France, so I could always have her at hand. I had sent her money at fairly regular intervals, taken out of the generous travel allowance given me by Arkadin. It was all to the good that Mily should be in a state of lover-like impatience, waiting anxiously for my letters.

I was at Salonika—from where I came back without having achieved anything—when she wrote to tell me how she'd heard from one of the dancers she met on board the *Raina* that Arkadin, encouraged by the exceptional autumn weather, was thinking of making a little trip after all; around the Spanish and Portuguese coasts, and calling somewhere in North Africa.

"I needn't tell you how I feel about the idea of a cruise. I'm getting sick of having three slices of salami for supper. You know how it is, when one's alone, one lets things go. . . ."

I was to cable her if I could see any objection. When I received her letter in Vienna, on my return from the Balkans, the yacht was already in the Balearics, from where I got a postcard with flowers on it, and the text, which made me laugh, read: "It's lovely here, all the nature and everything and it makes me think of you." Dear Mily, her heart is pure gold.

Why would I want to raise the least objection to her gorging champagne and chicken in aspic at the Boss's expense? It was even amusing. Arkadin did not suspect that I had first-hand information about his movements, and that it was only for my own amusement that I communicated with him through his secretaries.

I wouldn't be able to say why, after sending him so many negative reports on my previous attempts, I had concealed from him my discovery at Zürich. I wanted to press my advantage, to suddenly produce the skein completely unravelled, but I hadn't enough strength of character not to boast about my success to Mily.

My excuse for this, however, is that I had to show her my hand. It was essential, if I wanted to get anything out of her meeting with Tadeus. Without that, I wouldn't have got Trebitsch's address, and the half-dead trail would have stopped short. I was trying to kid myself that I had acted on my own, as I sipped a glass of curaçao in that little bistro in Amsterdam. Night was falling, every now and then a boatman would come in, bringing with him a sickly smell of fog. In the street a barrel-organ was still grinding out a love-song.

I had already drunk three glasses. It was a fine curaçao, which the proprietor kept for connoisseurs. The sailors threw sidelong glances at my china jug, and swilled down their Dutch gin in silence. A parrot, springing up from behind a barrel, and pulling at its chain, went round between their glasses pecking up the sunflower seeds which they took from their pockets. I was drifting into a tepid euphoria, wrapped in remorse. I had been through this same kind of torpor in Brussels in the ever-hospitable place of refuge where I had gone to await the results of Mily's visit to Tangier. I had an old friend there, a woman who kept an establishment behind the Place de Brouckère. There was a bar on the ground floor, and bedrooms on three other floors. Gaby told fortunes too, and provided useful addresses. She had become very fat, for she never left her chair behind the counter, which was decked out with a multitude of little flags. Each different flag recalled some adventure for Gaby, because in the past she had been at different times a model, manicurist, a masseuse, a whole heap of excuses for jobs in the course of which she had formed extensive acquaintanceships. There was even a little Costa Rican flag, which she hadn't collected in the course of business, and which she had painted herself on a square of cardboard. Certain flags, French, English, Belgian, German, covered many memories; but in my special honour, she had added a star (mine) to the American banner. Moreover, she received me always with the same unvarying good-humour, attracting me by this greedy, uneasy world of hers, with its smells of food and hair-oil, its monotonous babbling, like the murmuring of some stream under the ground, and by the soft, and long-since platonic, caress of her white, heavily-ringed hand.

She told my fortune with the cards, telling me that a dark woman wished me well, and I thought of Raina, but it must have been Mily because there was something about a sea-trip; she saw a man of uncertain age and . . . oh, hell, some serious trouble! There was a spade there; it came up three times. Gaby consoled me by saying that with the diamonds, which always came out in the same hand, this trouble could very easily be interpreted as a minor incident. "You're going to get a letter tonight."

The evening mail in fact brought me one of Mily's long epistles, posted in Malaga. She confirmed that the yacht would put in at Tangier, and this was good news. But the rest of it I didn't like at all. Mily said that when they left the Balearics there was quite a heavy sea. She had to drink a bit to keep her sea legs. "And you know me, honey, I'm really a one-drink girl. A glass of champagne and I've had it." This was a little exaggerated, but Mily certainly had no head for liquor. And as soon as she'd 'had it', as she said, you could be certain she'd do or say something stupid. I went on reading, a little worried, and what I learnt didn't reassure me.

It was that very evening that Arkadin, thawing out a bit for once from his customary reserve, had noticed Mily. He even made a pass at her; and the evening being a little tedious, and the other guests being all overcome by the pitching of the boat, he had invited her to come and drink a last bottle of brandy in his cabin.

"You can imagine it was an opportunity not to be missed. I thought of you, naturally, and I told myself you'd be quite happy about it."

Happy, that's saying a lot. For the crazy little fool, completely carried away by the champagne, the storm, and the date with Arkadin, had given away some very unsuitable information. "I don't know how it happened, honey, but suddenly we started talking about you. . . ." Me, who thought I was being so smart, fooling my formidable boss and having my mistress on board his boat all the time! He must have been laughing up his sleeve at me, that's certain.

The parrot had jumped on to my table and advanced slowly, teetering on its great stiff claws. In spite of its vivid plumage, it reminded me of the Professor. Maybe it was the round black eye under the white, crumpled eyelid. I tried to drive it away, and it burst into a roar of laughter that was almost human. The sailors at the other table started laughing too, and I felt alone and ridiculous, jerked out of the gentle stupor into which I had fallen.

It was Mily's letter which burst open the cocoon in which I had wrapped myself at Gaby's. "He's a queer character, this Arkadin. How can I describe him to you? He doesn't move, he doesn't say anything, and you feel like a prisoner. It was funny on the boat, there was a lot of shaking, and I was thrown all over the place by the roll—not only on account of the champagne, you understand; then suddenly a lamp overturned and the bottle and tray with it. But Arkadin seemed to be screwed to the floor. He had his hands in his pockets and didn't budge. When I accepted to go to his cabin I was a tiny bit scared; guys with beards aren't my type, and anyhow it's you I love, and other men don't mean a thing, no matter who they are. But I was crazy to be scared. To begin with, he only tried a little petting. Then as soon as you came into the conversation, he did nothing but talk, and seemed to have forgotten his intentions towards me. . . ."

I could picture him very well, massive and solid in the middle of the tumult of the raging sea; and Mily, half-naked, dishevelled, her cheeks flushed, dancing round him like a drunken butterfly. "I told him everything. Everything. And then he had to take it on the chin!" She had told him everything, in fact; the idiot. She wasn't content with throwing in his face all the various misdeeds of which scandal accused Arkadin. She had set herself up as a redresser of wrongs: the Chinese armaments, the Ethiopian roads, and the rest of it. He must have "taken it on the chin", surely, with shattering indifference. These were innocent, out-of-date charges. I had been thinking about the words of the Professor, and I was convinced that they applied also to Arkadin. He was much too intelligent to have stayed with the small-time crooks, the sort that get into their hide-outs and start shaking at the mention of cops. He had long passed the stage where you had to be crooked to get anywhere. The rackets he was concerned with were honest, or at least looked that way, and if they weren't always in the open, for reasons of security often demanded by the governments themselves, they were in no danger from the law. It needed Mily's candour to believe once more in the shameful adventurer, his hands steeped in dirty business. She was still basking in her role of accuser "and then out of the blue—bang, like that! I mentioned Bracco." This was the last thing she should have done. The lines of writing overlapped, "because this morning we are still three sheets in the wind, in both senses. He certainly is a funny character, just like I already told you. He didn't bat an eyelid when I brought in Bracco's name. Still planted in the cabin there like a post. Except that the other posts seemed to dance in front of my eyes. Not him. He stayed quiet, not moving. Then I had a cute idea. I asked him why he wore a beard, and if he'd had it since 1927."

As I read this I broke out in a cold sweat. She'd given the game away. She was so happy, poor little fool, to be able to show I had no secrets from her, that she knew everything. She had even talked about the tailor in Zürich. "He looked a bit taken aback, just the same, when I told him he was Polish. Afterwards he pretended to laugh, and told me I'd had too much to drink; but I could see by his eyes he hadn't expected that."

I read and re-read the letter, patiently trying, coward that I was, to find some loopholes. The meanderings of a girl who's been drinking, do they count for anything? Certainly they would with Arkadin. I had promised him to act with the greatest secrecy, and he'd found out that I'd confided in someone like Mily. . . .

Squatting by the counter in the dim light of the bar, I awaited the consequences of what she had said. It was true I could do nothing about it. Nothing except wait, and go each morning and evening to see if there was any mail. Two days later another letter arrived from Mily. Still as pleased with herself as ever. "I'm putting in some good work for you, honey." And indeed she'd go straight to the little café on getting off the boat at Tangier. Had Arkadin followed her? Did he know Tadeus? And above all, did Tadeus know him? Did Tadeus know as much as the Professor had intimated. "You know what Tadeus is. Doesn't talk much. Always very busy. It looks as though things are going well with him."

I could imagine that automaton sitting at his usual table, among the swarm of spivs, racketeers and pimps. Now waving away some importunate fellow with a little silent gesture, now putting his hand into his pocket, taking out the bundles of greenbacks and counting them on the sticky marble table-top. Mily waiting for her chance, smiling coquettishly, making eyes, and thinking of me.

"I thought of you; I was so proud that you trusted me with an assignment, a real one, and that I was able to carry it out. Because with Arkadin, it was really too difficult. Imagine, the next day after our conversation in his cabin, he went on as though nothing had happened between us. Not that he had his nose in the air, or anything like that. But he was just the same with me as at the beginning, when he got me mixed up with Nelly the Egyptian. Anyhow, he went ashore at Malaga and nobody's seen him since."

Actually, with Tadeus, she did a good job. She got the address of Trebitsch.

"I only told him you needed some information about someone called Sophie."

I should have gone myself to Tangier, and looked for the reflection of this unknown woman on the face of Tadeus, as I had found it on the parchment mask of the Professor. Particularly as the Pole, if Mily could be believed, wasn't sore at me. He knew very well that accidents could happen to anyone. . . . Had he really said that, or was it just a comment by Mily? He wanted to know if I had a new boat. "That proves he would be willing to work with you again if the occasion arose."

I didn't dare to believe it, but I was relieved. I was scared of Tadeus, scared of his judgment and of his power, which I regarded as limitless. The revenge of a man like that would be terrible; long premeditated, savoured, calculated. . . . But then he wasn't sore at me. He had given me the address. . . .

"He didn't want to say anything more. He wrote this name on a piece of paper and gave it to me. Of course there were other people around. I thanked him, and all that. Then he gave his funny smile and said: 'Don't mention it'."

Was it the liquor that was upsetting me as much as Mily? My temporary well-being had given place to a feeling of suffocation. It stank like hell in that dark Amsterdam bistro. And that barbarous organ which never finished. No, it was an accordion now. It wasn't cold, as it had been in Zürich or Copenhagen; but a soft humidity blanketed the canals, where the street-lamps made great oily patches on the water. The elm trees along the quayside spread out their branches like clenched fists raised towards the leaden sky.

Tadeus had said: "Don't mention it." Well, that's a formula. . . . Why should I imagine it had a hidden meaning. A threat.

Irritated with myself, I started walking again. I went on towards the fence's shop, and not wanting to think any more I pushed open the door. A bell on a rusty iron wire above my head made a clamorous din, and as an echo, other bells, hoarse, shrill and catarrhal, began to toll in the gloom of the shop.

It was enormous, or seemed to be, once my eyes had pierced the semi-darkness, punctured here and there by the gleam of some gilt object, or the pale shine of a polished vase, illuminated by a tiny lamp hanging from the ceiling among a multitude of heterogeneous objects covered in dust. Yes, it was enormous; full of corners, of shadowy recesses, of chaos, like a grotto.

And at the same time it was disturbing, because of the suffocating heat in the place, and also because of the kind of objects I was beginning to identify, and which had that inarticulate pathos of incongruous, abandoned things jumbled indecently together by mere chance. Where had that beautifully carved harp come from, that curious Chinese box studded with nails, that bath-tub painted in bright scarlet? And that chest, wasn't it a coffin?

The cascade of tolling bells had died away. The silence was stifling, punctuated by mysterious rustlings and nibblings.

"Anybody there?"

It was crazy, but my voice shook. Angrily I advanced a few paces. I stumbled suddenly against a treacherous step, clung on to a pile of books which collapsed in a cloud of dust, dragging with it a collection of pewter plates or bits of old metal. My forehead encountered some indefinable obstacle which gave gently, recovered its balance, and came back to grab hold of my hair. It was a large stuffed lizard, scaly and rough, with jaws like a saw. I bit back an impassioned oath.

"Oh, well, if there's nobody . . ."

But a fluty voice came from two steps away:

"I am here, sir."

In spite of myself I recoiled, only to get entangled in the meshes of a net which brushed against me, loaded with grating shells. I could now distinguish a human being, sunk in an old easy-chair which had given way at the bottom.

"Trebitsch."

The confused mass moved. A smell emanated from it which turned my stomach. One hand groped among the chaos, reached for a bulb which was hidden among the rags, and a second lamp, as poor as the other one, went on above our heads.

Trebitsch was standing up now, and I could see that he wasn't, as I had supposed, a little old wrinkled creature in his tattered clothes. On the contrary, he was a corpulent figure, taller than I, with a fat body enveloped in an ancient, shapeless dressing-gown. The face too was fat and shiny. A filthy hair-net covered the top of his head, from which escaped dirty grey curls that fell in ringlets on the triple rolls of fat at the back of his neck. A soft, plump, clammy hand was put out, and I shook it with revulsion.

"Don't mention it," Tadeus had said. Why had he sent me to this frightful junk-shop? I had known some strange, disturbing, wretched people in my life; but none had ever produced in me such a feeling of repulsion as this slimy, corpulent Pole. He was civil, leaning over to speak in my face, brushing against me, in the unbelievable congestion of the shop, his horrible garments encrusted in filth.

He began treating me as though I knew a bit about antiques, and walked me around to look at his miserable treasures with the pride of a collector. I immediately threw Sophie's name into the conversation. All my prepared strategy had gone out of my mind, and besides, it would have been superfluous. I wanted to finish with this gross creature. I wanted to get the hell out of this suffocating scrap-heap.

"It's an exceptional bargain, I can assure you. It's yours for a hundred and ten guilders."

He had put in my hand an old telescope, corroded with rust, which immediately came apart. One of the links broke off, rolled away with a chinking sound and lost itself on the murky floor.

"That's nothing," Trebitsch hastened to tell me reassuringly. "You can fix it with a little sticky paper."

I was burdened with this crazy object, but didn't know where to put it. The Pole had picked up a chipped ornament from the table and was polishing it with his damp palms.

"Trebitsch," I said, as firmly as I could. "I have already asked you three times if you ever knew a woman called Sophie. . . ."

The reply came, so quickly that it took me by surprise.

"Sophie Radzweickz? What an amazing woman!"

I had been sore at Mily because she was unable to recall that surname, which Bracco stammered out with his dying breath. Now, hearing it so suddenly, it had gone straight out of my mind again. I could not, however, without some excuse, ask Trebitsch to repeat it. Despite his apparently casual air, he was watching me as sharply as I was watching him.

"I didn't know her personally, of course," he said, rearranging his mangy ringlets with the gesture of an old maid. His yellow skull shone like rancid butter.

"Wait a minute," he went on in ecstatic tones, disentangling as he passed some nameless object. "This would be perfect, as a case for your telescope."

It was a leather bag, swollen with damp and filled with rat-dung. He shook it, tapped it with satisfaction and handed it to me.

"What happened to her?"

I didn't want to let the conversation slide and to lose myself in the insidious bog into which Trebitsch was trying to lure me.

"Where is she?"

His colourless eyes moved in the greasy folds of his eyelids. He bared his teeth, which were held together by some complicated piece of metal apparatus. But his cunning, oily smile vanished quickly, and for a second I could see anguish in his eyes. I had seen this look on the Professor, on Arkadin himself, on all those who, if only momentarily, are disturbed by doubts, or by fears. In fact, I had seen everybody look like that. Everybody except Tadeus.

"Where is she?" he repeated, like some funereal echo. Then he started to laugh, with a sweeping gesture of his soft hand:

"Where are we any of us if it comes to that?"

He had slung the horrible, musty leather bag on my shoulder by force.

"Do you know if she's still alive?"

I didn't have the strength to play his game. I was panting with irritation and impatience.

"If you don't take the case, I can let you have the telescope alone. But, that will be a weeny bit more expensive. . . ."

Oh, to hit him! To wipe out that great spongy face with my fist! "You haven't answered my question, Mr. Trebitsch."

He scratched the inside of his ears with his little fingernail, a greyish, immensely long nail like the Chinese have.

"You haven't bought my telescope."

Let's get it over with, whatever price he wants.

"I'll buy it, don't worry. . . . All right, what have you got to tell me?"

Something moved, under a table draped with an old, tufted rug.

It was a cat; I could make out its grey paw, playing around with the fringed edging. Trebitsch bent down and picked up the little beast, giving it a long, infantile discourse in Yiddish. Then, in the same tone of voice, scratching the back of the puss's neck, he sighed and said:

"Ah, those girls! Who would have believed it? Charming, most of them . . . and looked as though butter wouldn't melt in their mouths. They were Sophie's ruin, though. . . . Yes, her ruin. . . ."

He was still playing with the cat, whose claws scraped on the padded lapels of his dressing-gown. He punctuated his recital with reprimands and cajoleries.

"Imagine, my dear, these little wretches were hired by the Police. Oh, you would, would you? . . . You'll spoil it, now. Yes, by the Police. . . . Naughty one, look what you've done. . . ." He threw the squalling kitten on to the floor.

"They were to pose as pupils in her Dancing Academy you see. . . ."

I tried desperately to understand. A pseudo Dancing Academy in Warsaw, under Sophie's direction. What exactly did it conceal? The Police had one or two girls in their pay. . . . What had they found out? I was struggling to sort out the tangle of Trebitsch's inconsistencies, which made me even more impatient than his silences.

"Perhaps you might be interested in this magnificent aquarium, exactly what you need for your tropical fish. . . ."

He rooted out the tarnished glass bowl from a collection of rags and crumpled ribbons.

"Thanks. I already have a telescope."

"But you haven't paid for it."

Sighing, he replaced the aquarium.

"Pity. Never mind, we can always make it up on the telescope, can't we?"

I decided to be firm.

"Trebitsch, I am prepared to buy certain information from you.

And I'll pay you what it's worth. You understand? The price it's worth to me."

He folded the stained tails of his robe across his balloon-like stomach, and eyed me with the phoney dignity of a noble father in a melodrama.

"Sir, I have made it a rule for a long time never to give any information to anyone, for any reason whatsoever. To anyone, you understand. Even about people who are dead. And I'm not going to change now, naturally. In my profession I have to be careful."

How did he actually make a living? As a fence? Who would trust him? He was stagnating among the musty rubbish in his shop. Did he take himself seriously with this parody of dignity he was putting across for my special benefit? Or was it all a sham, a sort of pathetic slyness which caused him much amusement?

"You see, you've only bought a telescope."

My impatient fever had given place to a dull despondency.

"A telescope . . . and an aquarium . . . the whole shop. . . . What the hell, if Sophie's dead anyway?"

"Who told you she was dead?"

I regained a little ground.

"Nobody knows if she's alive. . . ."

Exactly what did he know? At times I would get the impression that his wide, waxy skull was more cluttered up with memories than his den was. At other times, I thought that he prolonged a futile conversation for want of anything better to do, for the pleasure of being taken seriously.

"I seem to remember that she got away, after they broke up the gang."

A gang of which Arkadin was a member? Or rather the guy who was to become Arkadin? What kind of gang? I hazarded:

"White slavery?"

Warsaw was the great centre of the traffic, before the war. They ran the white flesh into South America—young Jewesses from

Poland and the Baltic countries. Trebitsch shook his head, lost in his recollections. His soft lips gaped over his grey teeth.

"Yes. . . . The greatest racket in Eastern Europe. . . . Superb girls. If you'd seen them. . . ."

A senile emotion troubled his watery eyes. What had his job been in this gang? Pimp? I tried to imagine him, thirty years younger, less gross, less dirty. He lifted his filthy mandarin's nail:

"Oh, I just remembered, I have something for you."

He began his silly little game again. I lost my temper.

"No, Trebitsch. No. I'm not buying any of your filthy muck...."

He remained calm, his face brightened quickly:

"But you'll buy this, I'm sure. Because this will interest you . . . very much. It's an idea that's just come to me."

Leaning over me, conspiratorial, offensive, like a great unclean beast.

"These girls I spoke of you . . . you recall . . . the ones who acted as special police agents. . . . It so happens I've seen one of them again. Here, during the occupation."

A frantic excitement took hold of me again, but I tried to conceal it.

"Her name?"

Trebitsch blinked, flicked away a piece of ash from my cigarette which had fallen on his lapel.

"I'll pay you what it's worth, Trebitsch."

He went on again, rather pompously:

"She was a heroine of the resistance. She worked for some English network. I, for my part, was mixed up in certain clandestine activities. . . ."

That I could well imagine: black market, forging passports, God knows what infernal rackets.

"She spent the night here. It was . . . let's see . . . it was in '42. We went on talking about Warsaw all through the night. You know what we Poles are like, very sentimental."

He was becoming maudlin.

"The Baroness could tell you all you want to know about Sophie."

At last, at last, I was touching reality! I asked as calmly as possible:

"Fine . . . where can I find the Baroness?"

His face sparkled with guile.

"The Baroness Nagel."

Then once again he handed me the telescope which I had thrown on to an old stand.

"Don't forget your telescope. Really an amazing bargain."

I grinned:

"Bargain? There isn't even a lens in the thing. . . ."

He shook the tube, which made a noise like gravel.

"What can you expect for two hundred guilders?"

I was mad with indignation.

"Two hundred guilders!"

Gravely he examined the instrument:

"Anyhow, you can easily have the glass replaced. . . . By the way, if you can pay in dollars I'll give you an excellent rate."

With a deft movement, he had seized my billfold from my jacket pocket, calmly opened it and started counting out the money.

"And of course I'll have to charge you for breakages. You've broken several plates . . . all old Delft, of course . . . for a curtain . . . damaged several books . . . first editions. And we mustn't forget the little alligator, he's so fragile. . . ."

I clenched my fists. I had to go through with this to the end.

"You remember the name? Nagel. I'll spell it N . . . A . . ."

And with each letter he counted out a twenty-dollar bill.

"Nagel . . . I know that. . . . Is that all I'm getting? . . ."

"Baroness Nagel . . . B . . . A . . . R . . ."

I snatched the billfold away from him:

"That'll do. I know how to spell Baroness. It's her address I want. . . ."

Trebitsch regretfully watched me pocket the billfold and ostensibly button my jacket. He looked more than ever like a greasy old monk:

"I give you my word of honour, my dear fellow, I swear on my heart . . . I haven't the slightest, not the slightest idea where the Baroness is now, *or* what happened to her. . . ."

CHAPTER FOUR

I was determined to spare no pains in trying to seduce the Baroness. Apart from every other consideration, she would be worth the trouble. She had reached that uncertain age which I find rather touching in a woman, when she is fighting, with intelligence, against an enemy which she knows to be implacable, and stronger than she is. How does that famous French poem go?— "the irreparable ravages of time." The Baroness Nagel was certainly not a woman who would let herself be ravaged easily.

I had hoped she would like this Hungarian restaurant. The Polish cafés in Greenwich Village were not so chic. They served a very nice Bortsch at Gipsy's. Not interested in the Magyar specialities, the Baroness had chosen, after her caviar, a young partridge done with grapes. She knew how to eat, with the careful epicureanism of a woman who is used to having the best, but who has also known hunger. I watched her fingers, with their garnet-lacquered nails, dealing competently with a small bone, managing the crouton dipped in foie-gras without getting herself into a mess. She was obviously happy to be here; and it was that, and only that, which betrayed her. A more casual, more sulky attitude, and she could have passed for a genuine woman of the world. With me it was the same; I had picked up the manners of a gentleman, but some subtle flaw in me would make it obvious that I was more at home in hotels than in private houses. I signed to the violinist and once more he began to play in the Baroness's ear the old gypsy song which she had asked for. She hummed it very softly, moving her pretty, well-groomed head in time to the music, closing her eyes at the nostalgic sobs of the violin. Her neck was still very beautiful, round and lissom, and this made up for her eyes, which were large, but a little bruised. She had pretty ears, made for real rocks and not those clips, very ritzy but . . . only onyx after all.

She saw I was watching her, and seemed rather ashamed of her passing display of emotion.

"We Poles are impossible," she said. "A little liquor, a little music, and our souls shine out of our eyes. . . ."

I very much wanted to give the impression that it was an intimate evening, that we weren't interested in anything but each other. I had done things well. A corsage of orchids blossomed on the Baroness's rather flat bosom. They were putting a second bottle of champagne in the ice-bucket.

The Baroness, definitely not being true to her Poland, had preferred Veuve Cliquot to vodka. But then I was not dining with the Baroness for the sole purpose of making love to her. She was much too shrewd to make any mistake about the intentions with which I surrounded her. When I finally located her—after so many blunders, false hopes, questions with no answers, and answers that were no good—in the Fifth Avenue dress shop where she had been working since the end of the war, I didn't pretend to be interested for very long in the new mid-winter collection. I whispered to the Baroness between the showing of 'Little Igloo' and 'Frosty Flower' that I wanted to talk to her. She pointed out the very new line of '3 above o', which a pretty redhead with an elegantly-curved bottom was trying to show me, and went on in the same tone: "What about?" I brought up Warsaw, and one or two fairly glamorous Poles who were among my contacts—no mention of the Professor, nor Trebitsch, and certainly not of Tadeus. She had simply written on the programme which had the names of the twenty models on it, in a distinguished hand, these few words:

"Let's have dinner together this evening. I'll be at the Gardenia at 7 o'clock."

I picked her up at the joint in question, and the meeting was altogether a pleasant one. What kind of a life could this Baroness have? Incidentally, was she a Baroness in the same way the Professor was a Count? Or was she really of the nobility? It was doubtful, considering she'd helped to break up Sophie's gang. It was hard to imagine a young aristocrat letting herself be hired as a police informer in a phoney Dancing Academy. But after all, anything is possible. Particularly in the case of a Polish woman whose world had been turned upside down after the first war. The Baroness's activities in occupied Europe, which had won her a decoration, confirmed that she had enough courage and nerve to make her a competent agent of the Allied Intelligence Service, and to have made her, before that, a competent agent of the police vice squad.

Yes, she could be well-born. The way she held her head, proudly but not haughtily, the challenging way she sucked a grape with grace and elegance, and especially her hands with their narrow finger-tips—all this suggested class. Baroness therefore, but a decayed one. And desperately alone. I could see that from the way she leaned against me when we started to dance. The abandon of a woman who was still young, who has been long frustrated, and whose head was muzzy with the champagne and the vaguely mysterious circumstances of our date together. She recovered herself at once, however, and then was on the defensive. She flashed an occasional glance at me and kept on her guard. We had chatted idly about everything and nothing. Without dwelling on it, I touched on the subject of her exploits in the Resistance. Unlike so many so-called underground people that I'd met, she didn't go on at great length about the dangers she'd been up against, and the things she'd done.

"That kind of thing is much less glamorous, much less heroic and

128

much less exhilarating than they try to make you believe. Actually, my work consisted in lying, hiding out, watching, corrupting people. . . ."

I smiled, toadying to her:

"Well, it was all in a good cause, Baroness."

She crushed out her lipstick-stained cigarette in the ash-tray. "Come, let's admit it, I don't know anything about these things. They paid me for a certain job and I did it. Honestly and conscientiously, the same way as I sell my dresses. . . . I always had a professional conscience."

A challenge again. She wanted to make it quite clear that she made no secret of being mercenary. I went on, still being gallant:

"But you weren't prepared to do any old job. . . ."

Her look was a little hard, the colour of opal, as she eyed me with, maybe, a touch of irritation. She was wondering if I were stupid.

"I started earning my living at the age of eighteen," she said, in the way one might say 'It rained a lot today'. "My father was ruined, my mother sick, and my young sister looked like going wrong; and I'd had enough of wearing mended stockings."

She tasted her water-ice with maraschino, letting it melt slowly in her mouth.

"And what did you do? You were a mannequin, I bet. Or . . . interpreter . . . model. . . ."

"I was a police agent."

She had lit another cigarette. The smoke trickled out of her mouth, from which the lipstick hadn't come away in spite of her gastronomic efforts. Her look still challenged me. I pretended to be surprised, romantically interested. If she hadn't been so refined, she would have shrugged her shoulders.

"It was pretty sordid, believe me. And not in the least amusing."

The role of idiot had been quite a convenient one after all. Why not stick to it?

"Criminals are never very amusing, it seems. A bad conscience has the same disastrous effect on the temper as a bad digestion."

She made an effort to smile politely.

"The reason is," she corrected me, "that criminals, as you say, are always failures. Because, obviously, as soon as they are successful they stop being criminals, or sharks, or bad ... bad eggs, or whatever you want to call them ... and they become personalities. Financiers. Businessmen. It's purely a question of social class, not an ethical problem."

I had tasted the champagne. It was iced just right. I filled her glass and raised my own.

"Let's drink to crime."

My witty toast could scarcely have amused her, but maybe she would like to prolong the evening. Already of mature age, poor and proud, she wouldn't often have the luck to get a champagne supper from such an attractive bachelor! Dreaming all day of mink coats, diamond clips, basking in stories of European travel, yachts, frolics on Miami Beach? ... Poor Baroness. Or did she find perhaps that it added a piquancy to the evening, this digging-up of a forgotten past, of which she had been so long ashamed, and would she now, after the glory of her achievements in the resistance, feel in a reminiscent mood?

"Have you ever heard of Sophie Radzweickz?"

I couldn't help wincing as I said it. Perhaps she was smarter than I was, perhaps she'd seen this coming a long way off, clumsy bastard that I was. She didn't seem to notice the expression on my face.

"She was an amazing woman. She was the most important criminal in the underworld of Warsaw, back in 1925 ... but we managed to put her out of business."

What was she smiling at? At the picture of the young girl she was then? I tried to imagine her. Let's see, 1925 ... Chanel, the dress like a sack, the cashmere scarf thrown over the shoulder with an impudent air. Maybe a fringe, to complete her personality. She went to Mme Sophie's Dancing Academy to learn the tango and the hesitation waltz. I suppose they played 'Dream Tango' or 'The

Dance of the Dragonflies' or something like that. She must have been rather excited at the idea of venturing into that kind of world.

"It was so sad it made you cry. The girls were so silly, you couldn't even pity them. There were several of us employed as agents, all frightfully young, and I will not pretend to you that we were not a little thrilled at being part of the Secret Police. Also, in my case, my family needed the money. I was a sort of wooden duck . . . how do you call it? A decoy? It was rather a horrible business really . . . they masqueraded as a dancing school where the young ladies went to learn the tango."

The tango. . . . They were playing a kind of gypsy tango now. The sickly-sweet, repetitive rhythm of it was forcing her mind back to Warsaw, to the years when she craved adventure and learnt disillusionment. To the years above all, when she was young. . . .

"The victims, of course, ended up in Buenos Aires . . . also, there were drugs involved."

Her voice was brittle now, as she tried to disguise the impact of an experience which had once shattered her illusions.

"It was all quite sordid; one is not a prude, but one was glad to be useful in breaking it up."

I lit a cigarette for her, taking my time.

"The leader of the gang got away?" I asked.

"She was persuaded to retire, and has been living abroad ever since, in great style. She married . . . years ago."

The Baroness was nervous, decidedly. I would have to distract her mind from the bitter taste of this memory.

"Would you care to dance?"

I wanted it to look as though I'd listened out of mere politeness to her little story about a woman called Sophie.

"What did you say she called herself now?"

A haunting samba made us sway around along with the other couples, locked together on the narrow floor. The Baroness and I were dancing cheek to cheek. She pretended not to understand.

"This . . . this Sophie we were talking about just now. . . ."

The dance ended. I guided the Baroness gently back to our table, and to our gossip.

"I never told you her last name," she corrected me.

She sat down, took a gulp of champagne. It was lukewarm, at the bottom of the glass. Would I have to order another bottle? I hesitated. When Poles get tight they start weeping about themselves. I couldn't really get interested in the Baroness's life of failure and disappointment.

"The watchword of the dress house is absolute discretion," she said.

She was trying to be dignified on me, as Trebitsch had done. At least she didn't suggest anything else. I waded on:

"She's a customer of your dress house, right?"

"She's a very good client."

That made the thing clear. Decidedly it just wasn't by chance that the Baroness had let her hair down. She knew what I wanted out of her. She hadn't avoided it. From now on I could take my time. The final count would be just a question of price.

"If she comes to buy dresses, haven't you ever seen her? Did she recognise you?"

"Certainly she did. What does it matter? She's a rich, respectable woman now. What has she got to fear from me?"

Funny to think of the Baroness making a fuss of the rich customer and the latter being, maybe, just a little condescending towards the girl who, thirty years before . . .

"You are, in fact, very discreet. But how does she know that? And I've heard they're very strict in the Argentine about people with police records. . . ."

She interrupted me with a smile:

"She doesn't live in the Argentine. Nor in Brazil."

Then, quietly mischievous, she said:

"Did you think I'd fall that easily into the trap?"

Decidedly she played very skilfully, and had done so ever since we first met. I liked that.

"I bet you two hundred dollars I'll catch you out just the same."

"Let's say five hundred dollars, better stakes."

Cupidity suddenly made her ugly, for a second she was an ageing, embittered woman, harassed by financial worries. I would have given way to a baroness in all her glory. With this sharp-witted money-grubber I was going to haggle.

"Three hundred. That's good enough stakes for me."

In spite of myself my tone was less polite. It wasn't just a social occasion any more, it was business.

"Each one of us is going to write on the back of our menus what we think Sophie's address is," I went on, trying by at least a pretence of gaiety to save the remnants of our cordial relationship. "And we will compare them."

Accustomed as she was to selling things, she recognised this was my final price. Resolutely she took the propelling pencil and wrote some words on her menu. On the back of mine I did a little sketch of the Great Bear. She gave me the card. Her face was now hard, terribly aged. I was sorry for her. Lightly I kissed the dry hand which she brandished under my nose like a six-shooter. I wanted to soften the humiliation of the tip I was going to have to slip into her trembling fingers. When she lifted her head again, I saw that there were tears in her eyes. She took out a small handker-chief and dabbed at her mascara.

"I am being ridiculous tonight," she said in a voice which she tried to make casual. "All this is so . . . so sordid. I would like to have behaved properly about it. You're kind, though. It's so rare to find a bachelor of your age who isn't a . . . what do you call it? . . . a heel."

She blew her nose carefully. She had the refined gestures of an old maid. The natural simplicity of a woman of class had been overlaid by the mincing mannerisms of her profession.

"Honestly, I've no compunction about Sophie. She's got herself nicely established. She doesn't fear anything from anybody. Besides . . ."

She hesitated on the brink of another disclosure, which this time I hadn't asked her to make, which I hadn't promised to pay for.

"Anyhow, you aren't the first person to be interested in Sophie all of a sudden, after all these years. Last Monday there was that big man, with the beard. . . ."

I had called the waiter, so that she wouldn't notice my great agitation. I had been feeling like a million dollars. And all the time Arkadin had been there three days before me. He had found the Baroness and Sophie . . . and so he hadn't needed me at all.

CHAPTER FIVE

"Hullo," Raina said, as though we had parted the day before.

She was sitting discreetly on the bench in the little lobby. I liked this rather modest hotel, it was quiet. I had lived there for several months after my demobilisation. They gave me rather special consideration. With Arkadin's money I could certainly have gone somewhere more luxurious. But I didn't know exactly how long I would be in New York; and with the perpetual upheaval of my life, I had always needed to make a kind of home for myself; the quiet street, the elevator man who told me about his little girl (she had had a mild attack of polio three years back), the squeaking of the elevator door, the taste of a certain kind of dry biscuit they served with breakfast—all this made me feel I belonged there. Like at Gaby's, in Brussels. Or with Jennie, with my mother. However rootless a guy may be, he needs to have something, some place to hang on to. It's like the laurel, whose roots can only thrive near walls or the trunk of a tree; or those bulbs which send out their fragile roots, in the absence of proper humus, into moss, or into water. . . .

But how had Raina found out my address?

"Well," she said sweetly, "aren't you glad to see me?"

I didn't have words to express what I felt. She got up and came

135

towards me, even slimmer than I remembered her. I couldn't imagine how I'd managed to live without her all these months. Finding her again like this, so unexpectedly, was like being a long time out in the cold and wind, and then suddenly finding warmth and shelter. The thrill of it went to my head, like liquor. I took Raina's hand in mine, stupidly. I raised it to my lips. I recognised the hard, slightly nervous grip of her long thin fingers, with their pale, shining nails.

Raina, my darling! The elevator man watched us, no doubt amused by this continental hand-kissing . . . the kind of thing you'd expect from a pimp or a foreigner, he must have thought. I drew Raina behind one of the pillars. But then a mirror revealed us to the porter who was telephoning. He shouted to me from his desk, in the amiable, easy-going way which was part of the hotel's charm:

"I thought you'd gone upstairs. . . . It's for you. The airport."

I had Raina's hand clutched in mine as though I was scared she would run away; I didn't move, still under the impact of a paralysing emotion.

"They say they've been able to fix it. . . . You can travel on the 10.40 p.m. plane."

Less than an hour earlier, at the company's office, I had been insistant, thrown tips everywhere, telling them I absolutely had to be in Mexico the day after tomorrow. They promised to do the impossible. . . . But it would be difficult.

"Right. . . . Do I tell them O.K.?"

I had to say something, no matter what.

"Yes. . . . Wait a minute. I have to think. . . ."

Raina had drawn her hand away, and as with a magnetic current, when you release the lever which transmits it, I felt free again, more clear-headed.

"I'd better speak to them. . . ."

But the porter had hung up.

"They didn't wait for the reply, sir. But don't worry. They said they'd keep a place for you."

Since the day before, I'd been set on catching the first available plane to Mexico. I had to get there ahead of Arkadin. The Baroness had assured me that she hadn't sold him Sophie's address, as she had to me. But that could have been a lie. I was in a hurry to get myself on to the trail which at last, at long last, was going to lead me to the mysterious Sophie. I was nearing the target; and I was like somebody reading a detective story, turning the pages two by two to get more quickly to the solution.

But now, all that wasn't interesting any more. Raina was two steps away from me.

"As we have such a short time ahead of us, aren't you at least going to offer me a drink?" she asked.

Her voice was ironic. Maybe she was teasing me a little. She went towards the door. I held her back:

"No. Please. . . . I have so many things to tell you. Come on. . . ."

I led her to the elevator. As I pushed her inside, the operator tried to protest. Yeah, yeah, I knew the hotel regulations didn't allow women in the bedrooms. But still, in a place like this they couldn't start being tough about it. Firmly I made the jerk close his mouth, and turned my back on him. I only had eyes for Raina. Like everything else in the hotel the elevator was a bit old-fashioned, and dragged itself slowly up to the eighth floor. It was a narrow space; Raina was pressed against me and her breath caressed my chin. I had got hold of her by the elbows, forcing my hands into the wide sleeves of her fur jacket. I felt her skin and the scent of her. I began to feel dizzy again, and shut my eyes. I wanted her lips so much that I couldn't speak. She was disturbed too; I could see her bare throat throbbing, the hollow between her grey dress and the locket she wore was rising and falling, beating like the ruby heart of Salvador Dali.

I was shaking; overcome by tenderness.

"Raina!"

The presence of the elevator man was upsetting her.

She spoke reproachfully:

"I ought to be angry with you. You left me so many months...."

How could I explain my sudden departure, my silence? The reason for it all didn't make sense any more.

"I've been travelling around . . . Switzerland, the Balkans, Scandinavia."

She smiled.

"Why the European tour? The Monte Carlo Rally?"

"No. An important assignment."

She had put her head back to look at me better, leaning against the wall of the elevator, watching me with disturbing intensity. I turned my eyes away.

"An assignment . . . for my father?"

It was easy for me to forget that Raina was Arkadin's daughter. In fact, between them they occupied my entire thoughts, my life; but each on a different plane, so they never clashed. I had never seen them together, except during that brief and horrible scene at the castle. The taste of it was so bitter that I'd tried to reject it from my memory. I was very good at this kind of censorship of my past. The parts I didn't like, or where I had shown up badly, I had the gift of wiping out of my mind almost completely. And Raina only evoked moments of happiness, of ecstasy.

I lied, and said:

"No, not for your father."

But she wasn't convinced.

"That's funny, I thought . . . I would have expected it...."

"Of me?"

I didn't like that; my hands, in the warm shelter of the fur sleeves no longer caressed her arms.

"No. Of him. And the way you suddenly went off, your long absence."

I didn't want her to ask too many questions; nor did I want her to guess that I was hired by Arkadin. I needed her; but I wanted her relaxed and tender, so we could forget the rest of the world. I had recourse to a little blackmail; which was cowardly of me, and effeminate.

"Raina darling, why don't you trust me?"

With the others, that always worked. But Raina wasn't the others. Her interested look became critical.

"It's funny," she murmured.

At last we had arrived at my floor. Opening the steel door, which squeaked a little as usual, the elevator man tried to talk to me again. Irritated, I shut the door myself. With some defiance I took Raina's arm. She let me lead her away without resisting.

"My father is always asking me if I trust him." She gave a little laugh that was almost pitying. "That's really what's so funny."

I was annoyed, without knowing why. What was so funny about it?

"Simply that nobody in the world . . . anyhow, nobody with any common sense . . . could trust him in the slightest, nor you either."

My room was at the end of the passage, in a recess, which made it a bit isolated. I looked for the key but I was so upset that I couldn't find it immediately.

I had Raina blocked in the angle of the wall, in the same way as in the elevator. I desperately, almost painfully, wanted her tenderness. No questions, no insinuating remarks, no playing games full of wit and irony, which I wasn't capable of. I wanted to put my head on her shoulder, to breathe the warmth of her body, to kiss her mouth until I could kiss it no more. Go to bed with her? Maybe. Later on. After I had stayed a long time close to her, really close. It would be like a slow fusion, inevitable, the climax of a long intimacy in the silence, in the half-light. I crushed her desperately in my arms, covering her with light, rapid kisses, my lips not resting on any part of her, even where it was such heaven to kiss—the thrilling moistness of her eyes, the silky-smooth surface of her neck, near her ear, her mouth which trembled under mine, trying to hold my lips against hers. Trust me? She told me that was impossible. At any rate, she was there, in that little hotel; she was in my power, silent now, as I had wanted her to be, silent and acquiescent. I had only to push the door open. I hardly noticed that it opened without my even having found the key. No need to put the light on. The divan was immediately to the right. But as I was closing the door—Raina still held close to me, her heavy fur wrap open, revealing her firm and supple body—the room was filled with light, and I saw Arkadin standing in front of the fake fireplace.

The camera can catch with a flash-bulb certain secret expressions which would never be revealed in an ordinary photo. In the clear rays thrown by a weak lamp, which lit his face from beneath, I saw Arkadin's better than he could see mine. Anyway, he wasn't looking at me. His eyes were fixed on Raina; with a furtive, though acute, satisfaction, I saw that he was suffering. His voice, however, was calm and cold as usual, as he asked:

"Raina. What are you doing in this man's room?"

Had she gone a little pale, or was the matt creaminess of her colourless face due to the reflection of the dull lamp, or perhaps to our emotional scene outside the door? Whatever it was, her poise didn't seem to desert her.

"I'm the one who should ask that question," she said. "What are *you* doing here? Don't tell me you knew I was coming here. I didn't know myself. . . ."

Had she hesitated for a long time? Was it by some happy chance that she had learnt of my presence in New York, discovered my address?

"I have some business to discuss with van Stratten."

But it was clear that I was excluded from the discussion, that my role was that of supernumerary, that this was between the two of them.

"Business," repeated Raina; her voice was brisk and harsh. "You gave me your word as it happens. . . ."

He interrupted her, and you could feel the rage under the veneer of self-command which he imposed upon himself.

"He gave me *his* word not to see you again."

I watched the thoughts flitting across Raina's transparent face, the fantastic shadows, delicate and mobile. Her first reflex was of joy. So it wasn't of my own accord that I went away, and didn't get in touch with her. . . . But already another explanation succeeded that one. I gave my word to her father. . . . Why? What methods had he used to impose his will on me? The answer, alas! was too simple, degrading for her and for me. He had paid me, and without a murmur I had given up Raina.

"How much?" she asked dryly.

She had turned to me. Her fur wrap was still gaping open, revealing the lines of her close-fitting dress. But she who, just before, had been so near to me that we breathed as one person, was now detached from me, blinded by the pitiless spite of a humiliated woman.

Arkadin wanted to butt in, but it was he who was excluded from the conversation.

"I asked you a question," said Raina, hammering out the words. "How much?"

There is a certain pleasure, obscure as the bitter-sweet taste of a mango, in relishing one's shame.

I gave her the figure.

"Fifteen thousand dollars."

Then anger came over me suddenly—like when you have a chill and don't look after it, and you end up with a cold in the head—and I went right ahead, not caring about Arkadin's tricks, not trying to hide my annoyance.

"You wanted the truth. You have it. It can't be that much of a surprise to you. You never trusted me, you just said so."

Then I pounced on Arkadin, as a small infuriated dog will sometimes pounce on an enormous, stolid Great Dane.

"As for you, you can spare me the melodramatic scenes of the father discovering his innocent child in the seducer's bedroom. I didn't bring her here. She came here on her own to find me. Anyhow, even if you hadn't been here, she wasn't in any danger. . . ."

At this incredibly opportune moment, the telephone rang. It was the porter who wanted to know at what time I wished my baggage taken down.

"Because I haven't time to spare for either of you. I'm taking a trip. This very evening. On business. Business which might interest, you, however, Mr. Arkadin."

I always talk too much. My mother told me so time and time again. I throw away my advantages by drawing attention to them; I drain away all my energy in childish agitation. I always realise it too late. Yet another side of my immature character. Between Arkadin, still standing in front of the red brick fireplace, and Raina also motionless near the door, I gesticulated wildly, pushed my bags around the room; I would have liked to make a dignified, impressive exit, like in the movies. But just the same I had to go in the bathroom to get my tooth-brush, my shaving-kit, and my slippers, and close my large grip, which was so hard to fasten, with its long, shiny zip. My fingers trembled, and twice I stumbled against a stool placed in front of the radio.

"Fifteen thousand dollars," said Raina, in a low voice.

It was for her own benefit that she repeated the figure. I coloured violently as it occurred to me that this sum, to her, was ludicrous. She despised me not only for the deal itself, but because of the low price I had got for our romance. She was Miss Arkadin, after all. She judged people according to their weight, in dollars.

"Yes," said Arkadin, with insulting detachment, "he wasn't worth any more."

This time it was too much. I calmed down immediately. I threw down the things I was holding in my hand. I'd had as much as I could stomach; inwardly I was on fire.

"That's right. I'm not worth more. And you, Mr. Arkadin, what's your price? Two hundred thousand Swiss francs?"

Arkadin didn't move, but Raina came nearer, and stood between us; she was the stake. I waved her aside, but I got the expression in her eyes. Very, very interested. She was rather surprised, but glad to see that I was going into action at last; she was getting ready to keep the score in this ferocious fight to the death in which I had engaged with her father. And it was my victory she wanted. It went to my head like burning liquor.

"That's the basis of the fabulous Arkadin fortune. Did you know that, Raina? Two hundred thousand Swiss francs. . . ."

My sudden audacity carried me away. I no longer knew what I was saying. In Spain I had seen matadors lose all consciousness of danger in the same way, when a woman looked at them. Sometimes, after two or three almost miraculous feints, which brought the house down, they would get caught on the bulls' horns, and then nothing could save them. But it can happen, too, that their folly and their daring is rewarded, that the bull has at last no more breath and lets itself be mastered, conquered completely.

Arkadin made a riposte unworthy of him, which betrayed his confusion.

"If you think I'm going to give you that fifteen thousand dollars. . . ."

That was a shabby trick for this giant of a man to play! . . . I couldn't help smiling. I detected disillusionment and reproach in Raina's glance. Not for me. For him. I returned to my insolent manner.

"Look, we made a bargain, Mr. Arkadin. You're supposed to have integrity in business matters. And you know very well that dough is dough in any language. I only need enough to take myself off. . . ."

I was amusing myself, like a juggler performing a very difficult trick, made dizzy by his own skill.

"How do you think I can ask your daughter to marry me when I don't have a cent? It would look as though I were after her money."

Neither of them was able to suppress an ejaculation. With the father it was one of indignation. But the daughter cried out my name, stupidly right enough, but with an almost childlike joy.

Actually I had never thought of marrying Raina. The idea had not even crossed my mind. It was so absurd. Marriage, for a guy like me. And with a girl like Raina. But I flung the words at them without thinking, for effect. It was a red scarf waved under Arkadin's nose, speechless with rage as he was. But the impossible suggestion was gaining substance. With the same gesture as the señoritas make when they throw a rose from their shawls, Raina had thrown out my name. The colour was mounting in her cheeks. I swear she was as moved as a college-girl. She had taken the flight of fancy seriously. She thought I wanted to marry her. Well, why not, after all? She was attracted by me. How could I still doubt that? And I loved her, honest to God I loved her. I was crazy about her, I was ready to do anything, anything for her. The only thing I couldn't take would be to lose her again. It was funny. All these months I had treasured the memory of Raina. An ever-present, burning and very dear memory. But deep down inside of me I had put it aside, I had left the problem of Raina until later. In some obscure way I was counting on a lucky break. Like the break of our meeting this evening . . . now that I'd found her again, that she'd come back to me, I couldn't lose her a second time. And Arkadin couldn't do anything about it, about me. All he could do to us he had already written down in his famous yellow dossier, which she hadn't even bothered to read properly. What she had read made no difference. She missed me. She set out to find me again. She came to me without pride, and I only had to hold out my hand and she'd fall into it like a ripe fruit ready to be plucked. Poor old Arkadin, with his millions, his schemes, his power which was no good to him. It pleased me at this moment to be able to torment him with impunity, to insult him, because he had treated me with such icy contempt.

"Everything leads me to the conclusion that these two hundred thousand Swiss francs, your original capital, weren't honestly come by either. Very soon I'm going to know the whole secret of your brilliant career, and who knows, once I have the recipe, maybe I'll become an Arkadin, too."

Slowly, although it was warm in the room, Raina drew her fur wrap around her. Her expression was intense and glazed, as it had been at San Tirso, at the procession of the Penitents.

"You heard him, Raina," said Arkadin heavily.

He spoke in a low voice, recognising defeat.

"This is the fellow you think you're in love with. . . . A vulgar blackmailer."

How could this man so recently have impressed me? I felt like David confronting a Goliath who was vulnerable and easily defeated, after all. Raina shook her head:

"Did I say that I loved him?"

She said this in a strange voice, as though she were talking about something which touched her from a long way off. It was my turn to feel the chink in my armour, to feel that a hit had been scored against me.

"You're not in love with him?"

Arkadin became hopeful again, obviously. But what did it matter what Raina said? I had only to approach her, to take her in my arms, to dare to do what she wouldn't let me do in Spain. She was mine. . . .

"You don't love him, do you, Raina?"

There was anxiety in his voice again. She didn't reassure him, she had no pity. She was only thinking about herself, about me.

"Blackmailer, did you say? I don't see it that way. It looks to me as though you paid him to keep him away from me. . . ."

Hits below the belt aren't forbidden in a battle such as the one I was engaged on. I couldn't allow myself the luxury of having scruples.

I lied.

"I never said I'd given you up, Raina. I accepted this strange assignment which he gave me. . . . An investigation of his real past. Unusual, isn't it? Yes, because of the money, certainly . . . so I could come back to you, Raina, with at least enough to pay for the wedding trip."

145

This exciting investigation with its confusion and its thrills, which had absorbed all my energies for four months, I threw it away like a worn-out glove. The essential thing at this moment was to convince Raina, and I had realised that I could give her all the humbug and clap-trap that one normally gives to any little floosie and get away with it. She had no critical sense any more, no discernment. She wanted to believe in me. She wanted to score over her father. The telephone again. They wanted to remind me that the airport was a long way off, that it would be unwise to delay any more. But I was almost ready to leave. Now I was able to fasten the remaining straps on my grip with an almost ecstatic rapidity. Some good fairy had managed all that scene to perfection; even arranging a lovely exit for me.

"Must you really go?" asked Raina.

She was talking like Mily. One hour earlier the idea of quitting her had been unbearable. Now I fastened the wide belt of my overcoat like a warrior buckling on his sword, with a virile and joyous enthusiasm, before dispensing a few words of comfort to the one who must stay home with her spinning-wheel.

"I must, darling. But I'll come back soon, and this will certainly be my last trip. We'll meet again in Paris." She was leaning against the wall, huddled in her wrap, and her face was pale and hollow. She seemed apathetic.

"Oh," she moaned, "when are you going to be through with all these trips? I'm sick of being a kind of high-class gypsy. I do want to pitch my tent somewhere. . . ."

Arkadin, too, had noticed her lassitude, and in spite of his bitterness, he was overcome by the tenderness that was in him. He went to her almost humbly.

"My dear, why didn't you stay and rest a while in Capri . . . or San Tirso? You say you like it there. Why did you come? You know, it was you who insisted on spending this week in New York to do your Christmas shopping."

She had her hands deep down in her pockets, and looked at him from under her eyelids, sulkily, crossly, like a naughty little girl, her lip raised slightly over her small teeth.

"I came because I wanted to, and I wanted to come because I thought I might find Guy here."

It was the knock-out; Arkadin had hit the canvas.

The porter came for my baggage. I took a last look around the room. No passionate farewells. That would be in bad taste. What would be the point anyhow? Weren't we going to see each other again in a week or two? We would spend Christmas together in Paris.

"So long, kid."

I threw her a kiss. She acknowledged it by slowly lowering her eyelashes. Arkadin was still standing near her, awkwardly, as though for the first time weighed down by his massive body; and his legendary profile was distorted, as though fallen away, leaving nothing but a great bearded figure who was almost ridiculous.

I raised my hat to him with exaggerated politeness.

"Till we meet again, Mr. Arkadin."

And I couldn't help adding, even though I could already hear the friendly little squeaking of the elevator door from the end of the passage:

"Funny, isn't it, how sometimes, and more often than you'd think, certain things escape you . . . hopelessly."

At the airport, they had given me five minutes' grace. I failed to miss the Mexico plane. It would have been better if I had.

CHAPTER SIX

IT had all been very unpleasant.

I had given orders for them to put into the shore. There wasn't much risk, the flat coast seemed deserted. Besides, it was doubtful if Oskar would try to get away. He was lying prostrate on a pile of sacks in the stifling little cabin, sleeping, or had he passed out? His periods of coma were getting more frequent and more painful, I don't know which scared me the most; this half-dead state, or the nervous crises which made him grimace and beg for another shot, slavering all the time.

I'd always had a kind of superstitious fear of dope. Once or twice I'd tried it, so as not to look a fool. But obviously, I was bristling with mistrust of the stuff; I was not in a state of grace, and felt nothing except nausea and migraine. It's a lucky thing to be immune against certain temptations. Not to drink, not to touch dope. . . . I remember the comfortable feeling of security I had when the jerks looking for snow or opium came begging me to get it for them, no matter how much it cost. I looked down on them from the heights of my abstinence, with pitying contempt. Looking down on everybody, like Tadeus. . . . It was a very comforting sensation.

But with Oskar, I felt nothing but compassion and disgust. He wasn't a pretty sight, this poor sallow man, shivering with lust.

. . . It's a privation worse than either hunger or thirst, it seems. But I wasn't in a position to make comparisons.

This trip to Mexico had been very different from what I had imagined. It really needed the mean, conspiratorial atmosphere of my little hotel in New York—my proper environment—to make me feel so triumphant on my departure. Scoring over Arkadin had made me drunk; and I had used a coward's weapon—a hostage. Because Raina had let herself be kissed in a hotel corridor, I thought I could get away with anything. When the plane waited for me before taking off, it increased my childish sense of importance; I had flirted with the air-hostess, chatted with the co-pilot good-humouredly, and with an air of authority, I had reassured a little girl who was scared because the plane was crossing a storm-cloud. The soothing atmosphere, the feeling of being wrapped in cotton-wool and surrounded by every comfort and consideration, which is the role on these big airlines, had helped me to retain my feeling of satisfied well-being.

For a little I played with the idea that Sophie would be at the airport, waiting for me.

The reality was certainly different. . . .

There I was on this coast road, walking with long strides, breathing in greedily great gulps of ozone from the Atlantic wind. I had finished up, on board, by getting sick myself, my nerves were worn through. The Gulf is very treacherous. The water, which seems calm, shakes the boats with little sly jerks, worse than the ground-swell. On the bridge I couldn't hope to make Oskar talk. The strong air stupefied him even more, and his fishy, watery glance lost itself in the distance, eluded me. I had to keep him with me in the cabin, holding him upright by the lapels of his old velvet jacket, searching every expression on his bloated face, every furtive look in his bulging eyes. A stink of corpses came from him, and the heat was stifling in the little narrow place, which was like a cupboard. His hands remained frozen and stiff.

Occasionally I would shake him furiously, wanting to hit him. But maybe he wouldn't even have noticed the blows. He looked as though he was made of white gelatine. Then I bit my lip and clenched my fists, and tried gentler tactics. I made suggestions to him, I humoured him, I made promises.

"Just answer my question, old man. And I'll give you your ration. And then we'll both go back to Mexico."

What made it all the funnier was that I had no 'snow' on me. I had never been in Mexico before, I didn't know anybody there, and to get contacts among the dope-fiends would have been a long and dangerous business. I was paying for my stuffed-shirt attitude when I'd been mixed up in this kind of racket in the past. Which was really only once, in Spain, and it had left an unpleasant taste in my mouth. But this past prudery had cut me off from the supply networks, so that I had to dupe Oskar by showing him a packet of bicarbonate. He was so stupefied that he didn't even suspect me. I have never seen such an acute case of narcotic poisoning. When I saw him for the first time, however, at the 'Amor Brujo', he had appeared almost normal. At least as normal as any of the phenomena that you find in the night-clubs of big cities. Sophie's night-club, or rather the night-club financed by Señora Jesus Martinez, as she now was, seemed very ordinary. A few wood-carvings on the walls, Indian masks and headdresses and some pottery made an exotic background for tourists. One was offered a fantastic 'pulque', and drank out of pig-skin bottles of obscene shapes which rested on wooden racks. One ate tortillas, stuffed pimentos, iguana done on a skewer from enormous lacquered plates; and an orchestra dressed up as gauchos produced mournful, quivering guitar music. I was very bored, not knowing where to go, when Oskar appeared from God knows where, and sitting down quite at home, ignoring the musicians, began to play the concertina. He was like some drunken hobo. He had the serene impudence, the don't-give-a-damn attitude of a Gringo who's had more than his whack of tequila or whisky. However, he didn't play 'Susanna' or 'Star-spangled Banner', but some complicated, poignant piece, obviously Slav.

I looked at him more closely. Somewhere in the unhealthy, bloated features, without being able to define it I saw a fleeting but undeniable resemblance. But to whom or what? His hair had lost its colour; probably it had never been a very definite shade in the first place. His skin had the lack-lustre tinge of pewter, and beneath his pale eyelashes his eyes, too, were the colour of stagnant water. His velvet jacket was very old, but good; it had the aristocratic air which all things that are originally of good quality seem to retain, however decayed they may become. And Oskar himself, playing his lament in an absent manner, wore, momentarily, the fixed and tragic expression of an Indian mask; I knew that expression, the impassiveness of it. It could only mean the extreme depths of melancholy or of humiliation; or contempt.

And suddenly I recognised that dull stupefaction, at the same time full of contempt and of unapproachable dignity. It was like the exiled White Russian aristocrats, washing dishes with hands from which nothing could take away the elegance; hands that still had signet-rings with their coats-of-arms, worn on the little finger. Oskar must be Russian. Or Polish. Polish, of course; now I recognised the tune he was dragging out of the concertina. I had heard Tadeus whistling it one day, while a horrible little Arab ruffian was trying to explain how he had mislaid twelve boxes of nylons. The evening suddenly became interesting. I had invited Oskar to my table. He needed no pressing. But he didn't drink. He didn't talk. He sat opposite me, his concertina in his lap, looking indifferently into space, answering my questions absent-mindedly. Yes, he was one of the regulars of this joint. You could tell that from the way nobody paid the least attention to him, even when, like a cat stretching itself, mewing, in its corner, he would take up the concertina and draw out a long arpeggio or a few chords; with no reference either to the orchestra or the dancers. Yes, he knew Señora Jesus Martinez. He hardly seemed startled that I referred to the latter as Sophie. This familiarity did surprise him, of course; but the sensation of surprise had to cross heavy layers of inertia before reaching a vital centre, and the effect of it was diminished gradually, provoking in the end nothing more than a vague curiosity deep down in his discoloured eyes. It took me some time to understand the reason for this stupor which enveloped him like a fog. The place was badly lit by candles fixed in wrought-iron stands. Finally I leaned forward, and in the light of the yellow flame I saw his inflamed nostrils, dripping slightly. Then it was all crystal-clear; the pale, enamel look, the softness of his face and the veneer of indifference. He was stuffed with dope, embalmed like a mummy.

But he was my only point of contact with Sophie.

So I went back several times to 'El Amor Brujo'. I spent hours drawing bits and pieces of conversation out of Oskar. Gradually I became more and more convinced that he was deeply involved with Sophie, and had been even more so in the past. Otherwise he wouldn't have been allowed in this place, where a moustachioed manager kept very strict control beneath the atmosphere of picturesque friendliness which prevailed. He had his eye on everybody; but sometimes Oskar would suddenly start going round the tables holding out a large, battered hat or an earthenware bowl, and the guests, either amused or irritated, would throw money into it. Or else, becoming serious, he would take out of his pocket a dirty bit of paper containing the quills of a porcupine. An Indian witch-doctor had given them to him, he said, and they could cure heart diseases and snake-bites. . . . Sometimes the tourists would buy some, in the same way as they bought coloured postcards and fake Indian jewellery.

I used to wonder why Oskar bothered about money. I never saw him pay for anything. He would take some dish off a tray that was being taken to one of the tables, and without a word the waiter would go back to get another portion in its place. I suspected that he slept in some corner behind the kitchen. He invariably wore the same jacket, the same woollen shirt with the orange check. But he wasn't dirty; the poison seemed to conserve him.

Obviously he was never without dope. You could see that in the serenity of his face, scarcely disturbed by an occasional nervous sniff. So I had nothing to offer him; that is why I decided I must manufacture needs for him, as he obviously didn't have any of his own. The surest and quickest, though the cruellest, method was to deprive him of 'snow'.

So I hired an old Ford, and on the coast I got a little fishing-boat with a sailor who looked like a bandit. But that was exactly what I wanted, because I was going to have to use him for nothing less than a kidnapping. I paid him well, he never asked any questions. He told me the boat would be waiting for me in a little place on the coast half-way between Vera Cruz and Nautla, ready to put to sea. He understood that this was going to be some crooked deal, and he didn't give a damn.

I went back to the 'Amor Brujo', looking for some pretext to get Oskar out in the street with me. I had parked the car in an alley near by. It was very much simpler than I thought it would be. In the town I had seen posters advertising a Polish movie, 'Barska Street'. It happened that Oskar had actually lived in that street. I succeeded in getting him vaguely interested. I told him the movie was showing in the cinema at the corner. There were photographs outside the door. He let me take him away with quite a good grace. When I knocked him out by clubbing him lightly on the back of his neck, he seemed to collapse like a pricked balloon. I was hardly able to drag him into the Ford, not because of his weight, but because his body gave; it seemed to be soft and spongy.

A whiff of chloroform enabled me to get him on board the boat without incident; when he came round, in the open sea, he seemed scarcely surprised. He merely sniffed convulsively two or three times, put his hand into his pocket, and found what he was looking for. . . . I had been crazy not to search him. I had lost at least one precious day.

But the sea made him sick, so I was able to relieve him of his small portion of dope, and by the evening he was beginning to get very jumpy. Then I got seriously to work on him.

To begin with he resisted savagely. He shouted that he wanted to be on dry land again. Then he relapsed into an angry silence. This was followed by an astonishing flood of insults and threats in every language, particularly Polish. But these were nothing compared with the discomfort caused by his increasing convulsive twitching, his nausea and his sudden black-outs.

Paco, the sailor, stayed at the tiller, chewing a quid of reddish tobacco, and amusing himself by spitting long jets of brown saliva into the water. Twice a day he would bring us down an oily, burnt stew, or half-cooked fish, which I had to force down my throat. Oskar ate nothing; I was worried by his extreme weakness, which soon made him collapse on to the bunk like a grey jelly-fish. But I had to torment him unmercifully, poor devil, dragging out bit by bit the confused recollections of his past.

Often I was scared. Dripping with sweat in the fetid atmosphere of the cabin, bullying this pathetic figure shaken with convulsions and sobs, relentless in my need to torture him, I vividly remembered the many cases of hyper-intoxication of which I had heard. Some of them pass out suddenly, like a candle when there's no air. Others go raving mad.

This lasted three days and nights. The results were poor, a confused recital interrupted a hundred times. I badly needed a rest. Anyhow, Oskar was worn out. I would get nothing more out of him for an hour or so.

So I walked along the coast road. Paco had warned me that the coast was unhealthy in that part. That didn't matter, I was sinking into a bog anyway. . . .

I tried to assemble the facts I had so painfully collected. Oskar belonged to Sophie's gang. Not merely as a stooge. But he wasn't the boss either. She was that. Not even her right-hand man. But he would try, every now and then, to get back some of his lost self-esteem by saying: "If you'd known me in those days, you wouldn't have dared to treat me like this. . . ." More often he would whimper with senile cowardice: "You wait till Sophie hears what you did to me. . . ." He sniffed. "She was always good to me, Sophie was. Even now, if I didn't have it. . . ." He went on to say with his intermittent vanity, which was getting stronger: "I never wanted anything from her. The love of a woman like that is a great honour for any man. It can't last for ever." Or else maybe he would beat his chest with typically Slav emphasis and swear I wouldn't get another word out of him. "I'm a filthy swine, O.K. I didn't treat Sophie right, either. I've been a dirty, stinking blood-sucker. But I'm no stool-pigeon. I'm not Athabadze. Poor Sophie, she was always too good to me. . . ."

Other names were mixed up in the scrappy recital: Zouk and Simon and Chaskiel, who had only one eye. Once I thought I heard Tadeus' name also, but that must have been a mistake. Oskar stammered out the words quite unintelligibly; almost unconsciously.

I had managed, however, to isolate the name of Athabadze, which seemed each time to stir up great fury and indignation in the amorphous mass which was Oskar. It was certainly hatred which I detected; a hatred which had not lost its venom in spite of the passing of the years and the blunting of almost all the faculties of this poor, miserable wretch. Professional rivalry? A woman? Both?

I walked on with long strides along the dirty shingle. Sometimes I would crush under my feet the crabs which dragged themselves heavily through the mud, leaving behind them the shining trail of their spawn. That reminded me of Oskar.

On either side of the metalled road the ground was all swamp covered with rough greyish grass, where snakes glided in and out, disturbed by my approach. Everything was muddy, dirty and sinister, even to the heavy grey light in the sky, hanging over the motionless Gulf.

It was as difficult, exhausting and tedious to catch the fragments

I had squeezed, bit by bit, out of Oskar like a refractory tapeworm, as to try and catch the lizards which were running under my feet.

However . . . Athabadze, that was a valuable clue. Sophie had been in love with him. Without any doubt he had betrayed her. At least Oskar said so. But that could be the spite of an unsuccessful rival. If only I could date the facts which the Pole had given me. He got everything mixed up; from the good old days in Warsaw, where in one evening he would lose heaven knows how much dough without batting an eyelid, to his present miserable state, when he had to put up with being treated like a hobo by that dirty Yid Muller who managed the 'Amor Brujo'.

"Zouk was a Yid, too, and I never trusted him."

But it was Athabadze who split on them. "And all my miseries started then. All my bad luck comes from him, the son-of-a-bitch. A curse on all his children, if he has any !"

Perhaps Athabadze had talked for 200,000 Swiss francs. No, that was too much for a stool-pigeon. The Polish police wouldn't be that generous.

I tried to get more out of him.

"And Sophie was ruined by him?"

The sadness in his bluish eyes was touching.

"Yes, ruined. Imagine, I saw her actually weep, a woman like her. Only once, it's true."

Tears of rage: the tears of the Amazon who had let herself be licked by a small-time crook. The bitter tears of a woman who had loved. How old was she then? Oskar's age was impossible to define. Time had ceased to exist for him.

"However, I'm a generous man. Jealousy is a base emotion. I forgave her. But that little pimp Wasaw . . ."

Wasaw Athabadze. . . . If I could only cable to Wasaw and put someone on this trail. I had one or two pals there whom I met in London or in the prison-camps in Germany, when I was with the U.S. Army. Some of them had given me their addresses. But I didn't know anything about them any more. I didn't dare to contact them for a thing like this, because I was afraid of what the consequences of a mysterious long-distance cable would be for them.

I could ask the Professor . . . or Tadeus. Trebitsch, maybe, with the help of a cheque which I wouldn't allow to go through until I had received his reply. A miserable village was silhouetted in the distance. I started to walk faster.

The post office was hidden behind a clutter of prickly fig-trees. A man with a heavy face like gingerbread was sleeping among the flies behind a desk sticky with filth. Feverishly I wrote out a cable in English and while he painfully spelt it out, I noticed hanging on the low ceiling a large yellow and green lizard, with a long, greedy tongue, gobbling the flies and gnats which hovered in the sunlight and rolling its great lidless eyes. Greedy, like Oskar, like me. For poison. For vermin. . . .

What had happened between Sophie and Wasaw Athabadze?

CHAPTER SEVEN

I WAS lolling in a deep cane chair, and a purring ventilator stirred up a kind of ersatz fresh air under the awning. The ice piled in my long glass cooled the palms of my hands, and as I sucked busily at my straw, my mouth became filled with the good, re-freshing sourness of the gin fizz. I had only to put out my hand to reach the big porcelain dish full of papaws, bananas, enormous oranges and sweet lemons. I had only to make a sign for one of the pretty brown-skinned girls who passed up and down the terrace shaking their black locks, their petticoats and the fringes of their brightly-coloured skirts, for her to come and sit near me and offer me the pleasure of her company . . . and the rest. . . . The country-side which one could see from this vast flowery terrace, where the constantly watered flagstones maintained a green humidity, was of incredible beauty. The indigo sea, smooth as velvet, lying behind the high red cliffs, and the snow on the nearby mountain-tops sparkled like jewels against the intense blue of the sky.

I derived absolutely no pleasure in all this, not even the animal satisfaction which I had come here to find. I regretted not having taken the first plane for Europe. I had very little hope of reaching Sophie, in her aura of money and respectability, protected by her husband, the General, hero of some local revolution and now all-powerful in Mexico.

Besides, I didn't have to see Sophie any more. She wouldn't be able to add much to what I had finally succeeded in dragging out of Oskar. My report was almost complete now. I could face Arkadin, go back to Raina. Why, then, should I wait any longer on this baking beach, in this picture-postcard countryside, petrified by the brutal sunlight?

It was morbid curiosity that kept me here. It would be hard to abandon the trail without actually reaching Sophie. I wanted to know this astonishing woman who once had Arkadin on a string, like a poodle, for three whole years. He broke his chain, bit the hand that had fed and petted him. Yes, no doubt of that. The fact remained, however, that for three years the man who wasn't yet the great Arkadin, but the little Wasaw Athabadze, came to get his orders, quietly, like Simon, like one-eyed Chaskiel, like Ferencz, Herscheles and Jacob Zouk, like all the nine underlings in Sophie's gang. Mme Sophie, as they called her in the underworld.

Perhaps that was why I had come to Acapulco, why for two days I lay around in a luxury and idleness which had no pleasure for me. It could be said of Arkadin, that if he had not actually denounced Sophie and her gang, as Oskar maintained, he had at any rate slunk off with the dough when things got too hot, like a maître d'hôtel who takes advantage of a fire to remove the silver.

That, then, was his secret. A miserable, wretched thing! A figure who made governments tremble, who could break men of honour and distinction by a telephone-call, who loved the grand manner! In Spain they told me how—parodying the gallant gesture of some hidalgo who had bought a palace in Seville so that his lady could pick the rose that she had caught sight of through the openings in the door of the patio—he had bought San Tirso simply because Raina, driving along the road, had sighed out longingly: "Ah, look Papa, the original Sleeping Beauty castle."

Did he think he could keep his daughter for himself, protected by the high walls, the moat, the ravine, and by his accumulated riches and most jealous care? Hadn't he ever read the fairy-tale, didn't he

159

know that a Prince Charming arrives one fine day, inevitably, and wakes up the princess and carries her off on a white horse? Even if the prince is only a degenerate adventurer with more debts than titles, and who has fought against creditors and cops rather than dragons. . . .

I was lost in my reverie, with eyes half-closed because of the dazzling reflection of the sun on the white marble flags. I looked fixedly at a large plant in a bowl; its enormous flowers opened, fleshy, vivid red, damp with sap, pulpy and glossy as skin. And I thought of Raina's mouth. . . .

But I had to think. . . . There was nothing missing among the facts I had been told to establish. I even had the date and place of birth. A small town near Tiflis . . . in 1895. Quite a coincidence. When he left Poland, his pockets stuffed with booty, Athabadze was exactly my age. I had been at times a crook, and a confidence-man, I had fooled people, lived on them; but I had never stolen. So why should Mr. Arkadin turn up his nose at me? I sniggered stupidly to myself, with defiance. A girl who had passed turned back again, on the look-out for an invitation, winked with arch slyness, and as I relapsed into my torpor again, finally went away, shrugging her satiny shoulders.

What was Arkadin going to say when he learnt the truth about his past? In France, during the 'ancien régime', foundling children were always treated as though they came from good families; it was considered preferable, as nobody knew anything of their birth, to ennoble a peasant rather than run the risk of debasing a nobleman. So Arkadin, trading on the mystery of his past life, had perhaps imagined various exciting or tragic adventures; but certainly not this shabby story of white slavery, of being the lover and right-hand man of a female gangster, an informer, a pickpocket.

I chewed over the more sordid details of this affair with satisfaction and yet a vague disgust. Oskar had suddenly loosened up after nursing his grievances for so long, and I had been swamped by the fetid flood of his reminiscences. I learned how, for years,

Sophie had run the best organised gang in Central Europe. It all began in the troubled days after the first war; they decided to help Russians to escape from the Reds with their jewellery and possessions. Some of the refugees had been unable to bring their money out with them, and the gang would get them on their feet again. Gradually a kind of 'agency' was organised, consisting of pretty girls without resources and without too many scruples. In the end the real racket was started. Sophie took charge of this with great vigour and enthusiasm. She was known as far away as Rio and Hong Kong. She maintained a military discipline and efficiency throughout. She controlled the procurers, the entrepreneurs, the agents, the supervisors; for she didn't abandon her charges after sending them to the night-clubs and the brothels of Central America or the Middle East. She liked to get news of them, to know if they were happy, and some of them, who'd struck it rich, would come back to see her and thank her for what she'd done. "Like a mother . . . she was like a mother to us," said Oskar, sniffling.

As I listened, I imagined a fat mammy with hennaed hair, with finger-nails which were grey under the varnish, counting her money and wetting her finger to turn over the bills, sorting out cheques like a butcher's wife. And it seemed she indulged in caprices in the manner of Catherine the Great. She had to make sure for herself that her pimps were really convincing. No doubt she tried them all, except one-eyed Chaskiel. . . . Or Jacob Zouk, the book-keeper, who looked like a sheep with his mass of woolly hair.

Why had she married Oskar? For love, he said. More likely to avoid some irritating formality insisted upon by the Warsaw police. Sophie was of Russian origin, she needed a Polish passport. And they had been ignobly happy until the arrival of Athabadze. Could Oskar be believed when he said that the latter was as thin as a starving wolf and had eyes glistening with passionate greed when Sophie took him into the gang? In his leaky, moujik boots, he surrounded her with the most servile devotion and was ready to do whatever was required of him. He sang Russian songs to her which made her cry. Oskar had been indulgent of the little weaknesses in a wife who was also his boss. He had accepted the long evenings when Sophie and her protégé got roaring drunk on vodka and sentimentality. He even took it when she gave herself to him for a one-night stand. He was good-looking, if you like the cossack type, tall as a church steeple, with a chest on him like a cavalryman. Sophie had earned the right to amuse herself a little. . . .

Things went wrong when Athabadze started to act big, to think he could give orders. Above all, when he swaggered around the place in a skunk pelisse which made him look like a Russian aristocrat. Then Oskar got jealous. He complained to Sophie and she, very bitter, told him to mind his own business. From then on Athabadze's authority became stronger every day. Sophie neglected her affairs, spent hours closeted with her favourite, behaving like a love-sick shopgirl. It was at this moment that an anti-vice campaign started in Poland. It was a real clean-up. The police had agents everywhere, in bars, night-clubs, dispensaries, beauty culture establishments and dancing schools. Sophie didn't take the threat very seriously.

I didn't believe her young lover had denounced her. He had more to lose than to gain by such a manœuvre. But it's easy to understand how, when he discovered in time that things were getting hot, he thought primarily of pulling out as advantageously as possible.

Maybe it was Sophie herself who had been warned, and who entrusted him with her dough so he could take it abroad where she would rejoin him. It would be easy enough to go to Zürich, when they had agreed on Vienna or Hamburg. . . . Or else, why not? something intervened, unforeseeable, fatal, which freed Athabadze. To prove I was acting in good faith, and that I was giving him the benefit of the doubt, I would check, at his expense, of course, if there hadn't been a railway accident in Central Europe in that year 1927. A shock, a nervous disturbance, and there was a traveller fleeing through the night without bothering to pick up his grip or put on his overcoat. He walks a long time, he comes to a quayside, shivering, lost . . . with amnesia. . . .

I was more than half asleep, my thoughts rendered formless by the state of torpor of my mind. The page-boy had to call out three times that I was wanted on the telephone. He was dragging behind him a long flex which twisted like a snake on the wet marble. He put the phone on the little table beside my chair and went away, after pocketing his peso tip.

It was Arkadin, and I was hardly surprised. I sank back a little deeper on my damp cushions, and took time to swallow two or three gulps of gin-fizz. I didn't have to stand to attention in front of the old paramour of Mme Sophie. And without trying to hide my extreme amusement I told him I had excellent news for him.

"Your past, Mr. Arkadin. I finally got the goods on you. . . . The dirt ! . . . all of it, and pretty dirty some of it is, at that. . . ." I waited for him to speak. He must be breathless with curiosity, he must realise that what I'd found out wasn't to his credit. "Can you prove it?" he asked simply. How could I have thought he would take my word for it? Proofs, no, only evidence. But now that I had the goods on him, it would hardly be difficult to find documents confirming everything.

"I'm thinking of leaving on Tuesday's plane. You don't mind, I hope, that I took advantage of my first visit to Mexico to travel around a bit. Anyhow, I was tired and rather . . . depressed. I needed a change of atmosphere. . . ."

I half expected him to interrupt, but he said nothing.

"Don't be impatient, Mr. Arkadin. You'll find all the details in the report. I'm going to prepare it at my leisure."

"I don't need a report. You only have to tell me what you know. . . ."

I laughed insultingly:

"What? On the long distance telephone? . . . Sorry, Mr. Arkadin, but I really think . . ."

But he started to laugh, too, and such unusual gaiety grated so sharply in my ear that I jumped. It wasn't only the telephone that brought me the echo of it. I straightened up on my cushions, and took off the large straw hat that had been shading my eyes during my siesta. And I saw that they had removed from behind me a long trellis covered with potted banana shrubs. One could then see a second terrace, a continuation of the one where I used to spend my days. Arkadin was strutting along it, also ridiculously dressed in white linen and wearing, like myself, a peasant's straw hat. He was surrounded by his usual entourage: the secretaries in jackets and striped trousers, the Chinese chiropodist in a kimono; and two or three little tarts laughing with him in a sycophantic manner and sticking out their breasts. They were all laughing at me; and I felt so violently angry that I went purple in the face. The coolness which I had tried so hard to achieve disappeared, and I was dripping with sweat as I angrily hung up the receiver and went over towards the jeering group. I had something that would silence this untimely mirth.

Arkadin watched me coming without moving, draped in his white linen peignoir, his foot given over to the skilled hands of the chiropodist. He was playing absent-mindedly with the long, sleek silky hair of a little half-caste who was squatting beside him. He had never looked more like an Eastern potentate. He reminded me of that statue of the bearded and lecherous centaur caressing a young girl which is at the entrance to the big bridge at Berne. Funny how he succeeded in disconcerting me. Each time I met him he would be different from what I had expected. I left him at San Tirso in a threatening mood, and when I met him again he was ingratiating. In New York I found him vulnerable when I had expected him to be intimidating and omnipotent. And now, when I thought he would be uneasy, a wretched individual whom I could almost be permitted to insult, I found him sitting there, in all the insolence of his obesity, his wealth and his infernal impudence, surrounded by his collection of toadies and parasites.

He didn't seem to be affected in any way by what I had told him on the telephone. It didn't look as though he feared any appalling revelation from me. It was true that he didn't know what I knew, he couldn't imagine it. The feeling of superiority which this ignorance gave me made me tolerant. I decided to take the thing lightly.

"What a pleasant surprise. . . . I was beginning to get kind of bored. . . ."

He shrugged his shoulders in a reproachful manner.

"Bored . . . in a country like this, with such lovely girls? Their skin, my dear fellow. . . . Pure silk."

His hand passed slowly across the naked back of the little girl who was leaning against his chair, and I thought: "That's the gesture of a connoisseur; he's been in the flesh trade." I longed to throw the truth in his face.

"Could I see you alone?" I asked him.

I was annoyed to find that in spite of myself my tone was deferential. He leaned on his elbow on the wheeled divan, his dressing-gown gaping open, showing his hairy chest.

"I know what you mean," he said.

And as I looked around me:

"All these people scare you. . . . But you see I can't do without either the...useful"—he indicated the secretaries with their papers— "...or the ornamental," he added with a sigh, slapping the brown thighs of the girl.

She squeaked, threw her arms about Arkadin's neck, and started whining that she wanted to go water-skiing. This was becoming ludicrous, and I didn't try to hide my irritation. Arkadin still affected a disillusioned indulgence.

"It's a delightful sport. . . . I'll have to try it one of these days."

I laughed.

"Yeah, you'd look real cute on a pair of water skis."

But a secretary with glasses intervened.

"Mr. Arkadin would look exactly like Neptune."

It was really grotesque, the gravity of this boot-licker, and the satisfied air of the gross man, sunk in his fat, enjoying the exotic debauchery of the terrace. Another secretary arrived, carrying a bundle of papers, looking important. Arkadin indolently took the documents from him, gave them the once-over, and dictated some orders in cipher. That would be all part of the show. The big executive playing with millions while having his big toe-nail filed. . . .

In any case, it had gone on long enough. He probably realised that; he shook off the chiropodist and the girl like a dog getting rid of its fleas, then extricated himself heavily from his couch. His linen peignoir dragged behind him like a toga.

"Buy Chiquita a present," he said to the secretary with glasses. "Category 3A. . . . No, don't let's overdo it. 3B. That won't be too much. . . . And get some Chilean pesos, we're leaving immediately."

Then, almost amicably, he slipped his arm through mine and drew me towards the other end of the terrace. I was wearing a short-sleeved shirt, and the touch of his bare arm on mine made me sick. I side-stepped.

"Alright, let's go," he said. "I'm listening."

For forty-eight hours I had savoured my little story, yet when the moment came I told it awkwardly, as though it were something I had read in a newspaper.

"Up to 1927, a woman called Sophie had a certain racket. . . . You know what."

But he didn't play, didn't help me, I had to give him the whole thing.

". . . And of the nine men who worked for her, three are dead now. Three are behind the Iron Curtain . . . we can count them out, too. There remains Oskar, who's in Mexico, living on Sophie. And a certain Jacob Zouk, who's in Germany. And the last one . . ."

He didn't accept the obvious conclusion.

"Well? The last one?"

And I looked him straight in the face.

"I think he wants to go water-skiing."

I had expected various reactions. But not this overwhelming

flabbiness with which he dragged himself along, half-naked in this Turkish bath atmosphere among the green plants and the gungling jets of water.

"Do you have any proof? . . ."

The heat didn't make me dull and heavy; on the contrary it irritated me, as it irritates flies. I felt like a horse-fly buzzing round a bull, enraged by its placidity and the thickness of its hide.

"No need for proof. It all fits perfectly."

I told him his name, his birth-place, how he began in Sophie's gang, his luck with her and the way in which, undoubtedly, he had found himself with 200,000 francs in his pocket.

"And it was this . . . Oskar who told you all that."

"Nearly all. . . . I completed the details with logical deductions which it will be easy to check. If you hadn't always been so infernally camera-shy, I could have shown your picture to Oskar. He would certainly have recognised you, in spite of the beard. . . ."

He hitched up his gown which was sliding off his fat shoulders.

"And this guy . . . the one who's in Germany. . . . He would recognise me, too?"

"Sure he would. But you're in no danger of meeting him. He's in jail. Life sentence. White slavery gets a stiff one, you know."

He didn't seem to follow the allusion.

"By the way," he said, "they forgot to tell you there are two men waiting for you in the hall."

Perhaps this was a trick to interrupt our interview, so that he could pull himself together again.

"Let them wait," I said.

But Arkadin turned back towards his group of lackeys.

"I advise you to treat them with some respect. They're from the Police."

And since I couldn't hide the fact that he'd registered a hit, he added paternally:

"I've paid some more money into your account, in case you should need it."

We were quits once more. He was treating me like a salaried employee. Not a very smart one, but willing; better to encourage him. And I was disarmed; I had thrown all the dirt in his face, uselessly, like a kid very seriously firing a pop-gun under the nose of a passer-by, who is half-amused and half-irritated by the performance.

"One more thing," said Arkadin, going back to his chaise-longue. "All you've told me . . . this improbable story . . ."

"This true story, Mr. Athabadze."

"Alright, if that's the way you want it. . . . In any case, when you see Raina, don't say a word about it. I have your word for that?"

Yet another change of front? After treating me like some tiresome hanger-on, he was speaking to me as a friend.

"My word's worth nothing to you. You already said so."

He looked at me sadly and reproachfully.

"Van Stratten," he said, with a heavy sigh. "It's impossible for a man like you to realise what it is to have a conscience . . . and no memory at all. . . . To be ashamed of something you can't even remember. . . ."

CHAPTER EIGHT

I T's a funny thing. I'd been mixed up with the cops in a lot of different countries, but I'd never been extradited before.

"Just another new experience," I thought.

But it was no good trying to laugh the thing off, to tell myself that in any case I had decided to leave two days later, and that altogether my stay in Mexico had not been all that pleasant: I still didn't like the idea of quitting the country with a couple of cops.

At least they had left me a few hours of freedom, until the first available plane out of the country. The police sergeant, a little dry, yellow guy like a piece of kindling, had recommended me to be at the airport one hour before take-off. And he instructed me to go as quickly as possible to the residence of Señora Jesus Martinez, who wanted to see me. I had no reason to refuse.

In the taxi which took me all along the vast avenues towards the heights of Chapultepec, I tried to prepare myself for this interview which I had sought so long and which was now being granted me— forced on me, even—when I had given up hope of it.

There was no doubt that it was to the wife of the powerful General that I owed my expulsion from the country.

At first I had suspected Arkadin of a manœuvre which would ensure that I didn't meet his former mistress. Mistress in both senses of the word. But the insistent manner of the cop, the deference with which he pronounced Sophie's name, made it clear that it was from her he had received his instructions.

It was a beautiful amber-coloured evening, very sultry under the awnings. Women were cooking tortillas or offering bowls of dried water-melon seeds. Whenever the car stopped at a red light, ragged kids would crowd round the door holding out their dirty hands; then they would break up and start running in and out of the traffic like skinny chickens. As we passed I noticed the flaking domes like the flanks of a lizard, and great barbaric frescoes. These objects scattered my thoughts, my mind was a blank. I was tired, probably. The sudden changes of altitude are very trying for foreigners. And for some time my life had been fluctuating rather too frequently, too many contradictory cross-currents of hope, disgust, impatience and discouragement.

But I was nearing the end.

We were moving now between the green foliage of villas; lawns replaced the thickets and groves. The flowers were just too purple or too red, the walls too white or too yellow. I had an almost unhealthy desire for drabness and quiet colours.

The car turned in between two very high walls, straight through an iron gateway where there were two elaborately-uniformed guards. I noticed they had pistols in their belts.

But the rest of the place was reassuring. Two thick cedars threw a dense shade over a lawn where a Persian cat was dozing. A patio opened up, with its little fountain, under the drooping branches of a bougainvillaea. All the blinds were lowered and it was as dark as a cave in the great hall into which they ushered me without asking my name. Brightly-coloured crockery covered the walls, the floor was strewn with sweet-smelling branches; but two more armed guards were stationed on either side of an enormous door which was studded with nails like that of a Spanish convent.

The cat had followed me cautiously, and having had a look at me went over towards the guarded door. It seemed to open of its own accord, and I followed the animal into a still vaster room, darker than the hall. I could make out a group seated round a table by the light from two wrought-iron candelabra.

"Come in," said a woman's voice. "Your plane leaves in two hours. We haven't any time to waste."

A thick carpet covered the paved floor. A servant with long, plaited hair, her shoulders and armpits bare under her cotton shift, was sitting on the ground peeling oranges.

Sophie had her back to me, so that it was her companions I saw first. There were two officers, and an enormous guy as black as a stick of liquorice, whose unbuttoned uniform jacket and rumpled shirt revealed a fat, shining torso. He could only be the General. His teeth like a wild boar's, some of them with gold fillings, burst out of his thick mouth, forcing up his great coarse lip. He had very small, pig-like eyes, and his forehead was so low that his black mane of hair fell on to his eyebrows. His spatulate hand, a ring on almost every finger, was gripping some cards, and he was so absorbed in the game that he didn't give me so much as a glance. The other players didn't turn round, and Sophie herself waited to put down her cards and count her winnings before bothering with me.

This gave me a few minutes to study her.

I understood what the Professor meant, and Trebitsch and Oskar. A formidable woman indeed. Her hair was expensively done, and the curls around her forehead were mostly streaked with white, but the way she held her head was still superb, and the years hadn't changed the rather harsh nobility of her profile. Her jewels were perhaps a little ostentatious; the heavy drop ear-rings, the necklace, the bracelets which slid and rattled with every movement of her hands. But her dress was of monastic simplicity.

Having sorted her cards, she put them on the table, and raising her eyelids she looked me straight in the face with her clear, hard, blue eyes. She motioned me to a chair beside her. I sat down awkwardly. She hadn't held out her hand. The three men continued to take no notice of me. I was at the same time in the group, but not of it. Sophie looked at me, not saying anything, with almost unbearable concentration. A fat Russian cigarette, stained with dark lipstick, hung in the corner of her mouth, and the smoke from it made her screw up her eyes occasionally.

"Well?" she said at last. "What have you got to say for yourself?"

Her voice was harsh and raucous from smoking, or maybe from drinking, too much. Her question was not reassuring. But I managed to smile as casually as possible.

"Sorry," I said, "but I really don't have much of anything to say for myself, Madame Radzweickz. . . ."

She must have always had a cigarette in her mouth, and this had finally distorted her upper lip, giving her an expression of bitterness to which her large, beautiful, still sensual eyes gave the lie.

"Señora Martinez," she corrected me quickly.

And with a jerk of her head she indicated the gross, dark-skinned man.

"My husband the General."

He had picked up a hand, but hearing his name mentioned, he turned his head towards me, and I saw his cunning black eyes glistening, as stupid as an Esquimo's. He nodded vaguely, and didn't wait for an acknowledgment.

"O.K. I'm listening . . ." said Sophie.

As I always do when I'm horribly ill at ease, I decided to take the offensive.

"Sorry," I said, "but I've come all the way to Mexico to find out the answers to certain things. *I'm* the one who's got the questions to ask."

She threw down a card as though at random, but picked up all the ones that were on the table; and the General, furious, sniffed savagely.

"You're the one that's getting tossed out of the country, Mr. Wise Guy. For asking too many questions, and also because I don't like the way you get your answers. I don't go for people torturing other people. . . . Poor little Oskar—why did you have to pick on him?"

Her bracelets jangled on her wrists as she dealt the cards. I had lost all my self-confidence again.

"Believe me, I don't like these brutal methods either. But I had no choice. I'm involved in a serious investigation. . . ."

She shot me another look out of those clear blue eyes between black lashes clogged with mascara.

"A serious investigation! Why not leave people in peace when they're minding their own business and not hurting anybody? Me, I'm married. I got a legitimate business. I got an important position here. Nobody's got anything on me."

There was something irritating about this high-born-lady act, this smug and patronising manner of hers. All the same, she wasn't going to impress me with her worldly airs. I tore a leaf off the marker and scribbled a few words on it.

She took the bit of paper, hardly glancing at it, and passed it to the General who, surprised, read it conscientiously and, throwing it back on the table, went on with his card game—I was so shaken by this that there were beads of sweat on my forehead.

"Alright, so I'm a bigamist," said Sophie, sounding slightly amused. "Did Oskar tell you that?"

I felt like a fool; I stammered, I couldn't make my voice sound aggressive.

"It's one of the things I happened to learn from him."

"He told you we were married in Poland, and my marriage with the General isn't legal?"

The servant brought in some oranges dunked in powdered sugar. Sophie offered me one and began to eat, greedily, picking up the fragrant slices with the tips of her red finger-nails.

"I don't intend to use this information. . . . I wouldn't embarrass you for the world. . . ."

She eyed me up and down as her cat had done. With the same contempt. They had the same coloured eyes. They were alike.

"You won't do me any harm, Mr. Wise Guy, don't worry. I'm going to let you into a secret. It's Oskar I was never married to."

She was smiling, a smile that was a little distorted by her cigarette. She became very young again when she smiled that way, subtly malicious.

"Poor Oskar. You have to understand. . . . He's no good for anything any more, except living on me. A man's got to have a little pride. He's talked himself into thinking that our affair of a long time back was something different; so I let him blackmail me a little, just to keep up his self-respect. . . . Poor old Oskar."

There was a maternal tenderness in these last words.

"But what are *you* after, Mister?"

The orange was making my fingers sticky. Kindly she offered me her handkerchief. She had so many different facets, and yet she herself remained all the time as immovable as a statue.

"Just some names, that's all. The man who worked for you back in Warsaw."

She closed her eyes. Was she looking back over the past, or was it just the smoke from her lighted cigarette?

"Really? . . . That old stuff! So many of them dead already. Chaskiel and Schmruls died in '42 in the purge, and little Stas got T.B. For heaven's sakes, I don't see what . . ."

"There are the others. . . ."

This was the decisive interview. I couldn't let her mess it up idiotically; I wasn't going to be outsmarted by this woman.

But she wasn't trying to be smart.

"Yeah, the others. Simon and the Bulgarian went back to Warsaw, I heard. But Oskar must have told you all this. And Paco, poor kid, he's been sitting around here a long time. They shot his leg off in the Spanish war, so he thought, like a lot of others, that he could get a living in Mexico."

That shook me a little. Who was Paco?

She was playing rather carelessly now, and a growl from her husband pulled her up. She apologised.

"Yeah," she said at last; "Paco . . . Ferencz Bloch, I ought to call him. In Spain, and here, they call him Paco. . . . Francisco, if you like it better. . . ."

As bubbles rise up slowly to the surface of a tank and then spread out, there was a recollection bubbling around inside my brain. Ferencz Bloch . . . Paco. . . . Lost a leg in the Spanish war. . . .

"What happened to him?"

"Went back to Central Europe. . . . Alive or dead, I don't know."

"Dead, lady."

She was finding it difficult to follow the card game and the others were becoming bored.

"You're sure?"

"Quite sure. The guy that knifed Bracco in the docks at Naples, who was shooting at the cops; he was on the run, and he had a peg-leg. He was called Pacaud, according to the papers they found on him. François Pacaud. He had arrived with Bracco, on a freighter from the Balkans. I learnt all this right at the start of my investigation, I even went to Tirana, near Smyrna, following this little trail. But it didn't get me any place. So I thought Pacaud was nothing but a stooge. A small-time crook, like Bracco himself. Just an ordinary settling of accounts between the two of them. But if Pacaud was Ferencz . . ."

"I don't get it, quite," said Sophie. "You say your man with the peg-leg knifed this . . . Bracco, and then he tried to shoot it out with the cops. If he had a gun, why did he kill Bracco with a knife?"

"I wouldn't know."

I had never thought about it. In fact, it did seem rather strange.

Sophie was watching me furtively, at the same time sorting the new cards she'd just picked up; and in a flash I saw what was so familiar about her, and yet what worried me. Tadeus. The colouring was different, and the mannerisms; but still there was a family resemblance. That assurance, that way of appearing detached from other people and what they did, that impression of being invulnerable. With Arkadin, it was an attitude acquired by self-control, by power, by his great bulk. With Tadeus, a natural harshness, a latent bitterness had given to his regal detachment something inhuman, a morose hostility. While Sophie's detachment was natural to her, spontaneous, springing, probably, from tremendous vanity and egotism; but she succeeded in transforming it into fascination and even seduction. Like her Persian cat, which lost none of its dignity by squatting on its box of ashes, Sophie emerged unchanged from the most sordid adventures—the racket she ran in Warsaw, or her marriage with this appalling Mexican. I thought of the Duchess of Alba who, while she was posing for Goya, would summon her maid to help her with some intimate detail of her toilet, at the same time remaining always a really great lady.

And the less noble expressions which a human face can reflect—cunning, greed, cupidity—I surprised them all in Sophie's glance or her smile, without ceasing to feel for her an admiration which was at the same time respectful and . . . how shall I put it? . . . tender. Yes, I found that I was strangely attracted to this woman of over fifty summers, whom I knew to be a complete scoundrel. I would have liked to work for her, or at least leave her a good impression of me. I felt like an awkward kid with her, as I did with Tadeus. But with the one it was a painful and humiliating sensation; with the other it was an almost sensual pleasure.

"Tell me about Athabadze," I said.

My voice betrayed my anxiety; it wasn't just out of curiosity that I asked her. Her disconcerting smile kept changing, but the fat cigarette between her lips kept it at a crooked angle on her still impassive face.

"Wasaw. . . ."

In spite of herself, she had put a musical sweetness into the pronunciation of that name. That's how she must have said it, all those years ago.

"I was crazy about him, if you want to know. . . . But what's all this to you?"

She admitted having been in love, and I knew that this love

had been betrayed, but that this didn't hurt her any more. There are some people who try to hide a scar, others who show it off; there are still others who accept it so completely that one can't believe it hasn't always been a part of them.

But undoubtedly I had in my hand the secret weapon which could touch this smiling, impassive woman to the quick; this woman like a Hindu goddess, armed and adorned with precious stones.

"I ought to tell you I'm working for Athabadze. . . . Of course he has a different name now. . . ."

I was on the alert, expecting to see at least a change of expression in those receptive, sensitive eyes. But Sophie said simply:

"Sure . . . Gregory Arkadin."

She had disarmed me utterly with that one little phrase. I stuttered pathetically:

"You knew that? . . ."

Between their mascaraed lashes, her eyes were for a moment dazzlingly bright, like a flash of lightning. She shrugged her shoulders contemptuously, apathetically.

"I've known it for years. . . ."

The everlasting game still went on, with the three men sitting in silence, indifferent to everything but the cards. And Sophie, who never lost a trick, kept making the score; I was beginning to think that far from going on playing to distract the others' attention, she was just humouring me in a casual, friendly way as though I were a child, or some domestic animal.

"Didn't you realise what that information was worth?"

The shrugging of her shoulders moved the pendant between her breasts, which were sheathed tightly in dark satin.

"Money I don't need, Mister. I got all I want. But even if I did, that kind of money I couldn't use. . . ."

She shook her head, a gesture of denial emphasised by the sparkle and jangle of her long ear-rings.

"Not that Wasaw doesn't owe it to me; he does."

I helped her along.

"Two hundred thousand Swiss francs?"

She did a rapid mental calculation.

"Near enough. . . . It was in Polish roubles."

"He . . . *borrowed* this money?"

Her bright, complacent look emphasised very clearly that she wasn't going to let anything be dragged out of her, that she wouldn't tell me anything she didn't want to.

"Borrowed? . . . Yes, if you like."

A ferocious growl made me jump out of my skin. It was the General sweeping the cards off the table with one arm. He had lost. Imperturbably Sophie picked up the markers and added up the scores, tapping the table with the ivory mount of her propelling pencil. Still growling, the Mexican pulled from his belt a lizard-skin billfold, bulging with the thick wad of bills, and ungraciously counted out the amount he had just lost. Sophie swept it away with a neat and apparently indifferent gesture, rapidly but attentively counted the bills, rolled them up and put them in her small handbag. Once more I was conscious of one of Tadeus' gestures, checking over the banknotes and pushing them into the pocket of his grey trousers.

The men were having a drink now, excitedly discussing the card-game. Sophie drew back her chair, clapped her hands softly, and a house-boy dressed in white ran forward. She pointed out to him a green leather album lying among some others on a table by the window. She turned the pages rapidly, and beckoned me over. I saw the picture of a magnificent young man of about thirty. His shining hair was cut short, showing the natural curl, his head was bent so that one glimpsed his profile, but his eyes looked full at the camera; large, clear eyes, like a fawn's. The forehead was high, the chin well-formed and determined, and I recognised the mouth, the beautiful red, sensual mouth of Raina. His clothes, the necktie, and the pin which adorned it, indicated a rather flashy elegance, a satisfaction with himself. But the guy was undoubtedly handsome, and

I understood how Sophie, no matter how strong she had tried to be, had finally given way. . . .

"He has a beard now," I said.

But of course she knew that.

"Yes. He had a beard when I ran across him again in Deauville. It was just before the war, at the Casino. Sitting right next to me, and he didn't know me. Why should he, after all these years? . . ."

I longed to tell her that I would have known her, that I would never forget her expression, her face, or what was essentially herself. But I hadn't the courage.

"Not that he hadn't changed too, of course. All the strength and vigour he once had has just gone to fat. He doesn't look strong any more, just heavy. So heavy that it's weighing him down. And why the beard?"

She seemed very young and touching at that moment, like a little shop-girl wondering if she shouldn't tell her boy-friend to shave off his budding moustache.

I hazarded, rather treacherously:

"Maybe he's scared he'll be recognised."

"Maybe. . . ."

That misfired. I threw another dart.

"Unless . . . I think he's tried to create a new personality for himself. . . . The good-natured big executive, powerful but serene. . . . A cross between Buddha and Jupiter with the thunderbolts. . . ."

She thought that odd, she who had never tried to be anything but herself.

"All to impress Raina, of course."

This time the shot went home. She repeated in an interested tone:

"Raina?"

"Yeah. His daughter. You didn't know he had a daughter? In Berlin. The mother died when she was born. . . ."

Sophie didn't know Raina, hadn't seen Arkadin with Raina, which made it possible for her to discard this daughter of his as of negligible importance. Her maternal feelings can't ever have been very strong.

"I hadn't heard about a child. Anyway, I never saw Wasaw since . . . since he quit Warsaw. It was that night in Deauville that I found out . . . when he got up from the game somebody whispered: 'There goes the famous Gregory Arkadin.' So that's how I heard what happened to my boy-friend. I was going to talk to him. 'Hello, Wasaw,' I was going to say. 'Where's the money I handed over to you back in 1927. Remember?' He was that rich, he could have paid me back. . . ."

She passed her hand across her forehead; a heavily-ringed, well-kept hand, but still the hand of an old woman.

"But I didn't do it," she went on, for her own benefit, not mine. "No; because I saw his face in the mirror. He wasn't looking straight ahead the way he used to. He was heavy-eyed. There was that old hot, lonely kind of look in his eyes. The look of a guy who's always going to be alone."

I understood this absurd but keen feeling of pity which had affected me, too, several times when I was with Arkadin.

"I thought of all the fun we had together. A lot of things I wouldn't have known if it hadn't been for him. He made me happy sometimes, sometimes kind of humiliated. There were times when I'd cry. . . . You need all that if you want to feel you've really lived."

The wound was still there, secret, cherished with great care so that it didn't heal, but became, instead of a scar, a fragile, bitter-sweet memory.

"Besides, he was winning. I'd been playing his numbers and I was winning, too; a great deal more than what he'd got from me all those years ago. Even figuring the interest. So he didn't owe me anything any more. And I thought to myself: 'Here he's gone to all this trouble to be somebody else. Why spoil it for him? Why ruin this security he's been building up, this crazy kind of peace and quiet he's gotten himself deep down inside? . . . The big, silent guy with the beard and fur coat and all. . . . The mysterious guy. . . .

Alright, if that's the way he wants it. . . . Me, I got my money's worth twenty years before. . . .' I left him to it."

The men were through drinking and wanted to play again. They signalled to her to start dealing. Before closing the album, I saw, fleetingly, some more photos, and I recognised, in all the glory of youth, the thin face of the man with the peg-leg, and Oskar's too, ashen-grey and already soft. Sophie took the book away from me.

"Incidentally," she said. "Not that it matters . . . but who put you wise . . . to me?"

She had shown me that sometimes you have to keep certain things to yourself. And I didn't give away Arkadin's secret. I only talked about the Professor, and Trebitsch. . . . She listened dreamily, without interrupting, frowning slightly at the mention of the Baroness.

"There was Tadeus too. . . ."

"Little Tadeus, of Tangier?"

It was the one and only time I ever heard the Pole called 'little Tadeus'.

"He told you something? That's funny. Though after all . . ."

She knew him, then, she was surprised—as I had been—that he should be mixed up in this business. But it seemed she'd found the reason, though she didn't think I ought to be told it. And confusedly, I felt certain vague ideas beginning to crystallise in my mind; ideas which could be confirmed without any difficulty at all. But the Mexicans at the card-table were getting impatient.

"You can go now, Mister," said Sophie.

Subtly, but undeniably, the tone of her voice had changed. She didn't want to be bothered with this business any more. She was putting it out of her life. Anyway, it was nearly time to catch my plane.

"And when you see your boss, tell him from me he can leave well enough alone . . . Wasaw Athabadze doesn't exist any more."

I took her hand, which she hadn't held out to me, and raised it to my lips.

"You mean he has nothing to worry about? . . ."

She sighed, making no attempt to withdraw her hand, which I was still holding.

"He's the great Arkadin, a billionaire with a new name. . . . So . . . Oskar takes dope. . . . Why does anybody worry? Let them both have what they need. . . ."

She went back to sit down in her place at the table, not bothering about me any more. The boy in white showed me back to my car.

It was night now. The streets were crowded. The church-bells struck the hour. A drunk came out of a bar, lugging a bottle from which wine trickled, red as the blood from a wound. In a niche partially destroyed, at the top of a crumbling wall, I saw a little statue of the Virgin, with clasped hands, and I read the name of the square. Plaza de la Soledad. Place of Solitude.

I had never felt so alone as in this square full of people. That hopeless loneliness which one could read in the eyes of Arkadin.

The drunk passed in front of the statue, stopped to get his balance, and changed his hold on the bottle so that he could cross himself slowly and solemnly, finally brushing the big toe of the statue with his lips; and I envied him. I would have liked to be able to pray.

Book Three

The Ogre

CHAPTER ONE

I ARRIVED back from Mexico with a chill. Or was it perhaps the uneasiness within me that caused this chattering of my teeth which I tried in vain to overcome?

The cold hit me getting off the plane at Orly. Raina found me looking terrible. She was sleek and smooth and as fresh as a daisy in her great beaver coat, and her buckskin cap gave her the look of a cheerful urchin. She pretended to pout a little.

"I might have known it. You've come here just to go away again."

In fact I had decided to slip away immediately to Munich, to see Jacob Zouk. A mere formality. Then I could submit a reassuring report to Arkadin, collect the sum of money agreed upon, and start living my own life again.

At least that's what I had kept telling myself during the interminable hours of the journey; but the atmospheric conditions were terrible, and I alternated between nausea and anxiety; and I was unable to maintain either my equilibrium or an optimism which the circumstances certainly warranted.

And when I got off the plane this chill got me. . . .

The wind was sweeping across the field, whistling along the ground. It was a long way to the new refreshment-room, still badly equipped and smelling of paint. I ordered a consommé; it was lukewarm, and my teeth chattered on the spoon.

"Too bad for you. Bob's turned up again, in some miraculous way. Always available and ready to do anything for me, poor boy; and still as boring as ever, unfortunately. Still, if the right man isn't around, a girl has to make do with the one that is, doesn't she?"

She said this quietly, maliciously, but she noticed I was unusually silent.

"Jealousy seems to make you pretty dumb too," she said, crossly.

But she was wrong. It was a matter of indifference to me that young Rutleigh had taken up his role of gallant knight again, and anyway, as it seemed probable that I wouldn't be back in time for Christmas, I was glad he was taking her to San Tirso.

"Christmas week in Paris would be intolerable. I'll sit over there at my window in the tower and kid myself that my lord and master has gone crusading. . . ."

I tried to adapt myself to her mood:

"You still have your jester, who'll tell you all the latest scandals from Jermyn Street. . . ."

But I definitely wasn't feeling very well.

"You ought to be in bed," said Raina. "Or else put on your tuxedo and we'll go and have ourselves a really good time. . . ."

Neither the one nor the other. The loudspeakers announced that my plane was getting ready to take off. I had to go. Raina trotted beside me along the frozen concrete corridors. The great rooms full of windows were filled with draughts.

"Well, maybe you'll see my father; since he's in Germany, too. It's funny. . . . You're getting to be inseparable, you two. . . ."

She gave her little laugh, like a schoolgirl's.

"'Let's hope we never see each other again . . . I can't do without you! . . .' That's Dad's style. It's very Russian. . . ."

The official stamped my passport, checked my embarkation ticket.

"Russian? . . . Your father isn't Russian."

She came with me as far as the last gate. We were pressed close to each other in the line of passengers hurrying down the corridor leading to the customs.

"The fact that he told you he was doesn't prove anything, Raina. Don't you know he lost his memory . . . completely . . . back in 1927? . . ."

Why tackle this problem in such an unsuitable place, when we couldn't exchange more than a few words? Idiotically, to prove myself right on a point of detail, I was going to give away a secret which, like Sophie, I had promised to keep. But Raina didn't seem to be the least bit impressed by my revelation. She was still laughing.

"Poor sweetie, you certainly have a temperature," she said. "You'd better have the air-hostess fix you a hot drink."

Politely but firmly an official barred the way to Raina. We only had time for a brief farewell kiss.

"Who ever heard of amnesia lasting thirty years? . . ."

The sweetness of her lips. . . . Perhaps I had got over my 'flu. They told me to hurry up, everybody else was already on board. I didn't even have time to look back and wave my hand.

Once more the monotonous roar of the engines, the rarefied atmosphere of the pressurised cabin, the attentiveness of the hostess.

"Are you alright? Would you like a cup of tea? A cushion? . . ."

She was treating me as though I were sick, too. I must have looked pea-green or something. But it wasn't only the humidity, the cold . . . there were those words which Raina had said, quite casually, and which pursued me like a wasp, with its sting of suspicion.

"Who ever heard of amnesia lasting thirty years? . . ."

I would have given anything in the world to get my hands on a medical dictionary. Maybe there was a doctor on board. Get acquainted, and then lead the conversation around to problems of the human memory. . . .

I was crazy. It was the depression caused by extreme tiredness and this chill I had caught. . . .

At Munich it was worse. It had snowed, and after that the weather had become milder; one floundered in a morass like wet sugar. The sky was so overcast that by three o'clock in the afternoon they had to light the street-lamps. The shop-windows were all lit up, with their decorations—Christmas-trees, garlands and frosted chandeliers. The sidewalks were crowded, and nothing could have been more unbearable at that moment. All the insipid faces, muffled in woollen scarves, wearing the Christmas spirit like masks. And the raising of hats, the greetings, the shouts of "Happy Christmas" from one pavement to the other, the small parcels tied up with fancy twine that they dangled on their fingers. I was alone, a stranger in this crazy town, and nobody was giving me a Christmas dinner, nor even a present.

I had come to see an unknown man, an old crook who had always been disagreeable and dirty. And when I went to the jail to visit him, I learned that he'd just been let out the day before. Because it was Christmas. But there was another motive behind this unusual concession, and the warder didn't conceal it.

"The old geyser's sick. . . . So he'd better die some place else."

The more I thought about it, the more I found it really absurd to have come all the way to Munich to see this dying man. Sometimes I had, as my mother has often told me, "silly scruples which don't do you credit."

And so I hurried along in the brownish twilight, shivering. It had started to snow again, not the thick, friendly snow that you see on the calendars, or in those snow-scenes inside glass balls; but a thin, half-melting, sour and penetrating snow. I tried to find the street, of which the prison warder had scribbled the name on a piece of newspaper. He was an old man, and used gothic script, which I had some difficulty in deciphering. Twice already I had had to ask my way, and I felt as though I were going round in a circle.

I determined to ask once more. A big guy was blocking my way on the side-walk. He turned up the collar of his frightful greenish overcoat, and I saw the badge on the inside of his lapel.

"Police?"

Another plain-clothes man had joined him, and they both drew me under an archway, into the soft silence of a little snow-covered courtyard.

"We're sorry to have to do this, Mr. van Stratten."

The big man expressed himself in guttural and laborious English. Impatiently I told him I was in a hurry and he'd better speak in German. He seemed relieved.

"Oh, that'll be much quicker. We are acting on behalf of the Italian police. It's a question of an enquiry concerning a murder. . . ."

What? That old story? How had they found out I was in Munich? Above all, how had they nosed me out in the foggy, swarming anthill of the city?

"I know. . . . In Italy. . . . Somebody was knifed in the back. . . ."

I spoke impatiently. The big man seemed a little disconcerted.

"Yes . . . yes . . . that's right. How did you know about it?"

This was really ridiculous. I wanted to get to Zouk before night. I wanted to go back to my hotel and into bed, to forget Christmas, forget everything, plunge into the depths of a heavy sleep.

"Listen . . . this thing happened, in a way, right under my nose. But I've told all I know to the Italian police . . . I have nothing to add."

The two men hesitated, looked at each other doubtfully, turned aside to whisper together. I was exasperated.

"Look . . . it's cold and it's late. I'm expected at Mr. Arkadin's, he's having a party. . . ."

I said this to get away from them. They certainly seemed very impressed.

"Arkadin?" said the smaller of the two. "You're going to Mr. Arkadin's?"

I had almost forgotten that six months ago this name used to affect me the same way.

"But you're not going in the right direction for his hotel."

I couldn't help smiling. The proverb is right which says you can catch a thief quicker than a guy with a limp. But I told him I was lost. I knew the town so little. And with this wretched weather. . . .

"We'll come with you. . . ."

Devil take them ! . . . But there was nothing I could do but play along with them. Maybe it was better that way, after all. I had parted with Arkadin on the best of terms at Acapulco. And I had good news for him from Sophie. I would be well received; and knowing his opulent manner of living, I could count on a first-class meal. This would be perhaps the happiest Christmas dinner of my life.

My companions took one or two short-cuts, and soon I saw the brilliantly lit windows of the hotel. They were extremely polite and respectful, bowing and scraping outside the hotel entrance, and informing me that all they wanted was a simple piece of information. This was the name of the murdered person. It wouldn't mean going to the police-station. They would send me the identifying photograph c/o Mr. Arkadin.

They finally took themselves off, after wishing me a Happy Christmas. Already I was in a better temper, and I returned their good wishes. Out in the square the Salvation Army band was going round in a circle, starting off on a hymn, accompanied by a great deal of brass. I was surprised to find myself humming the tune in the elevator.

Arkadin occupied a whole wing of the fifteenth floor, and a waiter, stationed outside the landing-door, directed me without asking me for my invitation-card, without even asking my name, to a room from which emerged the roar and din of a party.

I couldn't distinguish anything at first but a fairly elegant crowd of people and, as far as I was concerned, anonymous. A blue haze of cigarette-smoke hung over it all. The pier-glass mirrors were misty, and they had put out the chandeliers, leaving only the flickering light from the candelabra, and the glitter of an enormous Christmas tree loaded with candles, glass balls, tops and candies.

Only there weren't any kids around the tree; and now that I could see more clearly, I discovered that the men in tail-coats and the women in low-cut evening dresses who were pressing round the buffet or dancing to the Viennese orchestra were quite different from those I had seen at San Tirso. It was the kind of party at which Raina would not be present.

I tried to pick out the host. It was not easy in such a crush. A glassy-eyed blonde put a necklace of paper roses around my neck, another planted a paper-hat from a cracker on my head. A big man was blowing up a red balloon, another was making a pretence of beating a tiny toy drum. I was beginning to wonder whether the party was going to be as amusing as I had hoped.

One group was playing darts with a board hung in the sculptured panel of a beautiful Louis XV door. I caught sight of a colossal Father Christmas, with black boots and a scarlet gown, lolling on a sofa between two rather showy lovelies. Under the white false beard I recognised the face I was looking for. I went through the groups of players, and a dart fixed itself in my sleeve. With a laugh I pulled it out. I was going to get a migraine any moment.

"Happy Christmas," said the big man in the red robe.

I didn't feel like exchanging festive greetings any more.

"Are you kidding?" I said without preamble, sickened by the prattling of the two little pin-ups.

Arkadin left them, and plunging through the crowd of guests like somebody threading his way among a herd of cattle, he reached a window-embrasure. He seemed in a very good humour.

"Well," he said, "did you find your man? That was nice, going to visit him Christmas Eve. I'll have to get busy myself on Prison Welfare. What's his name, your protégé?"

The headache had started to throb in my temples. Definitely no Christmas dinner this year. I tried to cut it short.

"Jacob Zouk. You know his name as well as I do. Anyway, I haven't seen him."

Arkadin had taken off his red cap and removed his false beard. He stroked the real one with his fingers.

"Why? Did he escape?"

"No. They let him out. Besides, he isn't going to last much longer. He's probably dying now in some miserable little room . . . 16, Sebastianplatz, to be precise."

Arkadin was still caressing his beard, carefully.

"Alright, that's fine," he said. "I wouldn't want to appear heartless, especially on an evening like this. 'Peace on earth and goodwill toward men'. But actually if your story is true, it might be better for me if this . . . Zouk? Is that right? . . . could be put out of circulation."

He signed to one of the waiters who was going round with trays, took a glass and offered me one. The champagne seemed bitter. Maybe it was the fever. I felt damp with sweat.

"To Wasaw Athabadze . . . lost and found . . . and, luckily, forgotten again."

What was there on Arkadin's face this time? Was it a malicious triumph? I thought of Raina's affectionate nickname for him: 'The Ogre'. I had read a story-book once in which the ogre really did have this bearded face, this expression of malicious glee. I had taken some pills to check my 'flu, maybe that's what made me so uncomfortable. I was suffocating in that smoke-filled room. I muttered some excuse and went out on to the landing.

A bell-boy came up at that moment with an envelope somebody had just brought for me. The porter downstairs was awaiting my reply.

Those cops again. I feared an endless interrogation. I would have been better off with Arkadin's noisy pleasantries.

"Come here," I said to the bell-hop, "I'm going to write a note for you to take."

I went back into the overheated stuffiness of the party. The darts game was in full swing. Arkadin was playing now. He hardly looked at the board, throwing the dart with a skilled hand. They applauded. I was pushed towards the corner of the room where the dart-board was. The bell-hop was watching the game round-eyed.

I still had the envelope from the cops in my hand. Mechanically I opened it. But when I finally glanced down at the photograph which it contained, the shock was so violent that I almost shouted aloud.

It was Mily. . . .

She was stretched out on a beach, hair dishevelled, her mouth wide open in kind of dumb horror. The incoming tide had made the folds of her evening dress wet, wrinkled and crumpled, so they clung round her legs, but you could see the knife which had struck her between the shoulder-blades. A dark stain, soaking into the wet sand, hid her bare flesh. . . . The sweetness of that flesh of which I knew the warmth, the fineness like old ivory. Mily . . . dead. Murdered. Knifed in the back, like Bracco. . . .

It wasn't only my 'flu, my temperature, which made me sweat with anguish at that moment. I raised my eyes and met those of Arkadin. He had been watching me the whole time. The others, all amusing themselves in their drunken way, hadn't noticed anything. They went on with their game of darts. It was Arkadin's turn. He took the dart, but broke it in his fingers. Then slowly, calmly he took a knife from the pocket of his scarlet robe, opened it, tested the blade and the point, and with an easy, sharp movement, threw it. The blade came to rest on the board, ripping the cork, ripping the embossed wooden panelling; and the hilt stayed there, quivering before my eyes.

Trying desperately to prevent my hand from trembling, I put the photo back in the envelope. Then I made my way to the door. I ran to the telephone-box. Could they get me through to Señora Jesus Martinez in Mexico? It was urgent, extremely urgent.

I was panting for breath, and felt so weak that I had to lean against the side of the box. I listened confusedly to voices at the other end of the line asking questions and talking. My God, if there were some priority I could use. . . . It would be hours, obviously. . . .

With an imperious gesture somebody grabbed the receiver out of my hand.

"Cancel that call, please. . . ."

Then he put it back on the hook.

"No use calling Mexico," said Arkadin in his calmest voice.

It was certainly a nightmare; this enormous man in the red gown, facing me in that narrow telephone-box. I felt suffocated.

"What's happened to Sophie? Knifed too, like Mily? And Oskar? I could call up the 'Amor Brujo'. No good either?"

In the background you could hear the laughter, the shouts and the music; the Christmas party continued in all its gaiety. Nobody was bothering about our intimate discussion.

"I'm beginning to understand," I said, trying desperately to see the light. "To understand it all. . . ."

The cops at Naples had got the man with the peg-leg, thinking he was Bracco's murderer. In fact, Bracco had been knifed by somebody else. By the man he and Pacaud were trying to blackmail. Pacaud, or rather Paco of Mexico, Ferencz of Warsaw.

"That's a theory," said Arkadin coldly.

He took a case from the pocket of his gown and lit a cigarette, with his usual precise, careful movements. I looked at his powerful, impassive hands, which he controlled so well, which never betrayed him. . . .

"It's more than a theory. I could prove it, if the blackmailers weren't dead."

He smiled, blowing out the flame of his gold cigarette-lighter.

"They're not all dead, Mr. van Stratten."

The whole thing was becoming frighteningly clear.

"There was Mily, too. Poor kid. . . . She doesn't count in this affair. She never understood what it was all about."

A frown appeared on Arkadin's face, and quickly vanished.

"You mean . . . she wasn't . . . in league with you?"

He must have been worried. As for me, rage and grief were overcoming my fear.

"No. It wasn't hard to understand. She was just a poor mixed-up kid; dumb, affectionate, over-enthusiastic, that's all. She didn't know what all those names meant that she threw out at you . . . Bracco . . . Sophie."

Until that moment Arkadin's face had had the frozen rigidity of a drunk's. But suddenly he seemed to sober up. He threw away his cigarette-stub, and crushed it out.

"Regrettable," he said.

"And Sophie," I went on. "What happened to Sophie?"

A hysterical fury was coming over me, overwhelming me. I was suffering physically, as much for the woman I only saw for one hour in my life as for the sweet kid that I had dragged to her death.

"Sophie knew what you'd turned into. You couldn't fool her. Not with a false name or a false beard. She recognised you. . . . After so many years. But she kept her mouth shut. She would never have talked. . . ."

Arkadin had regained his self-possession. Except that he was waxy white in his vivid scarlet gown.

"Why didn't you tell me?" he asked tonelessly.

Why? Did I have the time? And above all, how could I have suspected that she was in danger of her life?

"That should have been obvious."

Once again my fever, or my anxiety, was giving me the shakes. I had difficulty in breathing and there was a terrible taste in my mouth. Somebody seemed to be hammering inside my right temple.

"Bracco and the peg-leg guy . . . Mily . . ." I choked out. "Sophie and Oskar. There's only Zouk left. . . ."

The guests had finally noticed the absence of their host. The double doors burst open and there was a stampede of half-drunk girls on to the landing.

"Only Zouk left. . . ."

195

Arkadin let himself be surrounded and pushed around. He took a glass from the hand of a half-naked brunette.

"One left? Sure you aren't losing count?" he said, smiling. And he raised his glass, before draining it in one gulp.

"To *you*, Mr. van Stratten."

Then I understood. . . .

CHAPTER TWO

IT would be impossible to describe the smell which hung about the room; the smell of an animal's den, only there wasn't the living warmth of its fur. The stove was out and a glistening drop hung constantly on the end of the old man's nose, a broad nose covered with blackheads. He would wipe away the drop with the back of his hand, and sniff, but it formed again almost immediately.

He was sprawled out on an indescribable mattress, under a pile of covers and sacks. A shapeless overcoat was buttoned up to his chin, and on his head was a bowler hat. He was plunged in a kind of stupor, out of which he was sometimes jerked by a rending fit of coughing. Then he would spit slowly into a sticky rag which he pulled out of his pocket. He could hardly hear what I said to him. However, time pressed, the minutes were ticking away inexorably; his, and mine too, and I was getting impatient. Furiously I paced up and down the attic, I even bumped my head on a low beam as I did so; but I felt no pain at all. One idea kept me going, filled my entire being. To persuade old Zouk to come with me. Immediately. Without losing a second.

"I tell you, he knows this address. Like a crazy fool I gave him it, without thinking. . . ."

The old man scratched himself under his bundle of clothes, and looked at me over the top of his steel-rimmed spectacles.

"Why would he want to come here?"

I sat down on a chair with only three legs, making an enormous effort to keep calm, and to explain myself clearly:

"Don't you see, you're the last living member of the gang? . . ."

He wiped away the drop from his nostril and cleared his throat.

"So I'm alive, but that won't be for long."

"No, not for long. If you don't make up your mind to come along with me . . . and fast. . . ."

I leaned over the stinking mattress and took hold of the dying man's arm; but his body was rigid, as heavy as a corpse. I had to let him go. I must convince him.

But he didn't believe there was any danger, or else he didn't care.

"I don't want to go out in the cold. . . . Let me alone."

I tried to explain to him that I was in danger, too. He sniggered spitefully.

"What's that to me? I don't know you."

I attempted to awaken in him some semblance of human feeling. I talked to him about his old pals, about Oskar and Sophie. He would shake his head, mumbling all the time, and muttering phrases in Yiddish; but he didn't stir. What I told him about Athabadze left him sceptical or indifferent.

"So what? I don't want nothing out of him. . . . He don't want nothing out of me."

He wasn't completely sane any more, that was obvious. I had given him as rapid and as concise an account as possible of the extraordinary affair which had led me to him; I was on the run, in danger of my life, just as he was. He didn't follow it very well, he mixed everything up; already large chunks of memory had collapsed in his feeble brain.

"I don't know any more. . . . I seen such a lot, done such a lot. . . . Poland's a long way off, Poland . . . Sophie, oh yes, Sophie . . . lovely girl . . . the bitch. . . ."

And he launched off into a sentimental story about how she had accused him of stealing money. . . .

"Never mind about that, Zouk. Sophie's dead. You're going to be soon if . . ."

"If, nothing . . . we're all going to be, sooner or later. . . ."

He sank back under his rags, tilted his old greasy hat over his eyes. I pleaded with him.

"Zouk . . . Sophie and Oskar are dead . . . same as Mily . . . same as Bracco. A knife in their guts. I know who the killer is. I can prove it if you help me. Otherwise I've had it."

He laughed, scratched himself with his coarse, black fingernail and said:

"You can't do a thing. Your story don't add up. . . . You can't make me scared. . . . You're scared, though. Better start running. . . . What are you waiting for?"

Run where? Where could I run to in a world where Arkadin was all-powerful, where he must catch up with me sooner or later? I hadn't gone a step in months without him either following me or getting there ahead of me.

No, running away wasn't going to solve anything. I had to face him. Make accusations and prove them. It would be possible, as long as Zouk stayed alive.

How long? . . .

Across the thick snow I thought I heard the characteristic horn of Arkadin's car. I pressed my forehead against the cracked window-pane. I had not been mistaken. It was him alright, wrapped up in his black overcoat, with his broad-brimmed hat, advancing slowly through the freezing night. I saw his dark bulk looming up in the meagre light of the courtyard.

Then I hurled myself at the mattress, and heaved the old man off it. He had no trousers on, and you could see his grey, wasted legs in the torn, filthy underpants. I dragged him to the door, in spite of his kicks and protests. I seized a pair of pants from a chair on the way out, and wrapped him up as well as I could in one of the covers from the bed.

"It's him. . . . He's on the stairs. Come on. . . ."

199

I was strong, and so determined that I managed to drag him as far as the floor below. Arkadin's slow, heavy footstep made the old, worm-eaten stairs creak.

On the landing there was a door standing half-open. Without hesitation I pulled Zouk after me into a dimly lighted room. A fat blonde, wrapped in a faded dressing-gown, was cooking a sausage over an oil-stove. She turned round, astonished. I slid a bill into her hand.

"Shut up . . . I'll explain later."

There was an unmade iron bed, with a drab counterpane hanging down on to the floor, and a bolster with a greasy hollow in it where the woman's head had lain. She had obviously got up at nightfall and was dismally preparing to go and hang around the slushy sidewalks of some dark street. She was not young; her sallow face was bloated and expressed nothing, except perhaps surprise.

I pushed Zouk towards the bed.

"Get in there . . . fast. . . ."

He tripped over the coverlet, then gave a little sprightly, senile laugh.

"This ain't happened to me in fourteen years."

I shoved him, fully dressed, into the warm bed, and pulled the covers up over him. I could hear the footsteps on the stairs getting nearer, reaching the floor below. I went and closed the door behind me just as Arkadin's massive form emerged out of the flickering light thrown by the lamp in the courtyard. He looked at me without speaking. I stammered:

"You're looking for Zouk . . . so am I. He just went out . . . I don't know where he's gone. . . ."

He remained silent, immobile, just looking fixedly at me, and I was trembling like a kid that's been caught out doing something naughty.

I added quickly.

"I'll go and have another look upstairs. I must have got the wrong room."

I climbed up the steps which led to the attic, stumbling as I went. When I got there I bumped against the door, the low ceiling and the filthy walls, idiotically, like a fly knocking itself against a window-pane. Down below I could hear Arkadin crossing the narrow passage, turning the handle of the blonde's door and going into her room. I had to lean against the wall again; I was getting dizzy. I don't know how much time elapsed as I stood there in the silence of that top floor, my teeth chattering in the icy draught from the loft. From outside I could hear the clanging of the trolley buses, and motor horns, the angry barking of dogs, and, in the distance, a Christmas hymn. The Salvation Army. Wherein lay *my* salvation?

At last the door down below was opened again, the stairs creaked with that heavy footstep, and the silence seemed even more profound. I jerked myself out of the stupor which held me rooted to the spot, and hurried down into the blonde's room. Zouk was still in bed, the covers under his chin. The woman, trailing her loose bedroom slippers as she moved, was setting a place at the end of the table. The sausage had got rather burnt and was now growing cold, the sauce was congealing on the stove.

"What did he say?"

Zouk had lost his handkerchief and wiped his nose on the counterpane. The woman busied herself with the stove.

"Nothing. We just talked about the cold. He didn't insist."

Neither of them understood the significance of what was happening. I could accept the passive attitude of this blowsy woman; but Zouk was so contemptible and so filthy, wriggling about in the warmth of the bed, that I could have killed him with my own hands.

"Did he see you? Did he recognise you?"

Yes. He had come into the room. The woman had protested mildly, telling him she had company. He had pushed her away, gone up to the bed and dragged off the cover.

"But I had my hat on," said Zouk with an insane laugh. "He didn't see me so good. I had my hat on. . . ."

Was that all? Yes. He had a look round the room. The woman

grumbled about the cold. Particularly with the high rent they made her pay. He asked:

"You owe for rent? . . ."

And he took a bill out of his pocket. The girl showed it to me, folded in the palm of her hand, as though she was scared I'd ask for my share of it. Then he had gone away. Nothing else? Sure. He wished them a 'Merry Christmas'.

I felt so confused, so overwhelmed, that I had to sit down on the nearest chair, on which a pair of stockings was hung up to dry. The woman didn't like to eat her sausage, being rather put out by our presence; and also so impressed by the amount of money she'd received that she didn't know what to do or say.

I had great difficulty in pulling Zouk out of the warm, soft bed in which he had been lying.

I had him installed in my own room now. He was hardly able to move, the cold out in the street had started paroxysms of coughing. I had to lend him my scarf. We couldn't find a taxi. We had walked for a long time through the wet snow and every minute I expected to see the old man collapse. Every now and then he would stumble on a paving-stone and slip, so that I had to hold him up with all my strength. I had given up talking to him about danger. I tried another kind of persuasion.

"Zouk . . . you've been fifteen years in jail, you've had time to dream. There must be something you want . . . something you didn't have all those years."

He shook his head peevishly. He only wanted his bed, to be allowed to die in peace instead of being dragged through the cold night. . . . I promised him a steam-heated room, a feather eiderdown. He wanted his own bed. Just to be home.

While he protested and spat and stumbled along we somehow managed to make progress. I was scared of the hotel lounge. It was a second-class hotel, quiet and highly respectable. A big doorman with a moustache touched his cap to all the hotel guests. The district had been badly bombed; a number of mouldings and carvings were missing from the ceiling and the heavily ornamented walls, the electricity supply was poor and often came in erratic fits and starts from the winking lights in the chandeliers. I took advantage of one of these failures to go in and get as far as the elevator. I had at last found something which attracted Zouk. He had thought of it suddenly, and stood quite still in the middle of the street, among the traffic which was going by in all directions, splashing the slush on to the sidewalk.

He wanted a goose-liver, a fat one, roasted with onions and apples, garnished with mashed potatoes. And sauce with it. And a large glass of beer.

I had promised he'd have it. I would have promised anything. Obligingly I asked him to give me the details. Apples and potatoes are called in German 'heaven and hell'. And the old man slavered in greedy anticipation, thinking of the rich gravy being poured over the goose-liver. . . . This took him without too much difficulty as far as the hotel. He sat down in the armchair, but refused to take off his bowler hat. He always ate with his hat on.

I called down to the hotel restaurant. They were eager to oblige. Yes, of course. Certainly. There was an excellent Christmas Eve menu. . . . They served the best dinner in town. Old Bavarian dishes. . . . Goose? Certainly. Stuffed with chestnuts, garnished with red cabbage. Goose-liver? Of course. An excellent pâté, truffles, with a port-wine jelly. No, not roast liver. That had to be ordered in advance. 'Heaven and hell'? An ordinary dish like that . . . you couldn't expect it to be served in this class of hotel, particularly on Christmas Eve. . . .

I interrupted the maître d'hôtel. I tried to speak to the chef personally. He was up to his eyes in work and shouted at me to take a walk. There were three Christmas Eve menus, all different, all excellent, and I had to ask for 'heaven and hell' ! I beat a retreat. Zouk was getting impatient. I had hoped that the heat from the radiators would dull his senses, and that he would drop off to sleep in the armchair. But the thought of the food filled his entire being now, he had come out of his torpor in order to abandon himself to a greed which was almost touching. His jaws moved although there was nothing in his mouth, his lips were moist, his eyes half-shut, his whole face exuded gluttony.

"You stay here," I said. "I'm going to look for your roast liver."

But he started to protest. He refused to stay alone in the room. He wanted to come with me. I opened the window, and the cold night air calmed him. He merely shouted and kicked the door furiously, when I tried to lock it. He threatened to rouse the whole hotel. So I left the door open. He had promised to wait an hour. Not a minute longer. . . .

I began walking through the dark streets. The crowds were thinning out. There were still a few people peering into the brightly lit windows, but most of the shops were closed. Life had moved on to the cafés.

I tried two or three restaurants in vain. I certainly chose the moment to ask for a special dish, with all the restaurant staff tired out between the serving of dinner and supper. I tried some more modest establishments, small cafés, a kosher shop.

Time passed. The cold was going right through me, relentlessly. A whitish fog was coming up from the Isar. My feet were frozen, but my eyes were burning with fever. Sometimes, as I walked on, I caught a breath of warmth from an open doorway; people would go in carrying flowers or parcels, and would be greeted with laughter. In one of these houses perhaps they had prepared goose-liver with 'heaven and hell'. But I didn't know which one; I was condemned to wander through hostile streets, in despair. . . . 'Happy Christmas' said the streamers hung across the streets, between the wet fir-trees. And the trumpets of the Salvation Army broadcast a hymn into the indifferent air; a hymn sung by two or three old maids in bonnets, with quavering voices. Nobody passed except people who were late, who didn't stop to throw their coins into the collecting-box. The down-and-outs were beginning their nightly prowl.

Superstitiously, I put a substantial bill into the box. The musicians of God thanked me with a nod, and went on singing. Who gives to the poor gives to God also. Would God help me?

I found myself for the twentieth time in the same square. I didn't know which way to go. I was worn out. I had just decided I'd go back to my hotel, when a long black car brushed so closely against me that I nearly lost my balance. It stopped. The car window, operated by a button, came down noiselessly in its groove, and Arkadin's head appeared. He smiled.

"May I ask what you're doing now?"

I was as embarrassed as if he'd found me with no clothes on.

"Shopping . . . just a little shopping."

We were in the middle of the street, and an enormous cop, disgruntled at being on duty on such a night, came up to tell us to get moving.

"Hop in," said Arkadin. "It's crazy to walk in weather like this. . . ."

It was hot inside the car. In spite of myself I relaxed on the cushions and closed my eyes. Arkadin took a pigskin-covered flask from his overcoat and flicked open the gold stopper.

I swallowed a substantial gulp of brandy. The burning liquid half choked me, but immediately I felt better. I realised at once the absurdity of that despair I had felt a few minutes before. Arkadin and I were seated in a luxurious automobile which rolled silently through a town full of streets watched by cops very much on the alert, and where people were singing about the glory and loving-kindness of God. I had been imagining things. . . . Yes, it was a rather sinister joke at my expense. Arkadin had wanted to scare me . . . or take me for a ride. I hung on to this comforting theory. I thought if I could only smile, laugh at the situation, the nightmare would fade away. We would finish this Christmas Eve together. So, laughing about it, I told him my experiences with the various chefs and Munich delicatessen-keepers, and he seemed amused also. He gave an order to the chauffeur, and when he arrived at his hotel, sent for the manager to come out to the car.

It was all so simple . . . I didn't even have to leave my seat, I could give myself up to that all-pervading glow which the liquor had produced inside of me. With servility, the menials rushed to do his bidding, promised him what he wanted, and were all eagerness to please. . . . They could spare a goose-liver from the Christmas dinner, and they would certainly be able to find some 'heaven and hell' in the kitchens. They always made it for some of the staff. Five minutes only. . . . They were just going to prepare it. . . .

I was beginning to find the situation funny. One day I would have to order this dish, if only to learn how something tasted that I had taken so much trouble to get. Incidentally, I was hungry.

"Why don't we go in?" I said. "They said five minutes, but it won't be that soon. . . . I'd like to get a sandwich at the bar. . . ."

"No," said Arkadin.

There was something so definite, so peremptory about that 'No', that my precarious mood of optimism crumbled immediately. But I forced myself to maintain the light tone suitable to an exchange of pleasantries.

"Why? Don't you want to be seen with me?"

His smile was hidden by his beard, and it was dark in the car. I saw, however, the pitiless irony of it.

"You're getting smart all of a sudden, van Stratten. It's high time . . ."

This time it was he who tried to look into my face.

"You've been seen with quite a number of people, van Stratten. And it didn't do them any good. Bracco, for instance. Bracco died at your feet. . . . There was Oskar too, and Sophie. . . . They were killed just after you were in Mexico. . . . And that poor girl of yours, Mily. . . . You're a dangerous man to be seen with. . . ."

At that moment I felt the trap closing in on me. For months I had thought I could float along just where chance or my mood might lead me; I had played a game which I thought I was winning, sometimes angrily, sometimes with amusement. And all that time I had been just a fly caught up in Arkadin's web.

Now I was bound hand and foot, inextricably entangled in a net of circumstantial evidence. He had tried to frame me. And I had nothing to say in my defence. Nothing. Because my story was so absurd that nobody would believe it. Especially about Arkadin.

I had slumped back into the corner of the car as though I was scared of even touching the Ogre. Fumbling, I opened the door of the car. The cold night air gripped me.

"Yeah . . . I guess that's the way you planned it all along."

Sedately he closed the door, but put his head out through the lowered window.

"That's saying a lot. I had to check certain details, and you've been quite useful to me. I have to admit it. . . . But the difference between us, van Stratten, is that I know what I want. You, on the other hand, are constantly changing your opinions of people and your views on things. Very bad. . . ."

Carefully he stroked his moustache, on which his breath had left little drops of moisture.

"Look, there are two kinds of people in the world; those who give and those who ask, those who don't care to give and those who don't dare to ask. You dared, but you were never quite sure what you were asking for."

The doors of the hotel had opened, and a ceremonial procession was approaching the car, led by the maître d'hôtel. A waiter was carrying a dish with a silver cover. The bus-boys followed with baskets of bread, a bottle in its case, a dish of fruit. . . . With a brief gesture Arkadin cut short the flow of words which could be seen hovering on the obsequious lips of the maître d'hôtel.

"Now," he went on, "there is nothing more you could hope to get out of me, van Stratten. Even if you went down on your knees. . . . Nothing more. . . . Not money. . . . And certainly not my daughter. . . ."

I saw his cruel smile become accentuated.

"Not even your life. . . ."

And he called out to the collection of hotel servants who were all standing at attention:

"Give the gentleman his goose-liver. . . ."

I just had time to get out of the way. The car accelerated and disappeared silently into the night, the noise of the wheels still muffled by the soft, deep snow.

When I arrived at my hotel, with my load of food, everything was quiet. You could hear sounds from the dining-room, but the corridors were deserted.

Thank God, Zouk had waited for me! He was still in his arm-chair, wrapped in the counterpane, exactly as I had left him. And his ancient bowler was tilted over his eyes.

"I'm late. . . . But I got it," I said, forcing a note of gaiety into my voice; anyway I was relieved to find the old man still there. "Eat up quick, while it's still hot. Then we'll get moving. . . ." I had put the dish on the table. I went up to the armchair. Zouk still didn't say anything. I touched his hand.

Then all at once he toppled over and rolled on to the floor.

There was a knife between his shoulder-blades.

I shut the door behind me. I made a superhuman effort not to run the whole length of that dimly-lit corridor. The doorman touched his cap as I passed. I rushed down the steps of the hotel. The night, which had seemed so cold and dark, was now my refuge. I dashed into the first street I came to. . . . I was on the run. I didn't know where to find a hideout. I walked and walked, faster all the time, in spite of my exhaustion, in spite of the panic which took my breath away. . . . I wanted to put the greatest possible distance between me and that old man who was lying curled up on the floor of my bedroom with a knife in his back. The greatest possible distance between me and the hand that had wielded that knife. . . .

Once more I came to the river, and I ran, zigzagging, along the fog-enveloped quayside. But in the opaque silence I thought I heard a regular, musical note, menacing as the hissing of a snake in the undergrowth, the horn of Arkadin's car. . . .

Breathless and panic-stricken, I stumbled into a side-street, running towards a square which was full of twinkling lights.

It was certainly that particular horn, authoritative and at the same time insidious, the unusual note of which I had noticed that first evening at the Sporting Club in Cannes. . . .

I understood then how a stricken deer must find some thicket in which to hide itself when it hears the baying of the hounds.

I had just enough strength and nimbleness to avoid the car which turned silently but at full speed into the empty square. I got on to the sidewalk. The dark mass of a church loomed up like a black island in the middle of the houses with their brightly-lit windows. But the doors were closed; God's door is always open.

And I climbed up the steps and, knocking against a blind beggar, I pushed open the leather-covered door and flung myself in among the hymn-singing congregation, wet and chilled to the marrow. The candles were flickering, the censer-bearers shook the gilded censers, the crib was shining brightly, a great wave of faith and jubilation swept through the nave, where chubby-faced angels flew on high, and cherubs played their trumpets, where gilded bunches of grapes and pearl clusters embellished and enhanced every pillar, every embrasure and every arch. The gold, the naïve and touching, yet at the same time ludicrous, richness of the baroque ornaments, the music, the thick fumes from the incense and the candles, it all went to my head, so that I was like a kid on a carousel, made dizzy by the lights, the smells and the din of the fairground. I thought I was going to pass out. I staggered . . . I had to lean against my neighbour. Luckily he was strong. He caught hold of my arm.

It was Arkadin.

Bareheaded, very correct, he was looking at the crib. In the yellow light of the candles he had the face of an honest man.

"Happy Christmas," he said.

Then, quietly:

"Peace on earth and goodwill toward men."

I was shocked by this sacrilege. And yet he seemed to be sincere.

"Aren't you going to pray?" he asked. "Isn't that what you came for?"

"I came because the church has always been a sanctuary, and because I'd no place else to go. A car might run me down, if I stay in the streets. . . . And I can't go back to my hotel room because there's a corpse in there; in case you've forgotten. But me, I don't suffer from amnesia."

We were face to face, like animals who are going to fight to the death.

"It's a convenient affliction; it might be useful in your conversations with the police."

But it wasn't the cops I was scared of. Not at that moment.

A children's choir rose up from the screen. A supernatural peace came down from the high vaulted arches, and in spite of myself, it took possession of me. And suddenly, as in the car a little earlier, I was filled with renewed hope. But it wasn't a simple, irrational animal reflex. It was an inspiration which came to me, which forced itself upon me. The only way out.

The hymns rang out with redoubled volume around me. The priests in their shining raiment walked in a procession towards the crib. The congregation was on its knees, and from among the bright nest of candles the effigies of the Holy Family smiled upon it; Joseph, bald and bearded, Mary in her blue robe, and the blessed Child with great eyes made of glass. The Trinity of Bethlehem. In the adjoining chapel was one of those strange composite pictures which shone brightly in its heavy gilt frame. When you looked from the left you saw the Father. When you looked from the right you saw the Son. And from straight in front of it you saw the dove of the Holy Ghost. A Trinity again. Weren't we also a kind of small Trinity, linked together by the strongest feelings of love and hate? The three of us. Raina, her father and me. My life, my death and me.

I checked to see if I still had my billfold. It was still there, bulging, against my chest. It contained an airplane ticket. The plane leaving that night. I had made the reservation on the off-chance, rather reluctantly. It was unlikely that I would have been through with Zouk in time to take it. But the official had insisted: "It's our last place, sir. After that we have nothing for two or three days."

Arkadin was still standing next to me, attentively taking part in all the rites of this religious ceremony. I leaned towards him.

"Raina promised to think of me at exactly midnight," I said.

Perhaps it was that very thought which had reached me, bringing me salvation.

"Raina," said Arkadin. "Raina is lost to you, or you're lost to her. It's all the same."

He crossed himself, as everybody else did; perhaps to do the same as everybody else, perhaps to put a seal on his pronouncement.

"Besides," he continued, with a gravity which impressed me, "Raina has nothing to do with all this. Raina has to be kept out of it."

A Child is born, and the sins of the world are blotted out. Did he think his sins were absolved because he had had Raina, loved her, only lived for her? Some light was being thrown on the real secret of this gloomy, tragic man, this mass of contradictions.

"Raina doesn't have to know anything."

He was scared of her finding out. . . . Not of her finding out he was a criminal. At the beginning he wasn't one. Only a sordid small-time crook. It was exactly this that he couldn't take. That there was still somebody left who remembered Wasaw Athabadze, the greedy little sneak-thief, the unscrupulous pimp. Bracco had stirred up all this mud, and he had been terrified that a spot of it would splash Raina. If she ever found out that her father, the great, invulnerable, powerful Arkadin, had stolen two hundred thousand francs from his boss and patroness. . . . He couldn't bear the idea of it. Particularly as I myself seemed so like what he used to be, with the same desires, the same soft complacency, and that same charm of which he knew the power; when he saw me hanging around Raina it made him hate and fear the image of his youth even more. Wipe it out. Kill it. Find out first of all who was still alive, still to be feared, from his distant and forgotten past. Then liquidate the witnesses, one by one, as many as there might be. Finally, get rid of the tool; me. Raina would continue to smile and say: "Papa loves a mystery. . . . He's a real Russian." Raina would go on thinking: "My father is formidable. He wears his power as he wears his beard; it's all a trick, to make him seem like God, like Jupiter, like Bluebeard." He would offer her jewels, dresses, travel, so she would forget about me. She would forget quickly. "Papa is so good to me," she would say.

No. Because *I* wasn't dead; I, who was the only one left that knew the truth, the only one determined *not* to keep quiet about it.

Suddenly, before Arkadin could realise my intention, I broke through the crowd of worshippers and got to the door. The car was parked at the foot of the church steps. I leapt into it.

"Get moving. To the airport," I said, "Mr. Arkadin's orders."

The chauffeur hesitated. But he had seen me just before with his employer, on the best of terms. And my air of authority impressed him. He started the car.

I had nicely calculated the distance and the time in hand. The plane was on the airstrip. Having no baggage, I rushed quickly through all the turnstiles which separated me from the embarkation point. I had already handed over my embarkation ticket to the air-hostess, and joined my fellow-passengers who were docilely following her towards the plane and its throbbing engines. It was then that a voice was heard shouting from the far end of the hall:

"Wait!"

Arkadin was running. He had lost his hat, and his heavy overcoat was flapping round him like a bat's wings. He was out of breath. An official stopped him at the first turnstile. I wasn't worrying. The plane was full.

In fact, as I turned round, I saw the spectacle of the richest man in the world not, for once in his life, seeing a material obstacle swept away in front of him. He had brought out his billfold and he was brandishing dollars: he shouted and insisted to no purpose. The plane was full.

The last passengers were going through the door on to the airfield. From the end of the hall he started to shout despairingly:

"Listen . . . for God's sake, listen. . . . I have to catch that plane. I'll pay anything you like. . . . A thousand dollars. Ten thousand dollars."

I saw my fellow-passengers turn around, listen, and maybe hesitate. If one of them accepted the price I was done for.

"I am Arkadin."

I planted myself in the doorway and in a bantering tone I started to shout, too.

"No kidding. Me, I'm Santa Claus."

A shout of laughter came from the group of passengers. The hostess, surprised, turned back.

"Hurry along, please, ladies and gentlemen, hurry along."

The snow was thicker than ever, deadening all sound, and outside you couldn't hear Arkadin's voice any more. It was drowned by the loud whirring of the propellers.

CHAPTER THREE

RAINA wasn't at Barcelona airport.

I had sent her a cable from Zürich; but it was impossible to tell if she had received it in time. On Christmas night the postal services wouldn't be very efficient. Particularly as they would have had to send it on to San Tirso. Everybody would be sleeping on that white morning. The postmistress in her mail-office, the servants in the castle, and Raina in her beautiful Infanta's bed. The Sleeping Beauty castle. She had called it that one day in fun and her father had bought the thing. I hoped to find refuge there. The only possible place for me. But I couldn't get any nearer to it, because the spell hadn't been broken. First I had to find out where Raina was.

During the trip from Munich I had gone through the alternatives over and over again in my mind. Had she really stayed at the castle waiting for me, as she had told me she would? Bob would be with her. But Bob was such a bore that she may have suddenly had an urge to go down to Barcelona. Or maybe to attend the midnight mass at Montserrat.

If I couldn't be with her, the castle, instead of being a place of refuge, would be a kind of death-trap. A prison.

But I had a valuable head-start on Arkadin. I wasn't able to be sure of the importance of it, however; I could only wear myself out in calculations which had no foundation. It was almost a certainty that after my departure from Munich, Arkadin had done everything he could to catch up with me. He would charter a 'plane. But the charter outfits couldn't compete, over a long distance, with the commercial airlines. In the bad-weather conditions which prevailed over practically the entire route, he couldn't hope to reach Barcelona in less than a ten-hour flight. That was some consolation. That would give me time to go to San Tirso, to find Raina.

But he may have telephoned some instructions, so that I would be grabbed the minute I appeared at the castle gates, or even in the town itself.

Since I had made Llobregat my rendezvous with Raina, the best thing would be to stay where I was. My plane had landed there at seven o'clock in the morning; that would be the time the post-office would start functioning. I would need to give her time to get my cable, to slip on a coat and come down to the airport. . . .

I watched the hand of the clock moving slowly round, with little jerks, and I counted the minutes. I was mad with impatience; I felt that every passing moment cut short the start I already had in getting out of reach of the Ogre. Because something occurred to me, a fact which I had anxiously checked up on. Other airline planes had left Munich during the night. Maybe Arkadin had booked a reservation on one of them and travelled to Rome at the same speed as I myself had travelled here. Or to Milan. In that case there would be only half the trip to do in his private plane. Then I could only reckon on a head-start of two or three hours.

And one of those hours had already gone by, in the foggy solitude of this airport, in anxiously watching the flat road which led from the city. "Sister Anne, sister Anne. . . ." I realised then how fairy-tales can have the quality of nightmare.

I had so harassed the officials with questions and I had shown such morbid agitation asking for a cup of coffee which I couldn't drink, running to the door at the slightest noise, then going back to the buffet to get away from the freezing wind which swept across the airfield, watching the sky, jumping out of my skin at the least sound—that they certainly regarded me as a suspicious character. No baggage, either. . . . They checked my passport again, and once more I thanked my mother for getting me American nationality. It would be funny, just the same, if the cops were to get mixed up in this. . . .

After all, there was nothing to stop me asking for police protection. Strange I hadn't thought of that before. A long-standing distrust of them acquired in fifteen years of activities . . . not always respectable. And also a kind of pride. It was a question of ethics. I was no stool-pigeon. I couldn't split on Raina's father. She would never forgive me.

What good would it do to get myself out of trouble? I could never face up to Raina's contempt. I, who had always been able to sense it in other people, even in people more mediocre than myself; I couldn't take it from the girl I loved.

Arkadin had killed five people in cold blood, so that the daughter he loved would never know he used to be a small-time crook before becoming what he now was. And given the chance, he was going to kill a sixth. . . .

The thought jerked me out of the state of prostration in which I was drearily churning over in my mind various calculations, deductions and suppositions *ad nauseam*; and I began pacing up and down again like a caged beast.

It was already half-past eight.

The loudspeaker announced that the plane from Tangier was coming in, and then the voice resounding like a hammer through the glass-walled waiting-rooms, enquired if Miss Arkadin was at the airport. I had stood up, tensely, hanging on that inhuman voice which was shouting Raina's name.

"*Se llama la señorita Arkadin. . . . Atencion. . . . la señorita Arkadin*. Calling Miss Arkadin. . . ."

It was her father calling her, on the radio, from his private plane.

Taken unawares and reeling with exhaustion, hunger and animal fear, I stood there shaking, leaning on the cold marble table-top on which they had just put a bottle of brandy; the drink of the condemned.

I didn't see Raina's car turn and come through the barrier of the airfield. The official at the turnstile had to get up and rush forward to meet her.

"Señorita Arkadin. You're wanted."

Then I dashed over, towards Raina, knocking against the official.

"Raina, Raina. . . . At last !"

I was scared of bursting into hysterical sobs in front of the astonished girl and that dumb stuffed shirt Bob who was with her, and all the watching Spaniards. I drew Raina close to me, convulsively, hiding my agitated face in her coat-collar. A warmth, a familiar scent came from it. Antaeus regained his strength on touching the earth. I got a grip on myself.

"Raina, I've got to talk to you."

But some jerk in a uniform had come up to me.

"Señorita Arkadin. . . . Your father. . . . It's very urgent."

But I held firmly on to Raina's arm.

"What I've got to say is urgent too, Raina, I promise you."

She couldn't have understood what it was about, but she was scared by the look on my face.

"Your father will be here in a few minutes. But first, you've got to listen to me."

I drew her towards a bench at the side of the room. Bob was ostentatiously examining the airline posters.

"Raina . . . when you go and talk to your father you must make him think that . . . that we've been together for . . . an hour at least. He has to believe that I've had time to tell you . . ."

"Tell me what?"

It was impossible to tell her just like that in a few words, in the waiting-room. And the official was hanging around, pestering her.

"Señorita, if you will follow me to the radio-tower, I will put you in communication with Mr. Arkadin."

Mechanically she obeyed. I could only follow her, slow her down.

"Raina, if you care about me at all . . . tell him you know everything. I'll explain afterwards. . . . For God's sake . . ."

We got to the spiral staircase which led up to the control-tower.

"But what's it all about, Guy? This is so silly."

I caught her hand with the desperation of a drowning man.

"I want to save my life."

She climbed the winding staircase. In the tower you could hear the thundering echo of Arkadin's voice.

"He's in a little Italian 'Piper'," explained the operator, getting up with alacrity. "A few kilometres from the coast. He's been asking for you for more than a quarter of an hour already. He sounds very . . . Well, you'd better speak to him yourself."

He handed the mike to Raina. He took off the headphones, turned a knob, and Arkadin's voice filled the small room.

"My daughter. I want to speak to my daughter. At once."

She took the mike.

"It's me, father. What is it?"

She kept her voice calm, but her eyes, riveted on my face, were questioning.

"Have you seen van Stratten?"

I had caught hold of her other hand and was pressing it hard between mine.

"Yes, father. He's right here with me."

A short silence. Then the voice without a face; one could guess the confusion, perhaps the silent prayer.

"Don't listen to him, Raina. Don't let him talk to you till I get there. . . . I'll be there in a few minutes. Don't listen to him. . . ."

Raina's hand tightened round the polished surface of the mike.

"Tell him it's too late," I implored her.

"Don't listen, Raina."

"Too late, Raina. Tell him . . . *please*."

"It's too late," said Raina, like an echo.

There was a silence. A sudden silence, so complete that we stayed motionless, knocked sideways as if by an explosion. Then we could make out the crackling of the radio, the distant noises from out of the sky.

"Father," shouted Raina.

No answer, and the prolonged silence was becoming terrifying.

"Father. . . . What's wrong? For heaven's sake, answer. . . ."

It was her turn to shout, to entreat, to try feverishly to bridge the gulf which separated them. But there was no answer, nothing but a great emptiness, emphasised by the vibrating of the silent mike.

Slowly Raina put it back on the table. The operator, alarmed, got his headphones on again, and started calling, trying to make contact. The panic spread from the control-tower right through the airport. Hooters were sounding all of a sudden, there was bustle and confusion all over the field. From the height of the glass-walled tower, we took part in this weird, mysterious crisis.

Raina withdrew her hand from mine and went down the spiral staircase. Bob was waiting for her at the bottom. I didn't dare to follow her or ask her anything. I stayed standing there in the control-tower, trying to understand, in all the confusion of orders being transmitted, of plugs vibrating in the switchboard like the darts quivering in the board at Arkadin's party.

The Tangier plane was banking on to the airfield for a landing. All the personnel dashed towards the airstrip. The siren was wailing. The plane was nearly down. . . .

I was caught up in the flood of curiosity and anxiety which was pulling everyone on to the field. I heard snatches of their conversation.

"A 'Piper'. . . . It was Arkadin. . . . It nearly hit the Tangier plane. Crazy. . . . Drunk. . . ."

No. The pilots of the Tangier plane were positive. They had seen the Piper climbing in their path, less than two hundred yards away. The little plane was obviously in trouble. It was losing speed and spinning around like a kite in the wind. The pilot thought it was a slip-up with the controls; that often happened with amateurs. He had slightly altered course. But it was obvious the Piper was coming straight into the four-engined aircraft. A crash seemed inevitable. Then, by some miracle, an air-pocket, or a sudden shift of wind took a hand in the game. The small plane reared up, pitched from one wing to the other and slipped alongside the big commercial plane without touching it. And—on this point the pilots were absolutely positive—in the brief moment that the two planes were close up together, they had noticed quite distinctly that the cockpit was empty.

I was standing quite still. Around me there was a lot of coming and going, and conversation; the exclamations were dying away. I neither saw nor heard anything. I had only one thought, Raina.

I saw her walking slowly towards her car. I ran towards her.

Dry-eyed, she gave me a look, a fixed look, of such indifference that it turned my heart to stone. I trembled.

"Raina."

"Alright," she said. "I saved your precious life for you. I had to kill my father to do it. Anything else I can do for you, sir?"

Just before, when my life hung in the balance, I had hesitated to denounce Arkadin. It was worse now; it would mean denigrating a dead man. But I couldn't bear to lose Raina; that she should cry over her father and blame me for his death would be too unfair and too stupid.

"Raina . . . your father. . . . Don't you know what your father was? . . . "

She shrugged her shoulders.

"My father . . . was . . . my father. That's all. And I loved him. You ought to know better than anyone that I don't give my love as a good conduct prize. It doesn't have to be somebody great or noble or heroic or powerful, or even honest. I haven't wanted, I wouldn't ever want to know the whys and wherefores either with

220

him or with you. I couldn't care less about your past histories. . . .
Honestly. . . ."

The end of the affair was like the masked ball at San Tirso,
hidden behind a mask of mocking laughter, of farce. Derision. So
much trouble and trickery, so much brutality and patient waiting,
suffering and fear—for nothing. We had both risked everything to
win Raina's heart and mind, and she rejected her role of arbiter.
She would have refused to read the report on Arkadin just as she
had refused to read the yellow dossier about me. Maybe, like
Sophie, she had known all these years and said nothing. If it amused
her father to surround himself with an aura of mystery . . . so
what?

But Arkadin, who knew everything, who could do anything,
hadn't understood that. Like Tirso, who had doubts about divine
mercy and divine love, he didn't put his faith in the indulgence and
the tenderness of a daughter. Like Tirso, he threw himself into
emptiness.

And it was as though I had pushed him out of the cockpit. But
I was too much of a coward to be a killer. I had hidden behind
Raina's skirts; I had dictated to her the words which got Arkadin
as surely, as fatally, as the knife from his hand had got Bracco, Mily
and the rest of them. . . .

I thought about them at that moment, those people who had also
died for nothing. But blood cries out for blood and death for
vengeance. Arkadin and I hadn't stirred up the deep mud of this
world of intrigue and chicanery with impunity; this world in which
there are unwritten laws, and a rule of iron. A world in which scores
are paid off.

I thought of the tangled skein in which all the people I had
contacted were tied up together, at Copenhagen, at Amsterdam
and at Tangier. The professor, who knew more than he would
say. And the Mexican General with his small, fierce, gleaming eyes
and his porcine laugh. And, above all, Tadeus, 'little Tadeus' as
Sophie had called him, almost tenderly. Tadeus who would pocket

the dough or hand it out without speaking a word, who never forgave anything. . . .

But Raina wasn't even aware of all this accumulated bitterness which threatened her future. If she had known about it, she couldn't have cared less; honestly. . . .

I watched her walk away from me. The most beautiful girl in the world. The richest girl in the world. The girl who had loved me. Whom I loved.

I had killed Arkadin. And she had given me the brush-off, ruthlessly, and below me there yawned the enormous bottomless gulf of a life which was now without hope.

I knew I would never see her again.

The little marquis, who until that moment had been standing a little way off, with real British tact, came towards me. Either ironically or out of stupidity, he asked me if I was going to let Raina go off like that, all alone. I told him that if it wasn't too much trouble, I'd punch him on the nose.

He looked at me quietly with his childish blue eyes.

"That's very odd," he said. "I have a great desire to punch yours."

But he didn't condescend to do it. Shrugging his shoulders he went off with Raina.

STAR BOOKS BESTSELLERS

	MICHAEL CARSON	
0352316179	**The Genesis Experiement**	£2.50
	ASHLEY CARTER	
0352317264	**A Darkling Moon**	£2.50*
035231639X	**Embrace The Wind**	£2.25*
0352315717	**Farewell to Blackoaks**	£1.95*
0352316365	**Miz Lucretia of Falconhurst**	£2.50*
	ASHLEY CARTER & KYLE ONSTOTT	
0352317019	**Strange Harvest**	£2.95*
	BERNARD F. CONNERS	
0352315814	**Don't Embarrass The Bureau**	£1.95*
0352314362	**Dancehall**	£2.25*

STAR Books are obtainable from many booksellers and newsagents. If you have any difficulty tick the titles you want and fill in the form below.

Name _____

Address _____

_____

Send to: Star Books Cash Sales, P.O. Box 11, Falmouth, Cornwall, TR10 9EN.

Please send a cheque or postal order to the value of the cover price plus:
UK: 55p for the first book, 22p for the second book and 14p for each additional book ordered to the maximum charge of £1.75.

BFPO and EIRE: 55p for the first book, 22p for the second book, 14p per copy for the next 7 books, thereafter 8p per book.

OVERSEAS: £1.00 for the first book and 25p per copy for each additional book.

While every effort is made to keep prices low, it is sometimes necessary to increase prices at short notice. Star Books reserve the right to show new retail prices on covers which may differ from those advertised in the text or elsewhere.

NOT FOR SALE IN CANADA

STAR BOOKS BESTSELLERS

	DEAN R KOONTZ	
0352319860	**Strangers**	£3.95*
035231950X	**The Vision**	£2.50*
035231608X	**Voice of The Night**	£2.25*
0352314796	**Darkness Comes**	£2.50*
0352309350	**Whispers**	£2.95*
0352301643	**Night Chills**	£3.25*
0352314400	**Shattered**	£1.80*
0352314370	**Phantoms**	£2.25*
0352314893	**Chase**	£1.95*
	RAYMOND LEONARD	
0352318201	**Nostradamus Inheritance**	£2.50*
	GASTON LEROUX	
0352317167	**The Phantom of the Opera**	£2.95

STAR Books are obtainable from many booksellers and newsagents. If you have any difficulty tick the titles you want and fill in the form below.

Name _____

Address _____

_____

Send to: Star Books Cash Sales, P.O. Box 11, Falmouth, Cornwall, TR10 9EN.

Please send a cheque or postal order to the value of the cover price plus:
UK: 55p for the first book, 22p for the second book and 14p for each additional book ordered to the maximum charge of £1.75.

BFPO and EIRE: 55p for the first book, 22p for the second book, 14p per copy for the next 7 books, thereafter 8p per book.

OVERSEAS: £1.00 for the first book and 25p per copy for each additional book.

While every effort is made to keep prices low, it is sometimes necessary to increase prices at short notice. Star Books reserve the right to show new retail prices on covers which may differ from those advertised in the text or elsewhere.

*NOT FOR SALE IN CANADA